Heart in her throat, Cathy slid the shower screen open.

Lisa spun around, frightened. She had been cleaning her teeth but now stood stock still, toothbrush in her mouth and toothpaste foam wending its way down one side of her chin.

Cathy met the eyes of blue. Blood hammered in her ears, and her knees felt weak. Still, she held her gaze to Lisa's and broke it only for the time it took to lift her T-shirt over her head. It fell to the floor, and was soon joined by her panties. She stepped into the shower recess.

"You remember last night you said you had something you wanted to tell me?"

Whether Lisa remembered or not Cathy couldn't fathom. Lisa stood motionless, water streaming over the back of her head. A glob of toothpaste dropped from her chin to her chest and was immediately swept away by the stream of water.

Cathy pressed on. "Well, I have something I want to tell you, too."

"What's that?" Barely a squeak emerged, not at all aided by the toothbrush still firmly planted in Lisa's mouth.

Cathy reached to guide the offending implement away. "This." The toothbrush fell from Lisa's mouth as Cathy's lips met hers . . .

Visit

Bella Books

at

BellaBooks.com

or call our toll-free number

1-800-729-4992

Jane Frances

Bella BOOKS

2005

Copyright© 2005 by Jane Frances

Bella Books, Inc.
P.O. Box 10543
Tallahassee, FL 32302

All rights reserved. No part of this book may be reproduced or transmitted in any form or by any means, electronic or mechanical, including photocopying, without permission in writing from the publisher.

Printed in the United States of America on acid-free paper
First Edition

Editor: Pam Berard
Cover designer: Sandy Knowles

ISBN 1-59493-046-5

For Cheryl

Acknowledgments

Sincere thanks to all who provided me with advice, encouragement and support during the writing of *Reunion*. Some are current and some are past colleagues, and all extraordinary friends—Caroline, Don, Elise, Fleur, Jan, Joelle, Joey, and Lee.

And special thanks to Cheryl.

About the Author

If asked to describe herself, Jane Frances would say she was "an active daydreamer with a practical bent." A model student at school, Jane left home to attend university and subsequently discovered life outside the classroom. Many years later she graduated, with an ordinary degree but first-class memories of the journey.

Her studies took her to the marketing department of a city-based educational institution in Perth Western Australia, where she spent more than a decade working with a creative and supportive team.

Reunion is Jane's first novel. A first-time writer, she is pursuing a lifelong love of reading and self-expression through the written word.

Jane currently lives in Paris, where she is happily pounding the keys on her next novel and getting into all sorts of strife as she proves over and over her lack of aptitude for learning a second language!

Chapter One

Within minutes of stepping inside the warehouse, Lisa felt sweat trickle down her temples. It was unseasonably hot for late March, a month into autumn for Perth, a city renowned for its Mediterranean climate. For only ten in the morning, the heat inside was stifling and she wondered how on earth the staff managed to work a shift without keeling over from exhaustion.

Lisa could suppose only that the air-conditioning had broken down. She didn't recall the humidity being this bad on previous visits. But then again, on her previous visits she had been in the midst of buyer's fever, practically salivating at the sight of floor to ceiling terra cotta and stonework. Lisa recalled walking endlessly up and down the towering aisles of pots, urns, sculptures and anything that had ever been made from terra cotta or stone, visualizing the endless possibilities of having this or that in her garden, totally spoilt for choice and unable to make a decision despite having arrived with a preplanned design in hand.

Luckily, her friend Van—who was the reason Lisa made the trek to the wholesalers today—did not operate on the same level. Van needed two large pots for the entrance to her newly erected gazebo, and as soon as she spied the ones she wanted, she headed straight for them.

She nearly fainted at the cost. "This is the *wholesale* price?"

Lisa nodded. "Terra's not cheap you know. And these aren't your average petunia-sized pots."

"I suppose not," Van sighed. Indeed, these containers were huge. They had to be to take the orange trees she planned to plant them out with. "Okay, let's go make Visa's day."

"Hang on a sec," Lisa said, grabbing Van's sleeve before she could make a dash to the cash register. "They'll take them from up there." She pointed to the carefully packed pots stacked in piles of three almost twelve feet above floor level. "Don't you think you should check them a bit more closely first? You could get a cracked one if you ask for a blind delivery."

Van shot Lisa a look that implied no one would *dare* send her a cracked pot.

"A hairline crack gets bigger over time you know," Lisa continued, "and it would only get bigger during transit. You may as well check now and make sure they're perfect. Then, you can refuse delivery if you're not happy."

Considering the amount of credit she was about to clock up, Van agreed. She caught the attention of one of the staff by giving a sharp two-fingered whistle.

In the minutes it took the attendant to find and fire up a forklift, the heat began to really close in on Lisa. She pulled an ever-present rag from the depths of her shorts pocket and patted her face and neck. "I'm going outside for a few minutes."

"Okay," Van spoke skyward, too engrossed in watching the prongs of the forklift inch their way into a pallet to glance at Lisa's already retreating figure. "I'll give a yell when they've got them down."

Striding toward the entrance and the promise of air that was, if not cool, at least moving, Lisa shot her head around at the sudden crash that came from the other end of the warehouse. "Whoops," she said under her breath.

Lisa, along with a clutch of other customers, watched in silence as the young fellow who'd taken a liking to a pot at the bottom of a pot pyramid balefully surveyed the results of his impatience. Obviously he had never shopped with his mother for fruit and vegetables. One badly picked orange was a lesson learned for life.

The stunned silence was broken as staff rushed to the scene, most cursing, none looking in any way pleased with this most unpleasant interruption. Lisa followed, not to witness the effusive apologies of Mr. Impatient, but to more closely inspect an item which, prior to the pot topple, had been hidden from view.

Later, on the drive home, Lisa chirped happily as she stole another look through the rearview mirror at her impulse purchase, tightly secured with rope on the tray of her utility. "It must have been fate," she said. "I never would have seen it if that guy hadn't smashed all those pots."

What she had spied was part of a brand-new shipment, waiting to be located to the main floor of the warehouse. A thorough inspection through the wooden packing frame it was still suspended in, a quick swipe of her credit card, and the Grecian-style amphora was hers. It was going to look perfect in the arbor at the end of her yard. Lisa couldn't wait to get it home to show Janice.

Back at Van's place, Lisa declined the offer of a cool drink. Van folded her arms. "It's totally unfair you know," she said. "You get to take your purchase home with you. I have to wait a whole week."

Lisa grinned. Van knew there was no way they could have unloaded her pots; they were just too heavy. And even if they managed without breakage, there was the added problem of maneuvering them into place. It was much safer to leave it to the professionals.

"Thanks for your help today." Van caught Lisa in a quick hug before hopping out of the cab. "You saved me a fortune."

"No worries," Lisa said. She had been more than happy to help.

After all, getting items at wholesale price was one of the advantages she enjoyed as a small business owner. "You can repay me with bags of oranges for the rest of your life. Speaking of which, do you want to take advantage of me again to buy your orange trees?"

Van slammed the cab door and leaned on the open window frame. "I'll take advantage of you any chance I get, sweetheart."

"Promises, promises." Lisa threw the column shift into reverse and revved the motor. "Say hi to Steph for me." With that she pulled out of the driveway and headed home.

As Lisa approached home, she felt a prickle of annoyance. An old blue Commodore sat in her driveway. She parked on the street and prickled again at the steady thump that emanated from inside the house. Janice had promised she was going to get down to some studying today, and unless times really had changed since Lisa's student days, ear-popping music wasn't exactly conducive to mental gymnastics.

Spying old Mrs. Trimble heading in her direction, Lisa hurried her footsteps. Twice before, Mrs. Trimble—Lisa's immediate neighbor—had waylaid her on her way to her front door, complaining about the loud music played in her absence.

So twice Lisa had come to bear on Janice, and twice Janice had promised to keep the decibels to a reasonable level, both times muttering about how an old biddy like Mrs. Trimble could hear anything short of an atom bomb, anyway. Not wishing to argue, and feeling more like a mother than a lover, Lisa took Janice at her word and let the matter drop.

Once on the safety of the front veranda, Lisa stole a glance to the garden next door. Mrs. Trimble had returned to her stoop-style hoeing of the rose beds, obviously assuming Lisa's brisk walk indicated the *thump, ta da, thump* would soon be put to a stop.

Taking a moment to check the soles of her work boots and do a stamp dance on the doormat to remove any debris, Lisa pondered her best plan of action. To storm in and pull the stereo plug from the wall would only embarrass Janice in front of her blue Commodore friend. For all she knew, they may well have been hard at work and only paused for a break in the last few minutes. Alternatively, knowing how Janice was after nine months of living with her, it was more likely her visitor was not a friend from classes at all, but one of her large circle of nightclub buddies who had unexpectedly popped in to party before going home to crash. And Janice being Janice, she would have jumped at the opportunity to down pen and paper and spin a stack of discs.

Which is exactly what I did when I was Janice's age, Lisa thought to herself. She swallowed her annoyance as she unlocked the front door, vowing to be the hip older lover—not the nagging old mother.

The music hit her with a blast as soon as the door was opened just a few inches.

Lisa headed down the hallway, automatically poking her head into the main bedroom to make sure Janice had made up the bed. Again she scolded herself. It seemed she was forever looking to find fault. She partly blamed her friends for this emerging trait. They had teased her mercilessly when they found out she had slept with Janice (cradle snatcher was a term that came to mind) even though Van and Steph had been party to them getting together.

Thinking Lisa's three years of living like a nun were quite enough, they had dragged her to the local gay club, sent a drink to the first girl she thought was cute, and then bid a hasty retreat when Janice came over to say thanks. Two hours later Lisa and Janice were hard at it on the bench seat of Lisa's utility; then hard at it for the rest of the night on Lisa's queen-sized bed. It wasn't until breakfast the next morning Lisa discovered Janice was only twenty—eleven years her junior.

"You don't look thirty-one to me," Janice crooned in Lisa's ear as a tiny hand crept inside the folds of her sports shirt. "And you certainly don't feel it."

Not immune to the power of compliments—and as she had rediscovered the night before, even less immune to the powers of the flesh—Lisa succumbed to her first illicit sick day in years.

Van and Steph were all ears at lunch the following Sunday.

Then they were all mouth when Lisa announced she would be seeing Janice again.

"She *is* rather young," Van said for what seemed like the fiftieth time.

"I don't care." Lisa was sulky by this point. "I like her."

Despite, and sometimes in spite of, her friends' ongoing assault, Lisa decided she really did like Janice. Apart from her obvious physical attributes—although just over five foot two she was a green-eyed, fair-skinned brunette with all the right pieces in all the right places—Janice was like a whirlwind, racing from one idea to another and pouring all her energy into whatever project captured her fancy. When that project bored her, she was soon onto the next. Lisa's friends said she was flighty. Lisa argued she just didn't bother wasting her time on useless issues.

A casual remark while watching a gardening show one Saturday evening spurred Janice into another wave of enthusiasm.

"I was just thinking about doing something with the garden," Lisa had said. The next morning, she rubbed her eyes into focus and saw a set of elaborate garden plans laid out in front of her.

"Just take a look at them," Janice pleaded, sliding the plans closer. "I stayed up half the night doing them for you."

Closer inspection revealed the plans to be well thought out and workable, despite a few obvious exceptions. A heated argument ensued over the life or death of the Lilly Pilly tree. Janice was adamant it had to go. How else was there to be room for the hexagonal gazebo which housed a six-seater spa? Lisa was just as adamant. The Lilly Pilly added character and shade to the back garden. It was a fine looking tree with many more years of growth. It housed her rock doves. And how was Lisa's mum to make her Lilly Pilly jam without a supply of berries? Besides, there was no way even an old bath was in her budget, never mind a spa large enough for an entire basketball team.

Janice stalked off in a huff to the bedroom, but soon snapped out of it when Lisa announced through the closed door that they should do a nursery hike and check out some prices.

Numerous trips to the nurseries and Lisa's beloved terra-cotta warehouse later, Janice's vision took form, minus the spa and with the Lilly Pilly still intact. Their ensuing garden party was full of accolades. Even Van admitted Janice had done a wonderful job. Amazed at this unexpected compliment from her toughest critic, Lisa kept silent about the fact Janice's role had been purely of designer and supervisor. She hadn't actually done any of the physical work.

"I told you everyone would love it." Lisa and Janice lay in bed after the last guests had long gone.

Janice threw herself onto her back and stared at the ceiling. "Do you really think so? They weren't just trying to be nice?"

"Honestly Jan," Lisa reassured. "They loved it."

Janice turned onto her side, propping her head on her hand as she considered Lisa carefully, "What if I said I wanted to quit work and study building design?"

Lisa's eyes widened. "Building design? What's that got to do with laying out a garden?"

"I've been looking into it. There's a great course at the Tech in the city. It's mainly building stuff but it incorporates garden design. I reckon it would be really good." She curled her arm around Lisa's waist. "It beats the hell out of selling crappy phones for the rest of my life."

Exasperated—only a few months prior Janice had been full of the fortunes of flogging mobile phones—Lisa played devil's advocate. "Full-time study can be pretty hard going, especially when you're used to bringing in an income."

"So you don't think I can do it after all." Janice did a complete flip to face the window.

"I didn't mean that at all Jan." It took a few tugs to get them face to face again. "I just want to make sure you've thought this through. Are you sure it's what you really want to do?"

"Yes, baby." Janice snuggled in close enough that her breath washed over Lisa's face. "It really is."

Predictably, this new idea caused more raised eyebrows from

Lisa's friends during their rare but "we must do this more often" lunch at a local café. While giving her coffee order to the waiter, she overheard Van mutter to Steph, "I'll believe it when she actually gets her butt into the classroom and keeps it there."

"I have no idea why I even bother with you two." Furious, Lisa gathered her wallet and keys and tossed a note onto the table for her share of the bill. "You've done nothing but pick on Janice since day one. If you can't accept her as a part of my life, then I don't want you as part of my life either."

"Look Lisa, we're sorry." Steph followed Lisa outside, catching her arm. "You're right. We have been hard on Janice. But we just don't want you to get hurt."

Shaking Steph's hand away, Lisa spun to face her. "*You're* the ones hurting me. How do you think it feels when everyone hates your girlfriend?"

"We don't *hate* her." Steph tossed a wayward strand of auburn hair from her eyes. "We just don't think she's very . . . mature."

The flash of anger that crossed Lisa's face was enough to send Steph backtracking. "I mean—"

"I know exactly what you mean." Lisa spat. "Janice will prove all of you wrong. She's really serious about this course and I happen to think she'll stick with it." She twisted the key in the lock and tugged the door of her utility open. "If you don't believe me, call in a couple of months when classes are in session." Lisa climbed in, slammed the door, and left Steph in the wake of her Ute's exhaust.

Steph hadn't waited that long. She phoned the following evening to invite them both to the cinema. The altercation at the café was never mentioned, and Van or Steph no longer made disparaging remarks about Janice.

Lisa, for her part, let the matter drop. But she couldn't help gloating when Janice rolled home three weeks into term with a B+ for her first assignment. Lisa conveniently forgot to mention she practically had to chain Janice to the kitchen table to make sure the assignment got done.

"I don't need this crap." Janice shoved her texts away. "I can already design gardens. I've proved it."

"Well then, just go out and do it." Lisa had the sinking feeling she was going to have to explain another fleeting fancy to her friends. "There are heaps of landscapers around. Go and get one of them to hire you. I'm sure they'd love an enthusiastic trainee to boss around."

Janice was struck dumb for a moment, then pulled her texts back over the table.

In the weeks since, Lisa had not had to use her "study or work" tack very often. All in all, Janice appeared motivated, of late even spending a few evenings at the college library. The past weekend though, Janice had not even looked at a book. Lisa was partly to blame—she wanted to make full use of the last few days of swimming weather by spending them lolling on the beach. But she was met with a look of disbelief when she suggested Janice get down to work on Sunday night.

"I'm tired and sunburned." Janice aimed an accusing finger in the direction of the filling bathtub. "And you want me to burn the midnight oil while you soak in a cool bath?"

Chagrined, Lisa gave in. "Point taken. You've got the night off."

Soon discovering tepid water does not produce a mass of bubbles, even with vigorous hand stirring, Lisa stepped into a measly smattering of suds and beckoned Janice to follow. "But if I come home tomorrow afternoon and don't find at least a draft of your next assignment to proofread—"

"Yes, mum," Janice giggled, playfully splashing water over Lisa's head and shoulders. "I'll be good."

Janice's promise had been reiterated that very morning. "How am I supposed to get anything done with you hanging around and nagging?" She pushed Lisa to the front door. "Go have fun with Van. I'll see you later."

Now, standing in the doorway to her kitchen and seeing the activity taking place on the table, Lisa realized Janice had counted on her arriving home much later than this.

She gripped tightly onto the wooden doorframe for support. "Janice!!"

Despite the blare of the music from the lounge room, both Janice and her friend froze. Janice visibly paled when she lifted her head and turned around. "Oh fuck!"

Lisa watched for the millisecond it took the pair to separate. Then, shaking, she turned and fled to the lounge room, unable to witness the frantic scramble for clothes.

Resisting the urge to kick the life out of the stereo, Lisa pressed the eject button on the CD component. Doubly shocked by the sudden silence, she sank into the nearest chair, not knowing what to do or even where to rest her eyes.

It may have been a few seconds, or it could have been an hour—Lisa had lost all concept of time—when Janice entered the lounge room. She was at least fully clothed when she knelt in front of Lisa.

"Lisa?"

A shadow in the doorway momentarily captured Lisa's attention. The figure of a woman. It just as quickly disappeared. Lisa lowered her gaze to a point just above Janice's eyebrows. "I think your girlfriend is leaving," she said flatly.

"She's not my girlfriend," Janice whispered. "Look Lisa, I'm sorry. Things just sort of got out of hand."

"You'd better catch her. Maybe she can give you a lift."

Janice clasped Lisa's hand but then reconsidered, pulling away. "I love you Lisa. I really do. You have to believe me."

"Just go Janice. I want to be alone for a while."

"But Lisa!"

In the brief moment Lisa met Janice's eyes, she recognized her panic. It was the panic of an open wallet closing. She repeated, "Please. Just go."

Lisa didn't move in the time it took Janice to ferry armloads of clothes and a bulging carryall from the bedroom to the entry hall. Finally, the front door opened and closed. Lisa vaguely heard an engine start and a car reverse from the driveway. Then the house descended into silence.

Numb, Lisa pulled her mobile from her pocket and dialed. "Joel. It's me."

"Hey girlfriend." Joel's friendly tone boomed over the line. "That must have been some shopping spree. I was expecting you here over an hour ago. The brass edgings still haven't arrived though, so I haven't made a start on the stairs yet."

Lisa balked. She must have been sitting longer than she thought. "Sorry. I had to drop something off at home."

Joel chuckled. "I knew you couldn't resist once you got in there. You're the original terra cotta queen." Getting no response he asked, "Are you okay Leese? You sound kind of strange."

"I'm okay." Lisa clutched tightly onto the phone as tears sprang to her eyes. She swallowed hard, forcing them down. "But something's come up and I won't be able to make it to work today. I'll see you tomorrow." Not wishing to further explain her absence, Lisa turned the phone off and returned it to her pocket. Then she stared at the two red dots that blinked between the hour and minute on the stereo system's time display.

Somehow compelled into movement by the blinking dots, Lisa retreated to the street, reversed her Ute into the now empty driveway and opened both the front and rear doors of the garage, giving access to the backyard. Forming a ramp with a couple of planks she kept on the Ute's tray for just such a purpose, she carefully loaded the packing frame and its contents onto a trolley and wheeled them to solid ground.

The pneumatic wheels of the trolley made easy work of the cobbled pathway that wended its way to the rear of the property. Still, Lisa made the journey to the arbor slowly. Getting her amphora to its new home unscathed was the only thing she would allow on her mind.

She found a crowbar in her toolshed, and one by one popped the nails and set aside pieces of the packing. Once free of its confines, Lisa twisted and turned the amphora into position on its stand, stepping back after each movement to survey the results. For its size, it wasn't that heavy. The glazed terra cotta was reasonably fine and intricately carved at its broadest section with an aquatic theme. Satisfied, she sat cross-legged in front of the arbor.

In its new locale, the amphora looked just as she had imagined. Lisa sat there, watching its changing patterns of light and shadow as the sun made a slow westward decline. Briefly, she wondered if Janice had seen her purchase before stepping into the blue Commodore. She was sure she would have liked it if she had.

Chapter Two

Cathy alternated her glance from the clock on the far wall of her office to the empty seat on the other side of her desk. Only once a fortnight did she ask Toni to be at work at eight thirty instead of nine, and only once in a blue moon did Toni make it to their meetings on time. Today was obviously not one of those occasions. The minute hand shifted again, signaling that Cathy's senior employee was now fourteen minutes late.

Irritated, Cathy logged onto her computer and was in the midst of composing a scathing e-mail directed to the subject of her irritation when the office door flew open. In bustled Toni, looking flustered, but as usual, impeccably dressed in her standard warm weather office attire—tailored linen slacks and a short-sleeved blouse. Today's blouse was a sea green raw silk that accentuated the green of her eyes and darkened the olive tones of her Macedonian heritage. Cathy noticed she'd had her short, black hair trimmed since leaving the office yesterday, but didn't comment on it as she watched Toni struggle to remove a sheaf of papers from her briefcase.

"You should take a leaf from Julie's book," Cathy said, referring to the graduate accountant she had taken on at the beginning of the year. "She's been here since before eight."

Toni looked up from the papers she was still tidying. "She's just new and out to impress the boss."

"Something you should try one day." Cathy held up a hand as Toni opened her mouth to retort. "I'll give you until lunchtime to think up another of your colorful excuses for being late. But for now, we've got a pile of items to discuss in the *thirty-four* minutes before my first appointment."

Cathy launched into the agenda. Half an hour later they had discussed the usual round of business associated with Cathy's growing accountancy practice: new clients and their needs, overdue accounts, how Julie was progressing and which clients she could be assigned, the problem they were having with the recently upgraded spreadsheet software. Only one item remained on Cathy's list. But that would have to wait until later, maybe over lunch.

She glanced to her open diary. "Are you free around one?"

"I'm not sure. I'll e-mail you when I've checked my schedule."

Cathy hid a smile as Toni swept out of the office. Toni had a fascination with gadgets and insisted on using them at every available opportunity. Cathy walked to the front reception to greet her first appointment, confident it would be a good few minutes before her computer blipped a response about lunch. It would take that long for Toni to remember the sequence for accessing the diary schedule on her newly acquired Palm Pilot. Sure enough, even as she settled back behind her desk, her computer remained silent.

Later, seated opposite Toni at a table for two, Cathy asked lightly, "So have you thought of anything yet?"

"Sorry?" Toni glanced from her menu. Despite being a regular at the restaurant located just a few minutes walk from their office, she always dissected it fully before deciding on her usual Caesar salad.

"Today's lateus arrivalus." Cathy poured wine into Toni's glass. "What whopper do you have for me this time?"

"Oh that!" The menu was forgotten and Toni's eyes widened. "You wouldn't believe what happened to me this morning."

Cathy took an appreciative sip of her wine. "Try me."

"Well I was doing my ironing when there was a knock on the door. This was before seven mind you," Toni added, obviously assuming from Cathy's derisive snort that a late lie-in was being blamed. She took a quick sip from her glass. "Mmm, this is really good. Nice choice Cathy." Some of the contents slopped over the side as she illustrated her words with expansive hand movements. "Anyhow, I opened the door to find this woman on my doorstep. Before I could say anything she demanded to know if I had a mottled brown cat."

"Virgil," Cathy interjected, well acquainted with Toni's part-Burmese, part-moggie female cat with a male name.

Toni nodded, pausing to take another sip, this time a large one. "Of course I said yes, but before I could ask why, this . . . this *mad* woman starts yammering on about doves and a broken pot and hadn't I heard about protecting wildlife and cat bells and curfews and so on."

"But you *do* curfew Virgil don't you?"

"From sunset to when I get up in the morning."

"Which is *well* after sunrise." Cathy couldn't resist having a dig. Toni's answering glare was well worth it. "So does this woman live on your street?"

"If she does, I've never seen her."

Cathy frowned. Virgil wasn't one to wander. She had no reason to; Toni pandered to her every wish. "She must live close. Maybe she's seen Virgil hanging around in your front garden and mistook her for the cat that, what did you say, tipped over a pot?"

"I don't know." Toni shrugged her shoulders and shivered. "I tell you, she was bonkers. Said her piece then stalked off down the driveway. Poor Virg, I was so worried she might come back I locked her up in the house for the day. Which is just as well I suppose." One final gulp and her wine glass was empty. "Since she wriggled her way out of another collar sometime last night. That was why I was late by the way. I searched high and low for it and my clothes got crumpled so I had to iron them again."

Figuring Toni had probably bought a new iron and wanted to play with it, Cathy stifled a laugh and bent back over her menu.

A waiter who had been hovering in the background appeared as soon as their conversation lulled. Toni did a final skim of the menu and ordered a Caesar salad. Cathy nodded to make it two. She watched Toni pour herself another wine but shook her head when the bottle was tipped toward her own glass.

"Are you sure?" Toni protested. "I'll be on my ear if I finish the rest of this by myself."

"Don't worry. I'll have another one later."

"Oh dear." Toni placed her glass well into the middle of the table. "You have that look that says you have something you want to discuss."

"Stop fretting Toni." Cathy slid the glass back toward her. "It's nothing bad. Just an idea I've been tossing around for awhile."

It was late afternoon when Toni had the next break in her schedule. Armed with a coffee from the tiny staff room she had affectionately dubbed the "broom closet," she settled into her office chair and pulled out the Yellow Pages. There were literally hundreds of listings for tilers. How was she supposed to sort the wheat from the chaff?

Toni decided on a proximity strategy—figuring the closer the work was to the tilers' place of business, the more likely they would be to give a reasonable quote—and flipped from the general listing to the locality guide. There must have been a premium for inclusion in this section, because the suburb by suburb listing was much briefer. Only two businesses were listed for their immediate suburb. Toni duly scribbled down the details. Now, how to find a third tiler?

A scientific approach seemed best. Toni closed her eyes, waved her hand above the phone book and let it drop. Toni studied the details where her finger had landed, pleased with her choice. There was no address listed, but both the business name—Hawthorn Tiling—and the phone number prefix indicated she would be supporting her home suburb.

Toni pulled the telephone closer, hefting a square of tile in one hand as she dialed with the other. The tile was one of six samples Cathy pulled from her briefcase as she suggested an overhaul of the offices was in order. *Announced* was actually a better word than suggested; the paint swatches and catalogues of office furniture that magically "appeared" on the restaurant table indicated the overhaul was a foregone conclusion. Still, Cathy was the owner of the practice; she could spend her money on whatever she liked. That Cathy included her in the decision at all left Toni rather pleased.

By the end of lunch Toni had offered to do the ringing around to get quotes.

"Are you sure you don't mind?" Cathy had said, signaling to the waiter that they were ready for the bill. "I can do it tonight."

"I'm sure," Toni had said, gathering up the samples, placing her favorite on top of the pile and mentally noting that Cathy had no apparent plans for the evening. "I've got some spare time this afternoon and anyway, have you ever heard of a tradesman who takes business calls on a Friday evening?"

It seemed no tradesmen took calls on a Friday afternoon either. The mobiles she reached announced the phone was either turned off or out of range of the network. When trying their standard numbers, answering machines prompted her to leave a message. Annoyed she was unable to set up the appointments then and there, Toni left both her office and mobile numbers on the machines.

The lack of direct contact with any of the tilers meant her task was completed much quicker than expected. One more thing to do before getting down to what she was employed for. Toni's fingers flew over the computer keyboard. She trailed the mouse pointer so it hovered over the send button on the screen, hesitated a moment, then clicked.

It took only minutes for an answering e-mail to appear. Smiling broadly, Toni deleted the message and opened up a spreadsheet she had been working on earlier. She hurried through the rest of the afternoon, making a mental list of the items to pick up for dinner. Top of the list was a bottle of the wine Cathy had selected at lunch.

Dusk had well descended by the time Lisa and Joel arrived at Lisa's place. Joel had picked her up for work that morning so for the second time that day she enjoyed the luxury of sitting back and enjoying the ride. The motion of the Ute on the return journey lulled Lisa into near sleep, and it was with some reluctance she slid out of the cab. Tired, she dragged herself across the lawn and up the three steps that opened out to the front veranda of her home.

Home for Lisa was a cottage-style construction circa 1940, in a leafy suburb just a stone's throw from the city of Perth. It had been a rundown shack when she first moved in as a tenant nearly eleven years ago, the worst house on a well-established street. Its low rent—not the dream of living rustically—was the only reason Lisa signed onto the lease. One couldn't be choosy when trying to survive on unemployment benefits.

Initially Lisa had railed at the thought of joining an ever-increasing unemployment line; it was not a destiny she had ever entertained for herself. But it was surprisingly easy to slip into the routine of sleeping late, halfheartedly scanning the classifieds section of the newspaper and tossing it aside because nothing really appealed. And, as like is attracted to like, it didn't take long to collect a circle of friends equally lacking in ambition. Three others soon moved in and shared the rent, which came to almost nothing when divided between four, and so began six months of partying with the remainder of their welfare.

It was a scum-encrusted shower recess that proved to be her savior. In a fit of self loathing for the direction her life had taken,

Lisa donned her oldest shorts and T-shirt, grabbed a brush and pail and took to the bathroom with a bottle of bleach. Three hours later the bathroom was almost unrecognizable, but her frantic cleaning effort had stripped away a large portion of the already well-worn grouting. Added to this was a section of tiles that were dangerously close to falling off the wall.

Remembering the magazine-style program she had seen on television only a few nights previously—one where the ever cheerful presenters made building a house from the ground up look like child's play—Lisa decided there and then she was going to re-grout the bathroom.

With mission decided, she headed for the nearest hardware store. Four days later she proudly displayed her handiwork to her housemates, who not only "oohed" and "aahed" over the finished product, but heaved a collective sigh of relief as they could finally shower without having to take themselves and their cleaning accoutrements to the nearest pal's place.

Still bloated on her success, Lisa tossed and turned in bed that night. In the morning she took an inordinately long shower, much of which was spent admiring her lovely white grouting, and aimed her mustard yellow Datsun 120Y to the employment office to check the job boards.

After a month of scanning the papers, sending off resumes and daily journeys to the employment office, fortune turned in her favor. Lisa plucked the job card off the board, waited her turn and fidgeted nervously as the counselor—Judy, according to her nametag—made a call to the prospective employer.

Her spirits plummeted as she listened to Judy's half of the conversation. It seemed the fact she was twenty and female was not scoring her any points.

Judy placed the handset onto the base with a definitive click and a skyward roll of her eyes. But Lisa's sagging shoulders straightened as she watched Judy begin scribbling details from the computer screen. The paper slid across the desk. "This is the address. You have an interview with Mr. Giavanni at three today."

Beaming, Lisa thrust the paper into her back pocket, already mentally sorting through her wardrobe. *What on earth does one wear to an interview for a tiler's off-sider?*

Mr. Giavanni—George Giavanni to be precise—was a fiftyish Italian who lived in and ran his business from a white columned, red brick house that screamed of the old country.

George made it quite clear he had not been in the market for a female off-sider and proceeded to make the job sound as awful as possible. When Lisa nodded somewhat truthfully that she was an early riser (she *had* been prior to her days of sloth), that she didn't mind getting dirty, having rough hands, or working long hours, sometimes even on weekends, George returned to his "female equals lack of strength" theme.

"One must be tough." He flexed his own muscles, then felt Lisa's upper arm. "Got no time for weaklings eh." He must have found something promising in Lisa's arm as he kept on talking. "I give fair pay for a fair day's work." He then named a figure Lisa didn't see as very fair at all, but she nodded assent.

George lifted his large frame from his chair. The interview was obviously over. "I give you one-week trial. Be here six thirty tomorrow eh. If you late, you leave, no second chances."

So began a four-and-a-half year stint with George. Lisa still looked fondly over those years and acutely remembered the first two weeks, when she dropped into bed almost as soon as she got home, too tired to even eat. The mornings were worse. Every muscle ached, her feet were sore and blistered from the steel-capped boots she was wearing in, and true to George's promise, her hands were rough as sandpaper.

Over time Lisa's body became used to the rigors of its new regimen, and within a few months she felt stronger and fitter than ever before. She took as much pride in her work as her mentor, watching as George measured and cut, spaced and leveled, all the time guiding Lisa in the intricacies of his craft. George seemed, in his gruff kind of manner, to be pleased with her progress. So pleased that after three months he offered her a full apprenticeship. Lisa's time was then divided between work and technical college. Her wage was still paltry, but most of it managed to see its way into her bank account.

Two months before her apprenticeship finished, Lisa received a letter from the owners of the house she was renting. It announced they were putting the house on the market when her current lease expired—only six weeks down the track. Lisa was dismayed at this unexpected hiccup in her otherwise ordered life. She now lived on her own (her "friends" had moved out one by one, thinking she had turned into a "drag"). After receiving the letter, her mood at work the next day was sullen.

"Whaddya go wasting money on rent for eh?" George slapped a huge hand across her shoulder when he finally wrestled the truth from her. "You should be buying by now."

Lisa had to grin. How George had changed his tune in the last few years. His refrain had long been, "Whaddya want to work for? A young woman like you should find a man, get married, have da kids." Only after numerous attempts to pair her off with an endless succession of his nephews and cousins of his nephews failed, had George conceded Lisa was not interested in changing her single status. Or rather, her single lesbian status.

When she eventually told George she was a lesbian, he didn't speak to her for three days. He finally came around, although now he kept quiet about his numerous nieces and cousins of nieces.

Lisa adopted her "George" voice, "I can'ta afford to buya da house. I not got enough for da deposit."

George just grunted and went back to his work. Lisa went back to cutting tiles. They were both silent for the remainder of the afternoon.

George eyeballed Lisa from across the tray of his truck as they were packing up for the day. "This house you rent, you would like to buy eh?"

Lisa hesitated. Buying had not occurred to her as an option.

Renting a shack was one thing, owning one was quite another. It could promise to be a veritable money pit. "Well, it needs a lot of work—plumbing, floorboards, probably even electrical."

George rubbed thumb and forefinger together in the universal sign of money. "So, it should go cheap eh?"

"Well, yes."

"Anda the land, it in a good suburb eh?"

"Well, yes."

"You get da good price, I loan you da deposit."

On the day Lisa became part of the mortgage set she and George cracked open a few beers in her backyard. Also present were her parents, who had refused to give Lisa a cent as she whiled her time away on unemployment benefits, but couldn't wait to help as soon as she decided to help herself. They had been mortified at the thought of Lisa borrowing money from her boss, duly presenting her with a check for the deposit and waving away the promise to pay it back.

As dusk descended on the little group, Lisa saw her ramshackle cottage in a new light—an owner's light. And she loved it.

Eight years on, Lisa loved her cottage even more. She poured every available cent into either the mortgage or ongoing improvements and renovations. Major construction, plumbing and electrical work were left to the experts, while Lisa undertook the grunt work and the decorator touches. To save money, Lisa spent nearly every spare moment doing whatever work she could herself. Exterior and interior walls were stripped and painted, floorboards were lifted, replaced, sanded and polished, the living room fireplace had been restored, and the chimney was now used for smoke extraction as opposed to a comfy nesting place for a family of rock doves. To Lisa's delight, and probably aided by the seed she now tossed every morning, the said family took up residence in the Lilly Pilly tree in her backyard.

The kitchen had also undergone a major overhaul and of course, the toilet, laundry, and bathroom all benefited from new tiling. With the gardens now complete, Lisa's home had gone from being the worst on the street to—in her opinion—one of the best.

However, keeping her home in its now pristine condition was not currently high on Lisa's list of priorities. "Will you stop worrying and just get inside," Lisa said as she pushed Joel through the front door, stopping his third boot-stamping on the doormat midstream. "One bit of sand is not going to hurt."

"My, my, we've changed our tune. Haven't we, *Miss Take Your Shoes Off Before Entering*." Joel gravely studied the polished floorboards that graced the hallway of Lisa's home.

"I don't really care at the moment." It had already gone past seven and Lisa was tired. She and Joel had put in just under twelve hours of solid work, finishing a job which should have been completed the day prior. Lisa clomped down the hallway ahead of Joel. "How does a beer sound?"

"Like magic." Joel tiptoed down the hallway in his work boots, picking a set of security keys from the key rack next to the kitchen entrance. "It's a nice night. Let's sit in the yard."

Once outside, Lisa passed Joel a long-necked stubbie. In the time it took her to retrieve their beers and make a quick trip to the bathroom, Joel had unlocked the French doors, turned on the patio lights, and settled into one of two patio chairs he had moved onto the lawn. The citronella candle that usually sat on the patio table now flickered on the grass between the chairs. "Here you go. Make yourself at home won't you."

"Thanks. I will." Joel's tan face was dark in the dim light, making his teeth seem all the whiter when he grinned. He clinked his stubbie to Lisa's. "Here's to making it through another day."

"Hear, hear." Lisa leaned back in her chair, comfortable in the ensuing silence. Joel was not one who felt constant conversation necessary. It was one reason they managed to work together and also maintain their long-standing friendship.

Lisa and Joel first met during her apprenticeship studies. She was the only woman in their class, and Joel was the only person who made an effort to talk to her in the first few weeks; really talk, that is, without the leers and suggestive winks that the other, considerably younger, students made toward her.

Joel was also a late starter in the apprenticeship stakes—he was nineteen to her twenty years—and had draped his arm around her shoulder as they walked to their cars one afternoon. "They'll stop soon enough," he had said of the other students' behavior. "Once they realize what they're missing out on with me."

Lisa stopped walking only for a second. She'd had an inkling Joel was gay. "We may as well get them jealous then huh?" Lisa wrapped her arm around Joel's waist and they laughed all the way to their cars, fully aware of the small group of classmates following a short distance behind.

That day cemented their friendship. It also marked the end of the winks and leers; the other students assumed Lisa and Joel were getting it together. None of the apprentices, even those who looked too brawny to be only sixteen or seventeen years old, were willing to take on Joel's six-foot, broad-shouldered frame.

So when the time came for Lisa to branch out on her own, Joel was her first choice as a business partner. As in the purchase of her house, Lisa's decision to start her own business was not pre-planned. It was a result of George's decision to retire the following year, a couple of heart murmurs signaling it may be time to slow down.

Lisa didn't have the funds to buy him out. He had been in the business too long and built up too much goodwill for her to afford such a venture. She didn't want to be on-sold to the next owner; neither was there any guarantee the new owner would want to take her on at all.

"It could take quite a while before we bring in enough to turn a profit," Lisa warned as they spent yet another night doing their sums.

"Baloney." Joel's enthusiasm was not to be diminished. "With your brawn and my beauty we can't go wrong."

Lisa threw her writing pad at him. "Well, you'd better get your best frock ready for when we meet with the bank manager."

Joel threw the pad back. "And you'd better get your suit dry-cleaned and your jackboots polished."

The banks turned them down. Lisa's mortgage and Joel's poor

savings record worked against them. Six months later they tried again, this time with Lisa's parents as guarantors to her half of the loan and Joel with a nearing healthy bank account. Again there was a celebration in Lisa's backyard, this time with champagne and a framed Certificate of Business Registration that was passed among the little group.

Business was predictably slow at first. They walked a fine line between quoting low enough to get work and too low to make a profit. But their reputation as skilled and reliable tradespeople steadily grew, and with that, so did their profit margin. Joel had a creative flair that served them well with the resurgence in popularity of mosaics. His designs won many a client over, and they were able to charge a premium for the intricate work.

For Lisa's part, her lack of artistic ability was compensated for by her business acumen. Drawing from two years spent studying for her unfinished commerce degree, Lisa did all the business accounts, including their tax lodgments. She was also the initial point of contact for their clients, after she and Joel decided two residential and two mobile telephone numbers would be confusing to potential customers. To date, despite the occasional flare of temper, the business arrangement suited them both, as did their friendship. Lisa considered herself more than lucky for the consistency Joel provided in her life. Lovers came and went, but Joel was always there, often silent in his support, but always there.

Joel had been her rock the past few days, instinctively knowing when it was time to listen, time to give an opinion, or time to simply leave Lisa alone with her thoughts. He also seemed to know that tonight Lisa was in the need of some company. He offered to share a drink or six and crash overnight in the spare bedroom.

"But Friday's your big night out," Lisa argued. Joel rarely missed a chance to check out the talent at the one and only gay nightclub in Perth. Besides, she was reluctant to accept Joel's offer, it coming in the wake of Van and Steph's, which she had refused.

"Come out with me then," Joel countered, knowing Lisa, an infrequent visitor to the club at the best of times, was in no condition to face it at the moment, especially since the chance of Janice's presence there was high. With a glare from Lisa, Joel closed the subject. "It's settled then. Girlfriend, we're going to get sloshed tonight."

In keeping with his promise, Joel pried Lisa's almost empty stubbie from her hand. "Time for a refill."

"I'll get it." Lisa stood clumsily, a full day's work on nothing but a banana for breakfast sending one beer straight to her head. "I have to check the messages anyway."

"Let them wait." Joel called, content to let Lisa do the fridge run. "The world won't come crashing down if you leave them until tomorrow."

When Lisa returned with the beers, Joel was gone.

"Joel?"

"Over here." His answer coming from the rear of the garden, Lisa picked her way down the cobbled path. She found him on his haunches, examining the remains of her amphora. Not completely smashed, it lay in six or so pieces. "We could put this back together you know," he said.

He just nodded when Lisa said she'd rather not. "It's such as shame though," Joel said, fingering the carving on one of the pieces. He glanced up to the fence line. "Damn cat."

"Oh well, that's life, I suppose. I should have known it was too fragile to put in the garden."

Over the course of the day Lisa had become increasingly embarrassed about her reaction to the breakage. Another visit from Janice begging to take her back, followed by another sleepless night, found her with a fractured temper in the morning. So although the cat was a regular visitor to her yard, Lisa saw red when she spied it lying in readiness for her doves' daily feed. An unexpected squirt from the garden hose sent the cat fleeing for the fence, but in its fright it clipped a curved foot of her amphora stand. Lisa watched as the amphora began to wobble. Too far away to save it, she could only watch as its wobble gained momentum and it toppled. From its regular arrivals and departures, Lisa knew the cat lived in the house across the lane at the rear of her property. Still flaming, she marched around the block, said her piece to the dumbstruck woman who answered to her banging, marched back home again, and drove mad all the way to work.

"Oh come on Leese, stop blaming yourself for everything that happens. Had I been you I wouldn't have stopped at an ear bashing, I'd have demanded she pay for the damage."

"But even though I knew it was her cat, I didn't exactly have any proof," Lisa argued. "By the time I got there it was probably back inside, looking the picture of innocence."

"You want proof?" said Joel, who was still peering at the remains of the amphora. He reached to pick something from its upturned stand, then handed Lisa a red collar with a gold nametag. "Here's your proof."

"Oh no! Maybe," Lisa turned the tag over, holding it close to her face to read the name in the poor light, "Virgil hurt himself." Lisa popped the collar in her shirt pocket. "I should go and see if he's okay."

"Hold on a second girlfriend." Joel caught her by the arm. "For one, it's nearly eight. For two, if you went off half-cocked this morning like you said you did, I don't think Virgil's mum will be too receptive to another visit."

"But—"

"And for three, you're already a bit wobbly and you stink of beer."

"Thanks very much." Lisa shook herself free of Joel's grip. "And I love you too."

Lisa was adamant—she wanted to check on Virgil's welfare. "How would you like it if your collar was ripped from your neck?" she asked Joel. They locked up the house and set off around the block.

Giggling like a couple of schoolgirls and shushing each other every few steps, they crept down the old cobbled lane that divided the lines of houses. The lane was unlit. Both stumbled more than once as they had not thought to bring a torch.

"Can you see anything?" Joel whispered.

"Hang on a sec." Lisa adjusted her position on Joel's shoulders. "Move to the left a bit, there's a shrub blocking my view."

Clinging to the pointed jarrah pickets that comprised the fence, Lisa pulled herself a bit higher. "There's a light on. It looks like there's a sitting room at the back."

"I don't care about the architecture," Joel hissed from below. "Can you see Virgil?"

Lisa scanned the room as best she could. Only one of the two windows had the curtains open, so her view was restricted. "No. Hang on—" A mottled lump appeared on the back of an armchair. "I can see him."

"Well is he alright?"

"I think so." Lisa watched Virgil lift a leg to lick his nether regions. "His neck movement certainly seems okay."

"Good." Joel shifted his weight. "Can we go now? You're not exactly good for *my* neck movement."

"Better make it quick." Lisa's heart thumped as the woman she had bawled out appeared in the room, gave Virgil a scratch behind the ear, then frowned in her direction. "I think we've been seen."

"Bullshit. If the lights are on they can't see us." Nevertheless, Joel made quick work of dropping to his knees so Lisa could climb down.

They crept along the fence line, breaking into a run when the back door of Virgil's house creaked open. Once home they decided it was better to stay indoors for at least a little while, just in case Virgil's mum decided to investigate any farther than her back door.

Cathy knocked, then waited for what seemed an inordinately long time for footfalls on the other side of the door.

"Who is it?"

Surprised at the request to identify herself—surely Toni hadn't forgotten the invite for dinner—Cathy said simply, "It's me."

The door opened and Toni practically threw herself into a hug. "Cathy. It's you."

"It was last time I looked." Cathy laughed, pushing Toni to arm's length. Seeing the worry on her face, she sobered. "What's wrong?"

The door was quickly closed, but not before Toni had glanced from side to side, then down her driveway. "I think there's someone hanging around out the back."

"Oh." Cathy mouthed, in keeping with Toni's whispering. In the four years of their acquaintance, she had become well aware of her dramatics, her brilliant excuses for constantly arriving late to work testament to her penchant for exaggeration. "Maybe it was the mystery pot-tipping cat."

"I'm being serious here." Toni's eyes pleaded. "I was in the back room with Virgil when I thought I heard something. I peeked outside to check and I'm sure I heard people running down the lane."

Cathy took a long hard look at her friend. Toni was no shrinking violet, yet she seemed genuinely shaken. She tried for the obvious. "It was probably only a couple of kids, Toni."

Toni flew a withering look. "Yeah, and maybe it was a couple of axe-wielding murderers."

Cathy sighed, "And maybe not." She pulled Toni toward the kitchen. "Are all your doors and windows locked?"

"Shit yes."

"Well, there's nothing to worry about then." Cathy plopped into one of the chairs surrounding the large table that dominated Toni's kitchen. "What's for dinner?"

Momentarily forgetting her fear, Toni swelled and said, "Pizza."

"Let me guess." Cathy tried as hard as she could to keep a straight face. "You bought yourself a pizza maker."

"Not just *any* pizza maker. This is the best on the market. It's got—" Toni trailed away, a look of complete incomprehension on her face. "What are you laughing at?"

Later, after a meal of Toni's "pizza with everything," Cathy said, "I reckon this is an evening worth remembering. Good wine, great food, and not a soul within shouting distance."

"Don't forget the outstanding company."

"Of course," Cathy grinned, confident in her teasing. Toni was much brighter than before, her fears abated. And her new pizza maker—actually it was more of a mini pizza oven—providing results that surpassed any takeout. "Virgil has been a pleasure."

"As usual," Toni smiled sweetly, not biting, and said, "Now, how about dessert?"

"I couldn't." Cathy patted her tummy. "I couldn't fit another thing in."

"You sure? I'm thinking apple pie with double cream."

"Oh, God," Cathy laughed. "Did you buy yourself a pie maker too?"

"No." Toni shook her head gravely. "I'm talking *real* apple pie."

"Oh." The reply was just as grave. "Sara Lee."

Toni nodded. "Sara Lee." She took Cathy's plate and headed to the kitchen.

An hour later, Toni and Cathy lay flat on the floor. Toni had undone the button on her jeans. Cathy had pulled her T-shirt from her 501s. They were both clutching at their stomachs.

"I'm going to have to roll home you know."

"I'm going to be sick."

"I can't believe we ate the whole thing."

"You had most of it."

"Bullshit." Cathy couldn't help but notice the slight shifts Toni had made across the carpet. Barely discernible by themselves, their sum left them less than a few inches apart. "I saw you take that extra large slice when you thought I wasn't looking."

"I fed most of it to Virgil." Toni shifted again, this time to lie on her side, head propped by her hand. Her eyes moved quickly down the length of Cathy's body then settled on the ball of fur that sat at her feet licking its paws. "I don't think she'll be up to any mischief tonight."

Also moving to rest on her hand and watch Toni's much-loved companion, Cathy took advantage of the time to weigh her options. She knew Toni had a crush on her. Never mind the comments by Sue, her outspoken receptionist, when she scheduled their meetings ("Toni will *really* look forward to that,") every fiber of Cathy's being picked up on the vibes. Her plan was just to ignore it. Like every crush, it would eventually go away.

The trouble at the moment was Toni looked so damned attractive. Hell, she was an attractive woman. In Cathy's eyes it had never been an issue, just a fact. Cathy shifted, the weight of a full belly bringing her back to reality. Toni was a valued workmate and friend. That was a lot to lose for the sake of . . .

"Hey," Toni's voice was soft as it broke through Cathy's thoughts. "What's on your mind?"

"You," Cathy said without thinking, immediately feeling color spread up her neck, to her cheeks.

"That makes two of us." Toni's smile was as soft as her voice. Her hand reached to Cathy's face, a single finger tracing a line across her lips. Realizing what she had just said, a bubble of laughter emerged. "I meant, I was thinking of you."

"I know what you meant." Cathy laughed too, trying to rise above the tide of feeling sweeping through her veins. It was hard. For a long, long time she had worn the badge of celibacy. Now her awakening body was forming a mind of its own. Again she fought, "Do you know what we're doing?"

"Yes." Toni's eyes closed as she leaned closer.

"I don't want to ruin our friendship," Cathy said in between kisses—kisses that left her gasping for breath, but coming back for more.

"I don't want—" she tried again, but words escaped her as Toni slid a hand beneath Cathy's T-shirt and found a small, firm breast. "Please . . . Toni," Cathy gave in to her fight, pulling Toni on top of her, leaving Toni's lips only to wrench Toni's shirt from her shoulders.

Unbelievably, in the red heat that swam before her eyes, a picture of the two of them at work entered Cathy's vision. They were arguing. Toni was late again. Only this time there was no cheerful resolution, just a combined lover's sulk that sent them both to their respective corners.

Cathy's hands dropped from Toni's waist and fell to the floor. Still laboring for breath she forced out, "I'm sorry. I can't."

"Cathy?" Toni's flushed face was bewildered, as fingers that had found a taut nipple continued to stroke, tempting more life. They dropped away with Cathy's shake of her head. "Cathy. What's wrong?"

"This is." Looking directly into the eyes of the woman who had become her best friend, Cathy pleaded for some understanding. Finding none, instead feeling the rush of lust again shiver through her bones, she wriggled, sending a non-verbal message for Toni to move away.

Like the vision that had brought such a sudden halt to the proceedings, Toni and Cathy retreated to lean against opposite ends of the couch. Without a word, both readjusted their clothing. The tension was palpable.

Now unable to meet Toni's eyes, Cathy concentrated on picking at the cat hair that had drifted onto her clothes. She wished she could take back the last few minutes, either that or flee. Knowing an exit now would only make Toni feel even worse, she struggled to find something to say. A repeated "I'm sorry" was the best she could come up with.

From the edge of her peripheral vision, Cathy saw Toni give a slight nod as she stood, raking fingers through her hair. "Umm, would you like a coffee or something?"

The opportunity to flee came and went. "That would be nice. Thank you."

Toni headed for the kitchen, leaving Cathy to fidget in the sitting room. Virgil, who had witnessed the whole affair, fixed Cathy with a glare and padded behind her companion.

Cathy was not alone with her thoughts for long. Finding Toni's retreat was not to fill her bowl with more goodies, Virgil loped back into the room. She sniffed the hand held out to her but found it empty and thus uninteresting. Adeptly sidestepping Cathy's effort to pick her up, she jumped onto the stereo cabinet and disappeared behind the curtain. Almost immediately came the sound of claws scratching against the wooden window frame.

Jumping up to investigate, Cathy called, "Toni. Come here—quickly!"

Toni was at Cathy's side just in time to see a tail disappear through a loose flap of fly wire. "Why, the little shit."

"I nearly had her but she slipped out of my hands." Cathy turned an accusing eye to Toni. "I thought you said you'd locked all the doors and windows."

"I did." Toni pulled the curtain aside to reveal a window lock, bolt intact. "It's locked just a few inches open."

"Oh." Chiding herself for snapping, Cathy reached to finger the flap of fly wire. It had a covering of fur at its jagged edges. "It looks like Virgil has been using this as an escape route for a while."

"The little shit." Toni repeated. "She knows I keep that curtain drawn." She again raked her hair, a nervous habit. "What are we going to do?"

"I suppose we'll have to go and find her before she goes round annoying any more of your psychotic neighbors."

Toni paled. "Shit. It probably *was* Virgil this morning then."

"Looks like it. Come on. She may still be in the backyard." Toni hesitated, so Cathy pushed her toward the door. "Don't worry. I'll scare away any would-be robbers," Cathy said.

Once outside and with eyes finally adjusting to the darkness, Cathy pointed to the rear of the garden. "Look, there she is."

They crept toward the motionless shadow. The shadow came to life when they were less than a few feet away.

"Shit, shit, shit." Toni's vocabulary was still suffering its downward slide, this time as she witnessed Virgil disappear over the back fence. She plopped down on the grass. "Now we'll never find her."

"Don't be such a pessimist." Hands on hips, Cathy stood over her friend. "Get off your bum, and get me the key to the gate."

A look of horror crossed Toni's face. "No way."

Two minutes later they stood in the lane, scanning in both directions.

"Now what?" Toni whispered, their scan fruitless.

Cathy shrugged her shoulders. "You'll have to try calling for her."

"Like that's going to work." The sarcasm in Toni's voice was evident, yet she called in increasing whispers, "Virgil. Virgil."

A rustle followed by Virgil's unmistakable meow came from across the fence. "She's in that yard." Cathy pointed to the house immediately behind Toni's. "Keep calling."

"Virgil." Toni called a bit louder, "Virgil!"

"Trust you to have the most stubborn cat in the world." Virgil evidently thought this some new, fun game of hide and seek. Not another meow or rustle came. Cathy searched the fence for any sign of a hidden gate similar to Toni's. There wasn't. "Here, give me a leg up."

"You can't go jumping people's fences," Toni protested. "What if someone's out there? I can see the patio lights are on."

"This isn't shotgun country Toni. If someone comes I'll just explain we're trying to get your cat back."

"She'll run." Toni now looked thoroughly miserable. "Please Cathy, don't do it."

"Fine," Cathy said, folding her arms. Virgil wasn't the only frustrating member of their little household. "We'll just stand in the lane all night and wait until she's good and ready to come home."

Toni sighed audibly but cupped her hands.

"I really hate you sometimes," she whispered as Cathy placed a foot in the handhold and hoisted herself up.

Cathy grinned as she peered over the fence. She and Toni were already getting back to their normal banter. Hopefully they could put the incident in the house behind them. "Yeah, I really hate you sometimes, too."

Cathy lifted herself further, dangling one leg over the fence, holding herself upright as best she could. A pair of green eyes shone from under a bush directly in her new line of sight. "Virgil," she coaxed, making little clicking sounds with her tongue. "Virgil. Come here."

Echoes of movement from an unseen section of the garden silenced her. It was a human movement, the sound of irregular footsteps. And they were approaching. Despite her previous assurances to Toni, a knot of fear turned in Cathy's stomach. Ignoring it, she attempted a confident voice. Not much more than a squeak emerged. "It's okay. We're just looking for our cat."

Cathy held her breath as the footsteps stopped, then resumed, along with a female voice. "It wouldn't happen to be a cat called Virgil would it?"

The voice that came was so deeply ingrained in Cathy's mind she recognized it immediately, even with the slur that indicated its owner was quite drunk. *Lisa?* Cathy's brain made the connection but couldn't relay the information to her mouth. Speechless, she could only hang her jaw as a familiar figure emerged from the shadows, dangling a cat collar in one hand, clutching a stubbie of beer in the other.

Toni had not lost her voice. A desperate whisper hurtled upward, "Shit. I know that voice. That's the woman from this morning."

The next seconds degenerated into chaos. Virgil, having finally decided it was time to make her move, bolted from her hidey hole and sprang onto the fence. Lisa, already unsteady on her feet, lurched in fright and dropped her stubbie onto the pavement. The crash of glass was too much for Toni. She let out a shriek that so startled Cathy she fell from her precarious position on the fence into Lisa's garden.

"My God, are you okay?" Lisa rushed to her aid, her heavy work boots crunching on the remains of the stubbie.

Cathy nodded, shaken by her fall, which luckily had been into the relative softness of a lavender bush. She was more shaken by the golden haired woman who was pulling her to her feet. Once upright, Cathy dusted herself off and waited for the moment of recognition. It took a few seconds as Lisa blinked, either from disbelief, or to get her bloodshot eyes into focus. "Cathy?"

"Uh-huh." A million questions were running through her mind, but only the most inane emerged. "How are you?"

Frantic scuffling from the other side of the fence stopped Cathy from finding out. Two sets of eyes focused on the third set that appeared; Toni's knuckles were white from the effort of holding her head above the fence line. "You two *know* each other?"

Cathy nodded, bristling under the scrutiny coming from both sides of the fence. "I take it you two know each other."

In turn, Lisa and Toni nodded, Lisa holding up the collar she still grasped. "I think this belongs to you."

Cathy took it, Toni unable to let go of the fence. "Thank you."

"Listen," Lisa turned from Cathy to regard Toni. "I'm sorry about going off this morning. I kind of had a bad start to the day."

"I'm sorry about my cat." Toni smiled sheepishly. "She's a regular Harry Houdini." With Lisa's blank expression, Toni explained the broken fly screen and their subsequent chase. She trailed off toward the end of her tale, giving a pained groan, and saying, "My fingers are going to break off any second." Toni's head disappeared and her feet thumped to the ground. "Anyway—"

Lisa interrupted Toni's attempt to finish her story, asking, "Would you like to come over for a drink? Fresh supplies should be arriving any minute."

Cathy, already on the right side of the fence, took the invitation to include herself. She desperately wanted to stay—eleven years of questions she had—but, being Toni's guest for the evening, she waited for her to accept or refuse.

Her hopes were dashed.

"Thanks, but we really should see if Virgil has found her way inside."

Lisa appeared ambivalent, giving a slight shrug of her shoulders. "Okay." She turned back to Cathy. "Would you like a lift up or shall I get a ladder?"

"A lift would be good." Doubly disappointed at Lisa's attitude,

Cathy felt tears sting her eyes. Ashamed, she faced the fence, pretending she was just as eager to be gone. Her foot found Lisa's hands and she readied herself for the strain of the upward pull. *My God, she's strong, much stronger than I remember,* Cathy thought to herself as she found her head above the fence with little effort on her part. With a leg on either side of the fence, Cathy looked down. "Thank you Lisa." Her answer was a backward wave, Lisa already weaving unsteadily back toward the house.

Predictably, given Toni's irrepressible curiosity about anything to do with Cathy's life, Toni was full of questions even before Cathy's feet hit the ground. Her first question was asked in an ever so light tone. "How do you know her?"

"We went to Uni together."

"Oh." Toni hesitated. "You never mentioned her."

"She dropped out." Cathy swung open the gate and ushered Toni through. "We lost contact." Cathy closed and bolted the gate, then pressed the key into Toni's hand. "Do you think I could possibly have that cup of coffee now?"

Chapter Three

In the twilight between sleep and wakefulness shadows of noise entered Lisa's head then disappeared. As consciousness emerged, the noise became more constant, a drilling buzz. Lisa threw a pillow over her head but still the noise broke through. Rolling out of bed, she donned a long T-shirt and dragged herself into the kitchen.

"Hey girlfriend." Joel grinned and held out a glass of juice. In front of him were the remains of countless oranges.

"Hey yourself." Accepting the glass, Lisa threw a filthy look at the electric juicer Joel was putting through its paces, and retreated to her bedroom. Miserable in her hangover, she climbed back into bed, carefully sipped from her glass and cursed the day man invented beer and electric gadgets that made a lot of noise for little result.

A short nap, a long shower and a thorough teeth clean left Lisa feeling slightly more human. She returned to the kitchen, this time to find Joel searching through the fridge. After halfhearted apologies for the lack of produce (how was she expected to go shopping after the week she'd been through?) they fired up Joel's utility and headed for the local McDonald's.

"Now this is living." Joel scrunched up the wrapper of his bacon-and-egg muffin and reached for his sausage-and-egg muffin.

"Hum." Lisa idly toyed with her hash brown. Having not eaten since breakfast the previous day, she had salivated at the backlighted menu board and ordered profusely. Once the food was in front of her, she hadn't the stomach for it. Except for the piping hot coffee. She left Joel at their dinky little booth and headed to the counter for a refill.

"Are you sure you don't want these?" Joel's eyes focused on Lisa's untouched muffin and second hash brown.

"I'm sure." Lisa slid her tray across the table, content with her renewed coffee. "Although, I have no idea where you put it all."

"A growing man needs his energy." Joel made quick work of the hash brown and proceeded to demolish his third muffin. "And after last night—"

"Please." Lisa hid behind her coffee. When Joel had taken so long to make an emergency trip to the bottle shop located just a block away she knew he had finally gotten talking to the "cute" young attendant who worked there. Knowing Joel, and since his return had been long after the bottle shop's closing time, Lisa assumed his time away had not only been spent chatting. "Spare me the details."

Joel took the hint and kept quiet, concentrating on the remainder of Lisa's breakfast. When finished, he peeked into Lisa's Styrofoam cup. "I'm ready to go when you are."

"I'm done." Nearly half her coffee remained, but the dull thump in Lisa's temples was a sure sign she needed water and not caffeine. The hash brown she managed to swallow was not sitting well in her stomach either. When was she going to learn that day-after cravings for greasy food did not mean it wise to indulge? Still, it was so long since she had consumed enough alcohol to warrant a hangover, she had forgotten the day-after drill. Lisa edged carefully from the booth. "Let's go."

The roads were busy with Saturday shopper traffic. Joel thrummed his fingers on the steering wheel as he waited to pull out of the car park. "Any big plans for the rest of the day?"

"Nope. I've got that quote to do in North Perth at eleven, then nothing much." Sighing, Lisa added, "Although I suppose I should clean the glass from the path and see what I can salvage of the lavender bush."

With the smirk that crept over Joel's face Lisa asked warily, "And just what do you find so amusing?"

Joel chuckled. "Think about it. Here you are pleasantly single again and when a low-flying lesbian decides to drop out of the sky, it's one you've already had."

"You can be such a bitch sometimes Joel." The mental image his description conjured made Lisa smile in spite of herself. "And for your information I am not pleasantly single. I'm here under duress."

Joel gave Lisa a pointed look, and quickly diverted his attention back to the road. "If it's under duress, then take the sniveling little snot back."

"I didn't mean it that way," Lisa said quietly, her suspicions confirmed, Joel finally voicing what he thought of Janice. She always assumed he liked her, to an extent. At least he hadn't been as openly blatant as Van and Steph and . . . everyone else. "So it's true then, everyone saw through Janice except stupid old me."

"You're not stupid Lisa." Joel patted her fondly on the knee. "You just fell for the wrong person. You never know, the right one may be just around the corner."

"Not for me. You know the rule. Strike three and you're out." Lisa folded her arms and said resolutely, "That's it. I've had it with women."

Laughing, Joel turned off the highway to the side street that led to Lisa's home. "Honey, the day you turn hetero will be the day the Pope turns Protestant."

"Not hetero silly, even I'm not that desperate." Lisa held up her hand, placing thumb over bent little finger in the Girl Guide style. "From this day forward I'm the Emily Dickinson of the tiling trade."

"The what?"

"Don't worry about it." Lisa leaned into the headrest and closed her eyes. She quickly flew them back open, the motion of the Ute sending her head spinning. "Joel," she ventured, "You'd better hurry. I think I'm going to throw up."

Once back in Lisa's kitchen, Joel placed a tall glass of water on the table. "Here you are. Drink it slow."

"Thanks." Lisa gave a wan smile and followed Joel's instructions. They had just made it home in time, Joel running ahead to unlock the front door, then standing aside for Lisa to make the dash to the bathroom. Her stomach was now completely empty but the thump in her temples had gotten worse. She needed some Panadol.

Joel preempted her request, pushing two headache tablets from their blister pack into her hand.

"Joel," Lisa swallowed the tablets quickly. "I take back all the nasty things I ever said about you. You're the best."

"Hold that thought." Joel grinned. "The phone rang while you were head down and bum up, so I took the liberty of answering it."

"So?" This was nothing unusual. They took and made calls on each other's phones all the time.

"It was Janice."

"Oh." Lisa immediately sat up straighter. "What did she say?"

"Nothing much. I think she was a bit taken aback when I said you were unavailable."

"You didn't tell her why did you?" To date Lisa had managed to maintain her dignity with Janice, not budging an inch in spite of the pleadings and protestations on each of her visits. She didn't want Janice to know she had turned into a blithering, drunken mess in her absence.

"What do you take me for?" Joel grinned again. "I said I didn't think it was wise to disturb you since you had a big night."

"Good one Joel," Lisa said sarcastically. "Like Janice is going to believe I've suddenly turned into the party animal."

"I didn't say you had a party. I said one of your old girlfriends unexpectedly *dropped in* for a visit!"

Lisa groaned and placed her hands over her face. "What did she say to that?"

"Well, she went dead silent for a moment. Then she said to tell you she'd called. Then she hung up."

"Serves her right." Joel added when Lisa stared at him through parted fingers. "Let her stew for a while. See what it feels like."

"Well, thanks . . . I think."

"Anytime." Joel seemed quite pleased with his twisting of the truth, not realizing it would probably spur Janice into another visit, if only to check out what Lisa was up to. He pulled a piece of paper from his shirt pocket. "I also checked your messages. Steph called, and so did Dee. Both asked you to ring them back sometime soon. Your mum called to remind you about dinner on Wednesday. There was also another request for a quote—"

"Shit!" That reminded Lisa she had one to do this morning. She checked a bare wrist, her watch still on the bedside table. "What's the time?"

"Ten thirty."

Lisa relaxed. It would take no more than ten minutes to drive to North Perth. "Good. I still have time to make myself look human."

"Girlfriend," Joel sniffed. "The way you look at the moment it would take an army of cosmetologists to make you look even half human. I think you'd better give me the address."

"Are you sure?" Feeling a bit guilty, but not enough to turn down the offer, she pointed toward the hall stand. "It's in my diary."

Lisa studied her messages while Joel sought the address. It seemed he had already called the person requesting a quote, a person by the name of Tony according to the nearly undecipherable scribble. Along with the name was an address, a day and a time.

Lisa wafted the paper at Joel on his return. "As a return favor I'll let you do this one too." She lowered her voice as far as she could, "Tony. Monday. Six p.m. Be there."

Joel poked his tongue out and snatched the paper away. "Toni with an *i* dummy. It's a girl." He opened Lisa's diary to the coming Monday, passing it and the message sheet to her. "I think we should both go to this one. See the address? From the directions she gave it's in one of the posh office blocks on the South Perth foreshore." Joel rubbed his thumb and forefinger together. "Could be big bucks for the right people."

"The right people being us." Lisa grinned. "Okay. It's a deal."

Later, standing in the driveway next to Joel's utility, Lisa stood on her tiptoes to plant a kiss on Joel's cheek. "Thanks for doing this for me."

"You just take care of yourself Leese." Lisa was caught in a bear hug before Joel arranged his long legs behind the wheel. "I'll see you Monday. On site around seven?"

"By the way," Joel poked his head out of the window as he set the gears into reverse. "When I cleared the machine I also wiped the main message."

Lisa's eyebrows shot up. "Why?"

"It's about time it was changed don't you think?" With that, Joel blew her a kiss and drove away.

On her return indoors Lisa found Joel had not only wiped the message, but replaced it with his own. Deciding to keep it in case one day the machine had a chew, Lisa ejected the tape and inserted the spare one she kept in her stationery box. There was already a message on the spare, but on listening she realized it had her old mobile number mentioned. *Bloody hell*. Lisa erased it with a stab of the appropriate button. She wasn't in the mood for this. She hated speaking into the damn machine at the best of times.

Four times Lisa attempted to record a new message, but gave up, her voice sounding more and more flat each time she gave it a test run. The message Joel erased had been Janice's, recorded in happier times and done at Lisa's request, thinking such a bubbly tone would be a good first point of contact for any prospective customers. The garden aside, it was also the last tangible remnant Lisa had of her presence. Janice had moved in with only her clothes, a portable stereo and a hair dryer. Apart from a few odds and ends, all had been removed over the course of the last few days. Lisa had to admit, it was she who insisted on their removal, Janice reluctant as she obviously thought there was a chance they could renew their relationship. That was never going to happen, but the finality of wiping Janice's voice from her machine had been a task Lisa had avoided.

"Damn you Joel," Lisa muttered under her breath. The tears she had also managed to avoid finally spilled over as she replaced the tape with Joel's.

Lisa locked the doors and drew the curtains. In the relative darkness, her private mourning began. She realized she had forgotten to turn the answering machine back on when the phone rang too long, but she ignored it, letting it ring out. The early afternoon knock on her front door was also left unanswered. Finally, exhausted from so many tears, she fell asleep on the rug beside the couch.

Chapter Four

"Great Rod. I'll see you midday on Wednesday." Toni placed the handset onto its cradle, fired up her Palm Pilot and transferred the details scribbled on her blotter. That was the last of the tilers slotted in for their quotes. One due soon, in around ten minutes according to her desk clock, one at five on Tuesday and the third at lunchtime on Wednesday. Toni would have preferred to get them all in together and hence explain the requirements only once. But the picture Cathy had drawn of a bunch of blokes crawling around on the floor sparring with their tape measures convinced Toni separate appointments was the way to go, not to mention a lot less messy.

Toni swung her office chair around to face the expanse of window. Outside, the water of the Swan River glinted silver on blue, a cloudless sky providing the perfect backdrop to the city skyline on the opposite bank. There was plenty Toni could be working on, but with the limited time available there was little point starting on anything new. She rested her heels on the low bookcase that housed her volumes of the Master Tax Guide and an array of other accounting and financial texts, clasped her hands behind her head, and admired the view.

God I love this city. Without fail, this was Toni's first thought whenever she stole more than a fleeting glance from her window. She still remembered catching her breath when Cathy presented her with the office on her first day.

Attempts at acting blasé were all in vain. Her voice couldn't disguise her excitement. "This is *my* office?" She vaguely noticed the huge desk, the executive style chair and the other furniture, but she couldn't keep her eyes off the view from the window.

"Yes." Obviously pleased with Toni's reaction, Cathy nodded toward the desk, "Your computer's due to arrive in around an hour, but I'm sure you can find something to do until then."

Toni had. In between looking out of the window and counting her blessings, she managed to unpack a few books and her favorite coffee mug. It was only the arrival of the computer that captured her attention. Cathy had arranged a technician to assemble it, install the software and hook it up to the office network. Toni made him a cup of coffee then chatted away as she took over. She let him do the network connection, but was fully conversant with the procedure by the time he was finished. As she waited with him for the lift to arrive, he suggested she consider changing careers to work in the computer field. Toni gave him a derisive look, bade him farewell and rushed back to her office and her view.

Cathy caught Toni staring out of the window at the end of her first day, her head appearing around the slightly ajar office door. "How are you settling in?"

"Great." Toni swung around, a blush spreading. "I'm sorry. I just can't get over how pretty the city looks from here."

"It's quite something isn't it?" Cathy sat in one of the chairs meant for Toni's clients. "When I first took up the premises I had my desk facing the window. I had to change it round the other way because I spent all my time daydreaming."

Toni found that hard to believe. From her two interviews with

Cathy she just didn't seem the daydreamer type. Daydreamers didn't have their own accountancy practice in swank office buildings, especially at Cathy's age. Toni figured her to be in her late twenties at the most, not much older than herself. A covert check during her second interview revealed no wedding ring, hence no rich husband. Unless, of course, she chose not to wear a ring. Hell, who cared? No matter how Cathy got to where she was, Toni was now part of it—as long as she could get her mind on the job. She smiled at her new boss. "I think tomorrow I'll draw the blinds."

On Friday afternoon, Toni was greeted with a knock on her office door. "Are you free for a drink to celebrate your first week?"

Toni nodded. A newcomer to Perth, her social calendar was not exactly brimming. "That would be great. Thanks." She followed Cathy and accepted the champagne flute that Sue, the receptionist, handed her.

It was quite late by the time Cathy and Toni took the lift to the underground car park. Sue was long gone, eager to get home to prepare for some "hot date" she had lined up. Following Sue's departure, Toni found the conversation flowed. They talked of business, of Toni's previous life in Melbourne, of trivialities. Toni drove home knowing she and Cathy would be more than just business associates.

True to her instincts, they were soon fast friends. Friday drinks became tradition, more often than not followed by dinner. They discovered a local restaurant they liked and made it a regular lunch venue. Cathy was a lively conversationalist, quick to laugh and a good listener. In stages, Toni related her whole life story without even realizing the conversation had turned to her in the first place.

"You should have been a psychologist," Toni complained after one such episode, her latest revelation including her utter devotion to an actress named Sigourney.

"Why's that?" Cathy swished the remains of her wine before downing it in one swallow.

"See. There you go again." Toni held up her hands in exasperation. "Why don't you tell me any of your dirty little secrets?"

Cathy laughed. "Maybe I don't have any, Toni." An almost

empty bottle was lifted from the ice bucket. "Would you like another or shall we progress to the lattes?"

"Come on." Toni was determined to find out at least one snippet. "*Everyone* has a little secret. What's yours?"

"Well," Cathy rested her arms on the table and leaned closer. "Did you ever watch *Seinfeld*?"

"Every episode." Toni too leaned forward, her mind sifting through all the possibilities. Given the numerous indiscretions of the cast, something deliciously bad was obviously about to be admitted. She slumped back in her chair when Cathy announced she was guilty of eating the muffin top and discarding the bottom. "Thanks so much for sharing," Toni said.

Despite four years as colleagues and friends, Toni still found Cathy somewhat a mystery, and reticent to reveal details of the life she led outside work. The insights Toni had into Cathy's personal life were few. She knew Cathy came from a wealthy family, her offices and home due in no small part to the sizeable trust her parents bestowed when she was twenty-one. She knew Cathy had a brother she adored but rarely saw since he lived in the Eastern states.

And she knew Cathy was a lesbian. That discovery was made over her second glass of wine on the second Friday night of drinks in Cathy's office. Sue had declined the offer of a refill.

"Sorry to deprive you of my company again ladies," she said as she shot a winning smile at both of them, "but nature calls."

Cathy smiled a goodbye as Toni bid farewell.

"One can't defy the call of nature can one?" Cathy said as Sue's figure disappeared.

"Not at all." Toni had agreed. "Who's the lucky guy?"

Cathy cocked her head to one side, giving Toni a quizzical glance. "It's not a guy Toni."

"Oh." Toni took a quick sip of her wine, her mind racing. Should she tell Cathy or not? Why not? She certainly didn't seem to raise an eyebrow with Sue. And it certainly would be much easier if she could be out at work. A quick thought to life without her newly acquired office and window made her hesitate, but only for a moment. Toni steeled her courage with one more sip. "Well that's good. There's two of us then."

"Better make that three." Cathy raised her glass. "Welcome to the family."

A relieved grin spread across Toni's face. She really had come to like her office and her window. The view would be even better now she didn't have the nasty business of having to remain in the closet during office hours.

Although Cathy had no qualms about announcing her orientation, she kept the details to herself. Over time Toni became more than idly curious, trying in vain to eke out information. She knew Cathy lived alone and wasn't involved with anyone, indeed hadn't been involved with anyone in the four years Toni had known her. That there had been lovers in the past was a piece of information Toni did manage to extract, but details were undisclosed.

"It's such a shame Virg," Toni had said one night, as she squatted on the floor watching Virgil gobble dinner. "Today I caught Cathy in her office just staring off into space. She looked so . . . so . . . melancholy." Toni carried on talking although Virgil was not paying the least bit of attention. "It's not fair you know, someone with her looks and personality shouldn't be alone."

Toni's observation was an objective one. She adored Cathy as a friend, respected her as a colleague. As far as anything else was concerned, it just never crossed her mind. That was, until January 26 of this year. Toni remembered the date. It was Australia Day, the day of the annual firework display over the city.

Their offices in a prime position to view the spectacular, Cathy held an annual Australia Day party for clients and partners. This year, the offices were full to bursting, Cathy's decision to promote the practice as tailored to women's needs filling an evident gap in the market. Toni was talking with one of her more long-standing clients when the first firework burst into the sky.

All conversation lulled. Toni, along with a sea of heads, turned her attention toward the window. Cathy was directly in Toni's line of vision. She was settled on the window ledge, one foot tucked under a thigh, head and shoulders resting against the reinforced steel frame. Toni's breath caught in her throat when Cathy leaned forward to catch something said by half of the couple seated next to her. Then Toni's heart was in her mouth as she watched Cathy's profile back-lit in subsequent bursts of colored light.

Toni took an involuntary step backward. The feeling had come completely out of the blue. The feeling was so unexpected, but so strong she couldn't shake it. It was as if she was seeing Cathy for the first time. Gone were her good-looking boss and best friend. In their place was a woman who took Toni's breath away. Sleek brown hair, long enough to brush the shoulders, framed a lightly tan face and accentuated the deep brown of her eyes. Cathy was a good few inches taller than Toni's five-foot-six frame, and her loose fitting silk shirt and pleated pants hinted at the slim figure they contained.

As if sensing the gaze that was upon her, Cathy had turned and caught Toni's eye just as the final firework streaked skyward. There was a huge bang followed by a chrysanthemum of red and gold that filled the window. Toni took this on the word of other revelers' descriptions because she didn't see it. Cathy's smile crowded her vision and warmed her blood. With an equally loud bang she realized she was in love. Or lust. Or something. Whatever it was, Toni needed the advice of her confidante.

"Oh Virg." Once home, Toni had reached to the far side of the couch and scooped up the limp ball that complained loudly at the interruption. "What am I to do?"

Virgil wriggled from the embrace, complained again, yawned widely and did a three-hundred-sixty degree turn on Toni's lap. Claws exposed, she kneaded mercilessly into linen clad legs, staring into Toni's eyes with defiance at the pain she was inflicting. Suddenly she stopped, did another complete turn and plopped down. She purred as Toni stroked her from the tip of her nose to the tip of her tail.

"Life's so simple for you isn't it Virg," Toni said softly as she continued to stroke absentmindedly. "Just eat, sleep and stalk imaginary prey." As if in agreement, Virgil's purr increased to a low rumble. "No worries about mortgages, working for a living, or falling for your boss." Virgil stretched out a paw so it rested on Toni's forearm. *Poor human* the gesture seemed to say. But Virgil continued to rumble away, uncaring of how Toni managed to bring in the gourmet goodies, as long as they kept coming.

"You're right," Toni told the now napping feline. "Cathy's been on her own for a long time. She's not going to fall at my feet just because I give her a sideways glance. I have to stay cool on this one."

Toni's first act of staying cool was to trip over her own feet and spill a cup of coffee over herself and the carpet in Cathy's office the very next working day. Her initial embarrassment was overtaken by both the burning sensation of the liquid and the burning sensation of Cathy's arm around her waist as she was shuffled off to the broom closet for a wipe down. That Cathy just tossed her a wet cloth mattered not. Her cleanup unsuccessful—the blouse was ruined—Toni spent the rest of the day in a spare linen shirt Cathy kept in the private bathroom adjoining her office. The shirt had yet to find its way back into Cathy's possession.

The next cool act was to send Cathy a huge bouquet of roses on Valentine's Day. Ordered through a florist miles away from both her home and work, Toni figured there was no way anyone would guess the flowers were from her. She cemented the fact by being too cowardly to include a card. Toni was at the reception when the flowers were delivered. She saw the look of surprise as Cathy was presented with them. She also heard Sue's snigger.

"What?" Toni feigned innocence.

"Nothing." Sue sniggered again, looking pointedly at Cathy's retreating figure, head bent as she smelled the roses' perfume. "I just think it's *so* romantic."

"What is?" Toni picked up a file and hugged it close to her chest.

"Unrequited love." Sue smiled sweetly and leaned over to answer the phone. Toni stalked off with her file. She'd show Sue unrequited love.

It seemed she would show Sue just that. For weeks on end Toni walked the halls of yearning, poking into the crevices of Cathy's veneer, trying to find the smallest response. Each night she went home, dissected the day and came up empty. Finally, after a particularly trying Friday, she gave up. Cathy's e-mail blipped on her screen, suggesting their usual drinks and dinner.

Toni bit on her bottom lip as she typed: *Sorry. I have plans for tonight.* She slumped in her chair as the message was whisked to the next office. Half hoping for a response, Toni left her computer on until the last moment. None came. She packed up her briefcase and headed for the lifts, wondering what on earth she was to do with herself for the evening. She decided to visit Perth's gay nightclub and get Cathy out of her system once and for all.

"Do you want to go downstairs and get a kebab or something?" The crew-cut baby-dyke with huge, brown eyes Toni had been yelling at for two hours, yelled into her ear at the nightclub.

Toni nodded and yelled back, "Let's go."

Arm in arm, they descended the stairs. The nightclub was packed and hot from the crush of bodies so the cool night air hit Toni with a blast. She wasn't usually the nightclub type and the echo of music rang in her ears. Once outside, she glanced around. Kebab bars were on either side of the nightclub entrance. "Which place would you prefer?"

Baby-dyke's expression didn't change, all her emotions were in those big brown eyes. "How about your place?"

The following Monday Toni swung into Cathy's office and plopped into a chair. "Hi Cathy. How was your weekend?"

"Not as good as yours by the looks of it." Cathy tidied the sheaf of papers she had been working on. She smiled as she leaned back in her seat. "What did you get up to?"

Toni's own smile faded as Cathy's grew. A night tumbling in the sheets with baby-dyke was instantly shadowed by a mere glance from her boss. Toni knew she was long gone. She lifted herself from her chair. "Nothing much."

Ignoring all the voices that screamed she was heading for a fall,

Toni turned just before reaching the door. "Would you like to do lunch today?"

"Sorry, I'm straight through with meetings until six." Cathy flipped a page on her diary. "But tomorrow's good for me. How about you?"

Toni shook her head, more disappointed than she hoped she was letting on.

"Well, Wednesday's out," Cathy flipped another page. "But Thursday I'm free from 11:30 until one."

"You know I don't think that far in advance." Toni frowned, trying to visualize her schedule. "I'll e-mail you when I've checked my diary."

Once in her office, Toni swiveled round and round in her chair. She couldn't go on like this, catching the crumbs Cathy threw in her direction. Toni immediately retracted that thought, knowing it wasn't fair. Cathy was just carrying on with their friendship as usual. She was no doubt clueless about Toni's depth of feelings toward her, even with the presence of Sue—the eyes, ears and mouthpiece of the practice.

Despite being free, Toni sent Cathy an e-mail saying she couldn't make it for lunch on Thursday. Cathy's reply came later in the day, acknowledging the decline and reminding Toni of their fortnightly meeting on Friday morning.

I will get through this, Toni thought to herself. She bent to her work, feeling utterly miserable by the time she packed up her briefcase for the day. On Tuesday, she again kept to her office, buzzing the reception for her appointments and avoiding the staff room. Wednesday she spent most of the morning with a string of clients and all of the afternoon with Julie, the graduate accountant.

Toni had been assigned as Julie's mentor, a task she hadn't particularly wanted at first, but now found she enjoyed. Julie was an earnest worker, eager to please and in a constant state of panic that she was doing something dreadfully wrong. Many times Toni had to reassure her that the little mistake she'd made was not going to send a client into bankruptcy, nor was it going to get the pants sued off the practice. This day, unable to find fault with the accounts presented to her, Toni outwardly praised Julie, and inwardly praised herself for being such a marvelous teacher. She left for home feeling quite a bit brighter.

On Thursday, Toni hid in a café over lunch, but braved the broom closet three times over the course of the day. Cathy caught her on her third visit.

"Howdy stranger," she reached above Toni's head to grab a mug from the overhead cupboard. "I was beginning to think you'd run away to join the circus."

"Who needs to when I work here?" Toni quipped, passing Cathy the almost empty carton of milk. She quickly stirred her coffee and headed for the comparatively wide open spaces of the passage, doing a heart check as she went. True to form, it was hammering in her chest.

Toni kicked her office door shut, her kick hard but not enough for a true slam. *You are a pathetic piece of work Antonia Ljanjovich*, she thought to herself. Mug set aside so she could do her office chair swivel without incurring third-degree burns, Toni continued her mental flagellation: *So you have a crush on your boss. You've had crushes before and you've survived. Like every other crush it will eventually go away. So pick your misery boots off the floor and just get on with it before you lose a good friend, not to mention a good job.*

Toni let her chair lose momentum until it came to a complete stop. Tomorrow morning it would be back to the old Toni.

Once decided, it was easier than Toni thought to maintain her composure. She was late to her meeting, and was suitably scolded by Cathy. But that was normal. She hesitated over going to lunch, giving the excuse of having to check her schedule, but she eventually accepted and had a good time. The Virgil/madwoman/broken pot episode helped somewhat. Having a tale to tell almost kept her mind off those "come drown in me" eyes. Then there was the refurbishment of the offices—the paint swatches and tiles provided a whole new distraction.

Then there was the dinner. *The dinner.* Toni squirmed in her chair, swamped by the warm sensation she got whenever she dared think about it. Which, since Friday, had been every few minutes. Toni had not planned any sort of seduction. True, she had imagined what it would be like, but she'd been imagining that for the past two months. And true, her position on the floor next to Cathy had not occurred purely by accident. But when Cathy met her gaze, any self-control Toni had mustered disappeared completely.

The memory of Cathy's lips was seared into her own—just by cupping her hands she could imagine Cathy's breasts filling them. Cathy's response had been so passionate and Toni's own need so strong, she was left literally aching when their embrace abruptly halted. The minutes that followed were pure torture, but there was little time to gather her scattered thoughts before Virgil led them on a merry chase.

In retrospect, Toni thought Virgil's disappearance fortuitous. Without the distraction, Cathy would probably have gone home as soon as she could down a coffee. As it happened, once back inside, Cathy stayed for another hour or so. She seemed tense, but then, so was Toni.

"I'll see you Monday okay?" Cathy had stood at the front door, hands deep inside her jeans pockets.

"Sure." Toni was going to suggest doing something together the next day, but decided against it. Cathy's words were echoing through her head: *I don't want to ruin our friendship.* If Cathy was struggling with that thought, Toni was not going to push. She mirrored Cathy's hands-in-pockets stance, mainly to avoid pulling her in for a goodnight kiss. "See you then."

Toni waited until the midnight blue BMW pulled out of the driveway, then closed the door and leaned up against it. Virgil padded in to rub against her calves. "I know Virgil. I know." She bent down to scoop her into her arms. "I have to stay cool."

Over the course of a mainly sleepless night, Toni replayed the evening over and over in her head. The woman who lived over the back lane gained significance with each rerun. Cathy had been her usual noncommittal self when asked about the association, so Toni imagined the worst—that Lisa was an old flame, come back to stick her nose in at exactly the wrong time.

By morning, Toni had dismissed this idea as ridiculous. Although Lisa did not seem the obnoxious, crazy woman she originally thought her to be, she just didn't seem Cathy's type. Not that she knew what Cathy's type was, but short honey blonde hair and legs that would put a racehorse to shame surely wasn't it. Cathy's revelation they had gone to Uni together was no big deal. They probably sat next to each other in some tutorial and lost contact as soon as Lisa dropped out of study. And that was years and years ago.

Nevertheless, around midmorning, Toni took a stroll around the block, wallet in hand, with the excuse of making amends for Virgil's damage, and the intent of finding out a bit more about Lisa and Cathy.

Toni ground to a halt as she rounded the corner. A few moments later she literally skipped home. Lisa was no threat. Her affectionate driveway farewell to either her hubby or boyfriend was all the proof she needed.

Later in the day, still curious about the life Cathy had led before she met her, Toni made another trip around the block. Disappointed there was no answer when she knocked, Toni left the punnet of petunias and twenty dollars she had brought as a peace offering on the doormat. Attached was a note, which read: *I'm sorry about breaking your pot. From Virgil.* She didn't bother making any more attempts at contact. Toni had never really gotten into the neighborly thing. Chats over the fence and begged cups of sugar weren't her style.

Toni shook thoughts of Lisa from her head and glanced at her watch. It was two minutes to six. Toni took one last appreciative glance at the Swan River and the ant-like procession of cars making their homeward dash over the Narrows Bridge. Still enveloped in her warm Cathy glow, she checked her diary for a name.

Joel.

Toni strolled out of her office to wait for his arrival. Her timing was perfect, the lift sounding its arrival as she entered the reception.

"Shut up Joel." Lisa held her diary and notepad close to her chest, trying hard to keep a straight face. Throughout the wait for the lift at the lobby and the subsequent ride to the top floor, they had been trying to figure out the meaning behind the business name displayed on the building's directory board, CBW and Co— Chartered Accountant. Joel had hinged onto the staid and boring accounting stereotype, his last effort said in his deepest voice, *Crusty, Bald and Withered.*

Lisa smiled in spite of herself. "You forget I was going to be one of those."

"Yeah, but you had the sense to escape before the dust settled permanently on your ledger."

"And look what I ended up with." Lisa brushed at Joel's sleeves as the lift ground to a halt. They had come straight from a job, both covered in tile dust and smudges of grouting. She gave herself a last dust down and shake of her hair, as well.

"I know," Joel grinned, primping his dark, curly locks. "A pure Adonis."

"Prima donna more like it." Lisa did a sweep of the new surrounds as the doors opened. Because of her trade, she instinctively looked at the flooring first. Banker maroon carpet greeted her eyes. As did a pair of expensive looking black pumps. They were attached to—Lisa had to let out a laugh as her gaze lifted further— her back lane neighbor. This was just too much of a coincidence. So Toni was her name. She hadn't caught it on either of their previous meetings. At least she assumed it was Toni, her stance indicating she was waiting for their arrival. Lisa stretched out a hand. "Hi. Toni? Joel spoke to you on Saturday. We're here to do a quote for some tiling."

In turn Toni held out a hand to them, her expression unable to disguise her similar surprise.

Lisa got the feeling she was being openly scrutinized.

She was, and not only by Toni. The receptionist was staring at her like she'd never seen a woman in work boots before. Swallowing her discomfort, Lisa switched to business mode and said, "If you'd like to show us the areas you want tiled, we can start measuring up. We can get the other details after we're finished."

"Other details?" Toni gave a blank look, then Lisa's meaning registered. "Oh, you mean the tile." She took the few steps to the reception desk, picked up the samples and passed them over. "The two on the top are our favorites. We haven't quite figured which one yet."

"That's okay." Lisa flipped through the samples, turning them over before handing them to Joel. They weren't whole tiles, but at least stickers on the reverse gave their specifications. "We can advise on what will best suit your needs."

"Okay," Lisa said. Toni watched in silence as Joel placed the samples back on the reception desk. "Point us in the right direction and we'll get started."

"Well, we want all this done." A sweep of Toni's arm encompassed the whole reception. She led them toward the hallway, pointing as she explained, "Then there's the passage and the staff room. There's also the bathroom, which is just past the staff room, and the photocopying room which is next to that."

"And the offices?" Joel piped up, after he and Lisa had stolen a peek when passing an open office door. They had caught each other's eye, Joel mouthing a silent, "Wow." Lisa could almost hear the flutter of banknotes in his head. "Do you want them tiled as well?"

Toni looked a bit sheepish. "We haven't quite decided on that yet either."

Lisa sighed, wishing people would put a bit more thought into their needs. She couldn't count the number of times they quoted on clients' half-baked ideas, only to have them decide on something altogether different further down the track. "That's okay. We can measure the whole lot then submit two quotes, one with the offices, one without."

"Thanks." Toni gave a nervous little cough and raked fingers through her hair. "I suppose I'll let you get down to it then."

"Okay." Lisa was also used to this reaction, the client torn between leaving them to do their job, or to tag behind and keep talking. She generally preferred to be left alone for the process, not comfortable with having someone peer over her shoulder. "Would you like us to do your office first?"

Toni nodded, ushering them toward the office they had peeked at before. Once there she still seemed unsure whether to stay or go. She stayed, eventually moving to the entrance to avoid tripping over the tape measure.

"One down." Joel flashed his most winning smile, letting the tape snap back into its casing with a satisfying metallic twang. "Two to go."

"Umm," Toni glanced a bit further down the hallway. "Could you do the office right at the end of the passage next? I just have to check Cathy hasn't a client in with her."

Lisa was busily scribbling figures onto her pad. The lead of her pencil snapped off as she jerked her head around. Coincidence could only go so far. Surely it couldn't be *the* Cathy. But then again, it could be. Cathy had been with Toni on Friday night. And this *was* an accountancy practice. Cathy had been studying to be an accountant. As had Lisa. Lisa plunged into her memories, retrieving snippets of a conversation from many years prior. Cathy had said, "Think how good it will be Lisa. Our very own practice—Cathy Braithwaite and Lisa Smith: accountants extraordinaire."

They had spent many hours over many months discussing that dream to the last detail. These offices bore little resemblance to the picture Lisa found in the recesses of her memory, but some telltale touches were there. The Chesterfield lounge in the waiting area, the framed Escher prints which lined the hallway, and the stylized silver typeface of the business name on the wall behind the reception desk. Finally the name of the practice made sense. CBW. *Crusty, Bald and Withered* it was not. The use of the W was technically incorrect, but it had to be Cathy Braithwaite.

Joel waved a hand in front of Lisa's face as she stared at Toni's back. "Come on girlfriend," he said in a low whisper which held the traces of a laugh. "We'll be here 'til midnight if you keep perving at the customers."

"Uh." Lisa snapped back to reality. She hurried to the end of the passage, footsteps quickening as she passed the middle office, although Toni had already entered and shut the door.

The young woman frowning at some papers nearly jumped out of her skin when Lisa knocked on the half open door.

"Sorry to startle you." Lisa wiped a hand over her brow, disconcerted to find she was sweating. "We're here to measure up for the tiling. Can you spare a few minutes or shall we come back later?"

"No that's okay." The woman, Julie according to the name plate that sat at the front of her desk, stood and shuffled the papers into a pile. She placed a heavy text on top of them. "Toni said you'd be coming sometime this evening. I'll just get out of your way."

"She's quite cute too." Joel offered the end of his tape measure to Lisa. "Looks like this is going to be a good job. For you anyway."

"Shut up Joel." Lisa scowled as she pulled the tape and held it to the far wall. If her suspicions were correct and Cathy was the owner of the practice, there was no way she was going to take on this job. "I told you. I'm through with women."

Once they had finished measuring Julie's office, Lisa and Joel aimed for the third and final office. The door was still closed. Instead, they busied themselves with the other rooms and the hallway.

"Reception next." Joel strode off, unaware of Lisa's unease.

"We're going to have to check if they want this moved or if we tile around it." Joel was on his knees, examining the base of the curved reception console. "It looks like it may be fixed to the floor."

"Uh-huh." Lisa made a note of it on her pad, having begged another pencil from Joel. Sue, the receptionist, hovered a few feet away, openly watching her every move. Lisa took a quick glance at her watch. Twenty past six. Wasn't it time for all good receptionists to be on their way home?

"That's it I think." Joel lifted his frame from the floor. "Just the one office left to do." He turned to Sue. "Is it okay if we go and knock?"

"I'll ring through for you." Coming within a hair's breadth of Lisa's back, Sue reached for the phone. "The tilers are ready to measure up your office." Returning the handset to its cradle, she turned back to Lisa, "They'll be out in a minute."

"Great." Lisa shuffled sideways, moving away from Sue and closer to Joel. A roll of her shoulders relieved some tension. Lisa didn't know why she was so tense. She had managed Cathy quite well on Friday night, albeit with quite a few beers under her belt. Although their next meeting was to be in the cold light of sobriety, their one-time relationship was old news, eleven years old news, and nothing to get all steamed up about.

Two figures rounded the corner and crossed the carpet. Lisa quickly realized Friday's alcohol dulled eyes had left her unprepared. In the poor light at the end of her garden Cathy had appeared just as the day Lisa left her, right down to the jeans and T-shirt. Now, it was evident the years had brought changes. The drop-dead gorgeous nineteen-year-old student had matured into a poised and elegant woman. She was still gorgeous. No, that wasn't the right word. Cathy was . . . beautiful. Adulthood had defined the contours of her face and a light tan, not the deep gold of her younger years, drew the gaze to the eyes. Dark brown, almost black, they still shone with intelligence. That melting quality was also still in them, only tinged with something Lisa couldn't define. Aware she was staring, Lisa reached to straighten the collar on her sports shirt, feeling quite unkempt in contrast to Cathy's tailored pants and jacket.

"Hi Joel. Hi Lisa." Cathy didn't register surprise at Lisa's presence. No doubt she had been forewarned by Toni. However Cathy's palm was noticeably damp when Lisa clasped her outstretched hand. "I'm sorry to have kept you waiting."

"No problem." Joel was blissfully unaware of the flock of butterflies crashing around in Lisa's stomach, his smile easy as he accepted Cathy's hand. "It will just take us a few minutes to measure your office. Then, if you have time, we can discuss tiles and the like."

Cathy nodded, "Toni mentioned we had not quite done our homework properly. We're new to this. Any advice you can offer would be most appreciated."

"I'll do the measuring." Lisa hoped her voice didn't sound pleading. "Save everyone waiting for us both." She didn't give Joel time to argue, plucking the tape from his hand and hurrying toward the passage.

Once in the safety of Cathy's office Lisa re-orientated herself through a series of deep breaths. *So she's still beautiful.* Breathe in. *What did you expect? An old hag?* Breathe out. *She's just a part of your past.* Breathe in. *Been there, done that. Over and done with. Finished.* Breathe out.

Once steady, she glanced around, giving a long and low whistle. So this was where Cathy spent a large chunk of her time. The office was a good size bigger than Toni's, which was a decent size. As in Toni's office, plate glass offered a commanding view of the river and city. But the desk was bigger, the filing cabinets and bookshelves were more extensive and a peek through a doorway located to one side revealed a private bathroom. Lisa examined a business card plucked from a holder on the edge of Cathy's desk. It was plain white with black text, a green stripe at the bottom and the letters CBW blind embossed in the top corner. Another touch from the blueprint. Placing the card back on the pile, Lisa wondered if a BMW, either dark blue or black, was lurking somewhere in the garage level of the building.

Speculations were forgotten as Lisa got to the task at hand. She quickly scribbled down the office dimensions then stood with pencil poised over her pad as she considered measuring the bathroom. Assuming it would also be part of the quote—if not it could be discarded—Lisa stepped in. Immediately a familiar scent struck her senses. Yves Saint Laurent's Rive Gauche. It had once been

Cathy's favorite perfume. Maybe it still was. In the reception Lisa had noticed its slight fragrance. In the confines of the bathroom it lingered more strongly, evidence of a recent application.

Get a grip on yourself woman, Lisa thought to herself. She hurried through her task, forcing down the memory of inhaling that scent from an up close and personal perspective. Her professionalism demanded she ensure accuracy, not that it really mattered. There was no way she could do this job. Not when a whiff of perfume could make her heart pound.

The entire office contingent was in the reception by the time Lisa and Joel took their leave a few minutes after seven.

The doors of the lift had hardly closed before Sue swooned over the reception desk, fanning her face with one hand. "Did you see the legs on her? She could leave her steel-caps under my bed any day."

Cathy feigned interest in the phone message pad. Sue continued. "And those eyes. I have never, ever seen blue like that."

"Nice butt too," said Julie.

Three heads turned in Julie's direction, who immediately went crimson. "Well she has." Still glowing, she tossed a few papers into her briefcase and clipped it shut.

Cathy had to laugh, more than a little pleased Julie was finally loosening up. Even if it was to participate in a mutual admiration session of her ex. "Toni," she scolded, "It didn't take you long to corrupt the innocent did it?"

"Just doing my job." Toni smiled smugly and blew on her knuckles. "Anyway, you lot will have to keep your raging hormones under control. Lisa bats for the other side."

Sue sighed audibly, "What a waste."

"And how would you know?" Cathy kept her voice as steady as she could—what *would* Toni know? But, to be fair, Cathy hadn't exactly been honest about her relationship with Lisa. Not that it was any of Toni's business.

"Yeah Toni." Sue wriggled her eyebrows, "How do you know? Did you make a pass at her in your office and she turned you down?"

Toni flashed Sue a glare that would strike down many with weaker constitutions. "I happen to be Lisa's back door neighbor—"

"Ooh. Lucky you," Sue interrupted. "Can I come and stay at your place for a while?"

"And I saw Lisa and Joel being very palsie-walsie."

"What?" Cathy felt a ball of lead form in her stomach. Toni must have it wrong. The Lisa she had known would never . . . "When?"

"On Saturday. Remember I told you I popped around to pay for the pot?"

Cathy nodded.

"Well, Lisa was saying goodbye to Joel in her front yard. And I tell you—they are more than just business partners."

The ball of lead in Cathy's stomach grew larger and heavier. No wonder Lisa seemed so uncomfortable on her return to the reception. She probably hadn't told Joel about her past and was sweating it out in case Cathy dropped a bombshell.

"It's getting late." Unable to control her anger at Toni for telling her something she just did not want to know, she snapped at Sue, "What the hell are you still doing here anyway?"

Startled at the change in tone, Sue took a moment to reply. "I was just taking a professional interest in the office improvements."

"Well I hope I don't see it appear as overtime on your timesheet." Nodding a goodbye to Julie and ignoring Toni completely, Cathy turned on her heel. The whole floor reverberated with the slam of her office door.

Cathy paced the floor, immediately regretful for not maintaining her composure. Toni would be knocking at any moment, wanting to know all the details. Sure enough, a hesitant tap came only seconds later.

Cathy slumped into her chair. "Come in Toni." She nodded to one of the chairs in front of her desk. "I suppose you're wondering what all that was about?"

Toni nodded, settling carefully, as if any sudden movement would spark another outburst.

Cathy played with the mouse, rolling it in small circles on its pad. She looked at it and not Toni as she blurted, "Lisa and I were lovers at University. We were together for nearly two years. Obviously we broke up, and no, I don't want to go into the details. Lisa dropped out and last Friday was the first time I've seen her since she left me. As you can imagine, finding she's left the family was a bit of a shock. I didn't handle it very well and I'm sorry."

Breathing hard from her revelation, Cathy lifted her gaze to see what reaction it had received. Toni sat stock still, her eyes wide. "I had no idea."

"It was a long time ago Toni." Cathy tried to convey an insignificance she didn't feel. "I never saw the need to tell you, or anyone, about it."

Toni shifted in her seat, mouth opening and closing a couple of times before she spoke. "People change Cathy. I knew a lot of women who had lesbian relationships while at Uni. It was almost the done thing, you know, to experiment. But once they graduated, they went with men."

"I know." Cathy could name a few in her own circle of friends who had done just that. "But I was so sure Lisa was, you know, born and bred."

"You certainly don't think it had anything to do with you, do you?"

"No," Cathy lied, turning her attention back to her mouse. She didn't know what to think. She'd been Lisa's first girlfriend. Maybe she'd also been her last. "Like I said, it was just a bit of a shock."

When Cathy lifted her eyes again she found Toni giving her careful consideration. "Would you like me to phone and say we've changed our minds about the tiling?"

The hopeful ring in Toni's suggestion was unmistakable, despite its shroud of concern. Once again Cathy kicked herself for having lost control on Friday night. She dearly loved the woman sitting across from her, but she just didn't feel *that* way about her. Canceling Lisa and Joel's quote at this stage would only give Toni the wrong impression—again. "I don't think that's necessary. If Lisa hasn't told Joel about her past, I doubt they'll submit a quote that we'd accept."

Toni nodded slowly. "I guess so."

"Come on." Cathy retrieved her briefcase from under the desk and rose from her seat. Toni could keep her talking for the next hour if she wasn't careful and Cathy wanted to be alone with her own thoughts. "Enough of the ancient history. It's getting late and I want to go home."

Finally out of an atmosphere which she felt was closing in on her, Lisa breathed a bit easier.

A bit.

She knew she was in for a serve from Joel. As predicted, instead of heading to his Ute parked across the street, he followed Lisa to hers. "Okay. Fess up."

"To what?" Lisa unlocked her door and climbed in. She pulled at the lock on the passenger door and Joel climbed in beside her.

"To why you would make a suggestion that probably lost us hundreds of dollars. The *noise factor*—really."

Lisa shrugged. "It was a fair comment. I imagine accountants need to make their clients feel at ease when talking about money. I happen to think having chairs scraping against a tiled floor would make them edgy. Carpet is a much better option for the offices."

"I still don't get it." Joel threw his hands up in despair. "You've never done anything like that before. Don't you want this job or something?"

"Not particularly," Lisa said in a small voice.

"Why not?"

"You can be so dim sometimes Joel. Cathy is the ex that dropped into my yard on Friday."

Joel shot Lisa a look of disbelief. "That was *the* Cathy?" He grinned and patted her on the shoulder. "Girlfriend, it's nice to know you *used* to have good taste." His expression sobered. "So what's the problem?"

"I don't want to work for her—or her girlfriend."

"Toni is Cathy's girlfriend?"

Lisa nodded. Joel really must have walked through the whole hour with his eyes closed. "Think about it Joel. Cathy and Toni work together all week. Then Cathy and Toni are together on the weekend. And Cathy included Toni in all the decisions about the tiling." To Lisa it was obvious, she had cut herself out of the blueprint but Cathy had continued with her plans, filling the gap with Toni. "Didn't you see the way Toni looked at Cathy? She's head over heels in love."

"Maybe so. But if anything, I'd say Cathy couldn't keep her eyes off you."

"She was probably trying to send a message not to mention I was her ex. Knowing Cathy she won't have told Toni."

"Ooh. Do I detect a hint of sarcasm?" Joel's eyes narrowed. "Methinks you're not over this woman."

"Get real Joel." Lisa turned the key in the ignition, to signal that this conversation was over. "I'm way over Cathy. She's ancient history."

"So what's the problem with doing the work then?"

"Joel," Lisa pleaded. "Can we please just drop it? For once in my life I don't want to do a job. It's not like we're starving for work."

"I wish you women would get your act together. I don't have a problem with the men I've been with."

"Just as well," Lisa quipped. She could tell Joel was pissed off and she wanted to lighten the tone. "You'd have to avoid half of Perth."

"Ha ha." The cab door opened, and Joel slid out. "I'll see you tomorrow."

"Bye." Lisa spoke to an already shut door. She reversed out of her parking space without checking the rearview mirror. A passing car honked and an angry fist shook at her. Lisa waved an apology, cursing herself for her stupidity. Wiping her mind clear, she concentrated on making the drive home safely.

Chapter Five

Lisa hid the bunch of roses she carried behind her back and pressed on the doorbell. She still held a key to the Federation-style house that had been her parents' home since they migrated from England when she was a toddler, but she only used it if no one was home when she visited.

The lead-lighted door opened and Lisa was immediately hit with the smell of her mum's home cooking. Her initial apprehension at keeping this dinner date faded as her stomach growled. "Here you go." Lisa said, theatrically sweeping the bouquet of roses into view.

"These are lovely darling." Her mum gave the light pink blooms an admiring once-over. "From your garden?"

"Of course." Lisa swelled with pride. The Queen Elizabeth roses planted in her front yard last autumn had lived up to their promise of being vigorous growers, rewarding Lisa for her regular dollops of sheep poo with a continual flush of flowers. "They're about this high now." Lisa indicated a height around her mum's shoulder level, just a dash below her own. "But they're getting a bit leggy. I'll have to get dad to show me how to prune them properly this winter."

Lisa got the reaction she wanted, her mum huffing. It was common knowledge she was the rose expert in the family, a good amount of her time spent lovingly tending the heritage rose beds she had established in her own front garden.

"Go say hello to your father." Lisa was bustled toward the kitchen. "I'll find a vase for these."

Instead of doing as she was told, Lisa followed her mum into the combined lounge and dining room. "Mum," she ventured, wanting to get her major news over and done with.

"Yes darling."

"Janice and I broke up."

"Oh honey." Her mum spun from her vase hunt in the antique dresser, and folded her arms around Lisa. "I'm sorry."

Later that evening, once dinner had been demolished and the dishes done, Lisa and her mum sat at the kitchen table, cups of tea at their elbows. Muffled television voices came from across the hall, her father having begged the excuse of wanting to watch the late news. Lisa knew his escape was imminent from the time he asked of Janice's welfare over dessert.

"Dad hasn't changed." Lisa toyed with the handle on her cup. "He still makes himself scarce when he senses another one of my crises."

"He just knows what we're like when we start nattering." A warm hand was placed over Lisa's. "Give him some credit Lisa. He loves you very much you know."

"I know." Lisa sighed, knowing he was still struggling with her lesbianism. She couldn't blame him really. Since her coming out at age seventeen he had witnessed more than a few tears. Her flights home to cry on her mother's shoulder must have reinforced his view that a lesbian lifestyle could not be a happy lifestyle. But her mother was right. She had to give him credit. He may wish the "friends" she brought home would one day turn out to be of the opposite sex—his hopes had certainly been raised by Joel's appearance—but not once did he make any of them feel less than welcome. He had especially taken a liking to Cathy. Lisa could still picture them bent over the Sunday paper, arguing over the cryptic crossword clues. She quickly shook the image from her head. Her mum was waiting for the lowdown on Janice, and here she was thinking about Cathy. Again.

"So Lisa," Her mum said as she gave a slight squeeze to her daughter's hand. "How are you coping?"

"Fine mum."

"Really?"

"Yes . . . no . . . not really." Lisa shuffled her feet under the table. "Actually, life sucks at the moment."

"Do you want to tell me what happened?" she asked gently.

"There's not much to tell. Things just didn't work out."

"Okay darling." Questions hung in the air, but remained unasked. "I have a bit of news you might be interested in. I bumped into Mrs. Parkinson while I was out shopping the other day."

"Really!" Mrs. Parkinson had been Lisa's accounting and economics teacher for her final two years of school. One of the few non-nun teachers at the private Catholic school Lisa had begrudgingly attended, Mrs. Parkinson was soon Lisa's favorite. Actually, she'd had a queen-sized crush on her. Her devotion spurred Lisa onto a straight-A average for accounting and economics. Not having any idea what she wanted to do with her working life, her grades had been the major influence in her decision to study commerce at University. "How is she? Is she still teaching?"

"Yes. She's still at your old school. She asked after you."

"That's nice. I always liked Mrs. Parkinson. God," Lisa said as she did a mental count, "It's been over thirteen years since I've seen her."

"I know. She mentioned the reunion of your class was coming

up in the next few months. And she said she hoped to see you there—since you missed the seven-year one."

"Mum!" Lisa gave a derisive snort, and not only because her classmates chose such unusual intervals for their reunions. Once one of the popular girls, Lisa's final months at school were lonely and virtually friendless. It had been her own fault really. She let her raging teenage hormones get the best of her. In addition to her crush on Mrs. Parkinson, she harbored a secret devotion to her best friend, Simone. During one Saturday night party, Simone was distraught after having been dumped by yet another boyfriend. A deep and meaningful arm-in-arm talk on the back step drove Lisa to distraction. Unable to control herself, she pressed her lips to Simone's. There was one glorious moment of response, then a horrified look.

"You're sick." Simone said, and left.

After that fateful night, Simone refused to take Lisa's calls and turned her back on Lisa before class on Monday. Although Simone wouldn't speak to her, she certainly spoke to everyone else. As Lisa's infamy grew, her base of friends diminished. No one wanted to be associated with the "fucking dyke". Unable to give her parents a reasonable excuse for wanting to change schools so late in the piece, Lisa bent to her work, willing the exams to come so she could make her escape. When the final day did arrive, she emptied her locker, walked out of the grounds, and never looked back. "You know why I don't go to those things."

"Thirteen years is a long time, love. I think you may find attitudes have changed quite a bit since then."

"Mum!" Lisa couldn't believe her mum actually considered she might go. "Even if attitudes have changed I will never forgive those bitches for the hell they put me through. As far as I'm concerned, the chapter is closed on my school life."

"Okay." Lisa's mum held her hand up in surrender.

"And don't think you can answer the invitation on my behalf and expect me to go," Lisa warned.

"I won't."

"Good." Annoyed at the trend that was developing (why did everyone want her to reopen old wounds all of a sudden?) Lisa collected the empty cups, turning her back to her mum as she made a big deal of rinsing them out. The sponge was given a thorough squeeze and draped over the tap. The tea towel was also carefully rearranged so it hung neatly over its railing. Lisa's index finger stabbed at a crumb that had missed the wipe down. She flicked it into the sink. With nothing left to occupy her, an unexpected tear trickled down her cheek. Still facing the sink, she fought back a rush of tears.

The scrape of a chair was notice her mum heard her sniveling. Turning to reveal a tear-stained face, Lisa blurted, "I found her fucking someone else on my kitchen table."

If shocked at Lisa's language, her mum didn't show it. Again she drew Lisa into her arms, rubbing her back and making comforting little clucking sounds. "Oh honey."

Tears dried, but still clutching onto a tissue, Lisa stared into the steam of a fresh cup of tea. Alone with her thoughts—her mum had taken some tea and Tim Tams in for her dad—Lisa turned them to Joel and the ongoing saga of "to quote or not to quote." Joel thought she was being ridiculous. What was the problem with working for a past lover? Especially one from so long ago. Attempts to explain had been unsuccessful, Lisa getting twisted up inside and her words coming out all wrong. As a result, their working relations were suitably strained.

"God," Lisa voiced her thoughts out loud. "When things stuff up, they really stuff up."

"What was that darling?"

Lisa startled; she thought she was still alone. She tossed up the idea of landing another bolt from the blue on her mum. Hell, why not? Get everything out in one visit. "I saw Cathy on Monday."

"Really." Her mum sat down, genuine interest sparkling in her eyes. Lisa's dad hadn't been the only one to take a liking to Cathy. Her mum thought her the best thing since sliced bread. "How is she?"

"Fine. She has an accountancy practice in South Perth. She needs some tiling done."

"And she thought of you. Darling, that's wonderful."

"Mum," Lisa prickled. Had mum forgotten she and Cathy hadn't spoken in years? "She didn't know it would be me. I imagine we were picked at random from the phone book."

"Well, there's nothing wrong with that. When are you going to start? You have quite a full schedule over the next weeks haven't you?"

"Pretty much." Lisa agreed. "Actually, we haven't even put a quote in yet."

The mother instinct pulled Lisa up immediately. "You *are* going to put a quote?"

"I don't think so. It's a bit difficult."

"Why?"

"Come on mum. Cathy and I were going to be business partners. How do you think I'd feel working *for* her?"

"Lisa. That's silly. It's no different than if you went to Cathy to get your taxes done. Then she'd be working for you."

"It's not the same." Lisa folded her arms. Any hope of support flew out the window. She wished she'd just kept her mouth shut. "Can we drop it please?"

"Lisa," Just like Joel, her mum threw her hands in the air in despair. "Don't you think you're taking this flight thing a bit to the extreme?"

Lisa looked blankly at her mum, "What?"

"Fight or flight. Darling, life isn't a series of discrete compartments you can just put away once you're through with them. Every time something goes wrong you pack up your whole life and start again."

"I do not!" Lisa flamed. True, she no longer mixed with anyone from school. Who would want to? And true, she hadn't just dropped out of Uni when she left Cathy, but lost contact with that circle of friends, as well. "If I did that, I would have sold my house instead of just kicking Janice out."

"Darling, you're missing the point. I don't expect you to even want to see Janice after what she did. But what's the harm in doing a job, a *professional* job, for Cathy? You never know, you may find you can be friends."

"It's not that easy." Lisa pouted. Since she felt more like a child getting a scolding than a grown woman, she may as well act like one. "Cathy's latest girlfriend not only works with her, she lives behind me."

"Lisa, Cathy's girlfriend is going to live behind you whether you take the job or not."

"Okay, okay." Lisa couldn't fight that logic. "Point taken. I'll keep what you said in mind." She stood, stretching her hands high and forcing a yawn. "I'd better get going. I've got a big day tomorrow."

Lisa said her good-byes to her father, stooping to peck him on the cheek as he dozed in front of the television. Her mum met her at the front door, Tupperware container of leftover roast in hand. "Thanks mum." Lisa held her arms out for one more hug before she left. "Thanks for everything."

"Give my regards to Cathy." Her mum smiled in the way mums do when they assume their advice will be taken.

Lisa tugged the door open. "I'll give you a call soon."

The next day, Lisa followed the tinny strains of the transistor radio to the back veranda of the house they were working at. She had spent the morning affixing fittings in a bathroom they finished grouting the prior day. She found Joel sprawled out on the concrete, munching on his usual morning tea, two huge cinnamon buns and a carton of chocolate milk.

"All finished?" He glanced up to Lisa in between bites.

"Yep."

Joel picked up the piece of paper that fluttered onto his lap. "What's this?"

"That quote you've been sulking over for the last two days." Lisa plopped down next to Joel and eyed his bun. "I just wanted you to give it the once over. So you can't blame me if we don't get the job."

"I trust you implicitly Leese." Joel grinned, traces of pink icing around his lips. He studied the neatly handwritten sheet Lisa had worked on after she returned home from her parents. He shook his head and said, "You've missed something."

"What?" Lisa peered at the figures and frowned. "Where?"

"The extra two hundred and forty dollars Toni owes you for your pot."

Lisa laughed. "I must say I was tempted to put it in under sundries or something, but I'm just *so* honest I couldn't bring myself to do it. Anyhow, I imagine Cathy would be paying for the tiling."

"That's my Leese—beyond corruption." Joel offered his bun. Now that he had got his way about submitting a quote, Lisa was once again invited to share his morning tea. He had kept his buns to himself the past two days. "What made you change your mind?"

"Why, your marvelous powers of persuasion of course." Lisa tore off a section thick with icing. "And cinnamon withdrawal."

Joel pocketed the sheet. "I'll drop this in now." With Lisa's look he grinned, "It's not that I think you'll forget to post it or anything. I just want to make sure we get it in on time. We promised it by the end of the week."

With nothing left of the buns but crumbs, Joel stood, brushing down his hairy thighs. "Do you want to come for a ride?"

"No thanks. Someone has to keep the wheels of this machine turning."

"Are you sure?" Joel batted his eyelashes. "I'm sure Sexy Sue and Jumpy Julie would loooove to see you."

Lisa gave him a withering look, and said, "Just go—before I change my mind again."

Chapter Six

Toni flipped through the stack of mail on her desk. An envelope with the distinctive logo of her credit card company was set aside for later. She was not looking forward to opening it. A very late night in front of the television had introduced Toni to the joys of home shopping. How could she refuse the promise of equipment that would give her tight buns and abs of steel in just thirty days? Or the copper-based stainless steel cookware guaranteed to turn crap into cuisine, thus making the exercise equipment even more necessary?

Ignoring all the other correspondence, Toni ripped open a small white envelope, unfolded the enclosed sheet and did a quick scan.

Frowning, she searched through her in-tray for the other two quotes. Laying them side by side, Toni frowned again. Two hovered around the same figure. One was vastly lower in price. *Damn.* Instead of exulting over the price difference, Toni cursed under her breath. On the previous Thursday she had hardly been able to hide her delight when Sue presented her with a quote personally delivered by Joel. The cost was far above the figure given by the second tiler. Toni initially thought Cathy's prediction had been spot on. Lisa and Joel did not want the job. Which suited Toni just fine.

The appearance of this final quote exploded that theory. The figure was within a hairs breadth of Lisa and Joel's, indicating the other was either desperate for work, or had no idea what he was doing. On reflection Toni assumed it to be the latter. Unlike the others, this fellow, Brett, gave a quote on the spot, measuring up in double quick time, punching a few buttons on a small calculator and presenting Toni with a single figure scribbled on the back of his business card.

"So this includes everything, including the removal of the carpet?" Toni had peered at the card, impressed Brett was able to give a figure so quickly. Lisa and Joel wanted until the end of the week to do the same.

"That's right." Brett dropped the calculator into his shirt pocket, at the same time digging into his trousers for his keys. "Of course, you'll have to arrange the moving of the furniture yourself, but everything else is included."

"And how long do you think it will take?" Lisa and Joel estimated six full days, given the offices were vacated. Something to do with not being able to walk on the tile for twenty-four hours to let the adhesive set.

Brett shrugged, "It depends on what other jobs we've got going. But I'd say it should take about five days all up."

The one-day differential had seemed another plus in Brett's favor. Now, comparing the figures before her, Toni realized the danger of his comment. Both the other quotes included a statement assuring the project would be worked on exclusively until completion. Brett and his unseen team may take less time, but if it was done in a piecemeal fashion the renovations could stretch out for an unknown period.

Toni tossed the quotes on top of her credit card envelope. Like her credit card bill, they could wait. Turning to her other correspondence, Toni prayed the accountant in Cathy would come to the fore when making her decision. Eighty-five dollars might not be much, but why spend it unnecessarily?

As if instinct told her the quotes were in, Cathy knocked on Toni's office door not ten minutes after Toni had placed them aside. Color crept up Toni's neck when Cathy asked if there was any news. "The last one just came in the mail. I was going to talk to you about them later today."

"No time like the present." Cathy drew a chair to Toni's desk, hesitating before she sat. "You haven't anyone due do you?"

Toni shook her head, since her next appointment was not until late afternoon. She groped blindly for the papers, watching instead the not at all unpleasant sight of Cathy molding into her seat.

"I don't think this is for me." Cathy handed back the credit card envelope Toni had also mistakenly given.

"You're welcome to it if you like." Toni mustered a smile. She crossed her legs under the desk as Cathy bent to study the papers.

A few minutes later Brett's card was tossed onto the desk for filing in the wastepaper basket. Toni tore it into shreds as she watched Cathy look from Joel and Lisa's sheet to Rod's.

"They certainly are close aren't they?" Cathy said at length. She placed them onto the desktop. "I didn't get to meet Rod. What was your impression?"

"He seemed nice enough." Toni was careful not to appear too eager. "Middle-aged. Twenty or so years in the trade apparently. He had a young off-sider with him. He also seemed decent."

"Okay," Cathy said slowly, "When you showed him the samples, did he offer any advice or suggestions?"

Toni thought back. Rod agreed the tile and grouting recommended by Lisa and Joel was fine and noted the diagonal lay of the tile with an offset border (another Lisa and Joel recommendation). Then he did his measurements and left. "No. But what was there to advise? Lisa and Joel basically set the specifications for us."

"And he didn't question them at all?"

"No." Toni bit on her bottom lip. She knew what Cathy was going to say.

As predicted, Cathy placed her index finger on Lisa and Joel's sheet. "I think we should go with them."

"Okay." Toni resigned herself, unable to come up with any rational reason why Lisa and Joel shouldn't do the job. The term *ex-lover* bounced around in her head, but that wasn't a rational reason. It had been so long ago, and Lisa was now out of the running. Besides, people became ex-lovers for a reason, usually because they didn't like each other anymore. Toni was dying of curiosity over the details, but no opening had yet occurred for her to pop in a few questions.

"Great." Cathy smiled as she stood, "Do you want to ring and tell them the good news or shall I?"

"You probably should." Toni knew Cathy was the logical one to make the call. "You're going to have to discuss dates and the like. I'd end up having to pass you on anyway." She slid the quotes over the desk. "They're all yours."

Once alone again, Toni let out the sigh that had nearly escaped in Cathy's presence. *May as well totally ruin my day*, she thought to herself. She inched the credit card envelope closer and slid her thumb under the flap. As expected, the balance had skyrocketed. A bit rude as her cookware and exercise equipment hadn't even arrived yet. But it should any day now. Toni consoled herself by imagining presenting Cathy with some spectacular home-cooked creation, dressed in a crop top that showed off her fabulous abs.

Cathy hesitated over the phone keypad before resolutely pressing numbers. She hesitated again as it made the connection and began to ring. Even she was unsure why she had decided to go with Lisa and Joel's quote. By all accounts Rod was a competent tradesperson with years of experience over Lisa and Joel. Why spend extra money, albeit a paltry amount, when there would probably be no perceptible difference between his work and theirs?

When the ringing ceased and a familiar voice called in greeting, Cathy finally admitted to herself the truth behind her actions. The truth was simple; it was a safe way to see Lisa again.

"Hi Lisa, it's Cathy." Cathy knew she was being cowardly, that having Lisa in her temporary employ greatly reduced the chance of having a door slammed in her face at the invitation for coffee and a chat.

It wasn't too late to change her mind. A coffee offer was innocent enough, plus it was an activity considerably shorter than the tiling time span. Six days could seem an eternity if things turned frosty. However, the words spilled out, "I'm calling to let you know we've decided to accept your quote."

Twenty minutes later Cathy was busy tapping out a general office memo. Work would commence in two weeks on Thursday, concluding the following Tuesday. All staff were to clear their schedules from the Wednesday afternoon so the areas to be tiled could be emptied. No appointments were to be made until the following Thursday, to allow some leeway and also to allow the premises to be put back into order.

A whoop came from reception not thirty seconds after Cathy clicked the *send* button on her memo. Obviously Sue had read the bit about the enforced extra long weekend, which would be at the company's expense instead of being deducted from annual leave balances.

"Glad someone's happy." Cathy muttered. Her initial elation at the setting of the appointment had been fleeting. Over two whole weeks to wait. Thoughts of ringing back to ask for a coffee get-together were quickly dismissed. Lisa would think Cathy had turned loopy, or that Cathy still liked her *that* way. Which of course, she didn't.

Cathy turned her attention to her diary, flipping pages until she reached the Thursday when work would commence. She drew a line through the page. Underneath the line went a reason for the blanked out day. Cathy stared at the words. Without knowing why, instead of *tiling* she had written *Lisa and Joel*. The line and description was repeated on the Friday, and again on the Saturday. Before Cathy could turn the page to Sunday, she threw down her pen. *Lisa and Joel.* The words stared back at her from the page, taunting her with all the implications they contained.

It just couldn't be. If the past was any predictor to future behavior, there was just no way Lisa would be in a relationship with a man. Toni didn't know what she was talking about. And knowing Toni and the way her stories ballooned with each telling, a friendly good-bye at the gate would eventually morph into copulation on the front lawn.

Cathy reached for her previously discarded pen to scratch out the offending words. She worked back through the pages, confident she was right. After all, she'd been right about Lisa before, picking her as a kindred spirit almost from day one.

They met the first day of the first year of classes. Cathy was walking across the University's main car park when she spied a very lost looking Lisa struggling with a campus map. Cathy knew the campus pretty well, because her brother finished his own studies there the year prior and Cathy had graced him with frequent visits. She veered from her course to see if she could help.

Lisa blushed profusely but gratefully accepted Cathy's offer, a slight *I'm going to be late* panic in her voice as she named the University's largest lecture theater.

"No kidding." Cathy exclaimed, mesmerized by Lisa's eyes. They were a dazzling blue. Sapphire, she decided. "That's exactly where I'm headed."

By the time they reached their destination, Cathy discovered they were not only going to be studying the same course, but their first semester units all matched up. However, this wasn't such a surprise as all students studied the same base program before selecting their major at the end of the first year.

"But that *is* creepy." Lisa peered at Cathy's timetable, after they settled in adjacent seats in the back row of the lecture theater.

"Sure is." Cathy agreed. That all their lecture times were the same was coincidence enough, but to have four out of five tutorial sessions also coincide—that was downright spooky. Cathy pulled a writing pad from her backpack and glanced a little dubiously to her companion. Lisa certainly seemed pleasant enough now, but Cathy didn't relish the thought of a whole semester sitting beside her if she turned out to be a boy crazy pain in the butt.

Cathy soon discovered her initial doubts were unfounded. She found she enjoyed Lisa's company immensely. Lisa was funny, outgoing and intelligent, and it hadn't escaped Cathy's attention that she had the sporty good looks she found so attractive. More than this, Cathy also noted that if Lisa was boy crazy, she kept it well hidden. If anything, she was dismissive of boys.

By the time the second week of classes had drawn to a close Cathy no longer wondered about Lisa's orientation. Despite the lack of any direct evidence, she was almost one hundred percent sure she was a lesbian. Cathy's thoughts were more focused on how to reveal to Lisa the fact that she was almost one hundred percent sure she was in love with her.

The opportunity appeared to present itself the following week. Lisa, Cathy and a group of friends from classes were going to the University tavern to see a band. To Cathy's elation, Lisa agreed to her invitation to stay overnight at her apartment. After all, it was a perfect opportunity to get an early start on an assignment due in a few weeks. Once home and alone she could reveal her feelings and then . . . Cathy shivered at the possibilities.

All had not gone according to plan. Midnight saw Cathy hauling Lisa up the stairs. Lisa wobbled unsteadily as Cathy fumbled for her front door key. "Cathy," she slurred, throwing a limp arm around Cathy's shoulder. "There's something I want to tell you—"

"Hold on," Cathy guided Lisa toward the door. She was so drunk she was likely to fall over at any moment. "Let's get you inside first."

A few minutes later Cathy stood over the bed, hugging herself as she watched Lisa sleep. She had not found out what Lisa wanted to reveal, the woman half-unconscious even before her head hit the pillow. Cathy stripped down to her T-shirt and underwear, crawled into bed, and promptly turned to face away from Lisa. It was more than frustration at her thwarted plans that made her flip over. No matter what her feelings, beer breath was really putrid.

The sun was already high in the sky when Lisa stirred. Cathy had been awake for a short while, head propped on her hand as she again watched Lisa's sleeping form.

"Morning sleepyhead." Cathy shifted to sit up against her pillow.

"Morning." Lisa stretched, then groaned, "I feel like shit."

"I'm not surprised. You really pulled a bender last night." Cathy cocked her head to one side and asked, "Do you remember what you did?"

"Oh God," Lisa placed her hands over her face, in preparation for the expected humiliation. "What?"

Cathy suppressed a giggle, enjoying watching her suffer. "You threw a drink over that poor guy." Actually she was more enjoying the thought of Lisa's reaction to the fellow's attempt at a pick up. It further cemented her belief that Lisa was interested in women.

As did Lisa's reply. She looked at Cathy through her fingers and snorted, "Humph. What a waste of beer."

Before Cathy could think of an appropriate response Lisa swung her legs over the bed and tugged her shirt to her nose. "Pheew. I stink. Do you mind if I go have a shower?"

Following Cathy's directional nod, and overnight bag slung over her shoulder, Lisa retreated, leaving Cathy alone to digest her comment.

Although very much encouraged and somewhat emboldened by Lisa's statement, Cathy could not, even to this day, believe just how bold she became. Before she knew it, she was up and out of bed, padding softly on the hallway's carpeted floor. She stopped at the bathroom door. A try of the handle revealed the door unlocked. Quietly she pushed the door open, the rush of water from the showerhead masking her presence. Doubts suddenly crowded her mind but she pushed them aside. She'd come too far to pretend she'd wandered in there by accident. Heart in her throat, Cathy slid the shower screen open.

Lisa spun around, frightened. She had been cleaning her teeth but now stood stock still, toothbrush in her mouth and toothpaste foam wending its way down one side of her chin.

Cathy met the eyes of blue. Blood hammered in her ears, and her knees felt weak. Still, she held her gaze to Lisa's and broke it only for the time it took to lift her T-shirt over her head. It fell to the floor, and was soon joined by her panties. She stepped into the shower recess.

"You remember last night you said you had something you wanted to tell me?"

Whether Lisa remembered or not Cathy couldn't fathom. Lisa stood motionless, water streaming over the back of her head. A glob of toothpaste dropped from her chin to her chest and was immediately swept away by the stream of water.

Cathy pressed on. "Well, I have something I want to tell you, too."

"What's that?" Barely a squeak emerged, not at all aided by the toothbrush still firmly planted in Lisa's mouth.

Cathy reached to guide the offending implement away. "This." The toothbrush fell from Lisa's mouth as Cathy's lips met hers . . .

Lisa pulled away and immediately Cathy wilted, fearing the worst. But her fears were put to rest when Lisa spit out a mouthful of toothpaste and giggled with a mixture of embarrassment and nerves. "Sorry . . . foamy."

Cathy's responding sigh of relief was cut short, when Lisa resumed their kiss with an intensity that took Cathy's breath away.

And so began two of the happiest years of Cathy's life. The initial days and weeks were still vivid in Cathy's mind, although at the time she seemed to float through them in some sort of ecstatic blur. It was a time when they emerged from the bed only when absolutely necessary, either driven by hunger, the need to go to class, or the need to keep Lisa's folks at bay.

Lisa was not out to her parents. Neither was Cathy, but the five hundred kilometers between her apartment in Perth and her parents' home in Albany made explanations of her activities unnecessary. Lisa enjoyed no such luxury and had to make enough appearances at home so as not to raise suspicion.

However, Lisa's mum was no fool. Not more than a month into their relationship she waylaid her daughter on her way out of the house. Cathy was frantic by the time Lisa finally landed on her doorstep. She was nearly two hours late.

"She still loves me," Lisa twirled Cathy around the lounge room, triumphant in the success of her coming out. "And goodness knows why, but she kind of likes you too."

"Of course." Cathy laughed, caught up in Lisa's jubilation. Her chest tightened as she met eyes sparkling with happiness. How she loved this woman.

It was at that moment Cathy decided it was time she finally told her. Immediately she began mentally planning. Lisa's eighteenth birthday was only a few weeks away. She'd tell her then.

"Thank you for such a wonderful birthday." Lisa lay on her side, idly running the tips of her fingers up and down Cathy's bare thigh.

The touch made Cathy quiver. She smiled into Lisa's sleepy eyes. Her own felt heavy lidded, maybe from their rich meal of crayfish and champagne, but more likely from the extended period of lovemaking that had preceded it. She wasn't yet ready for sleep however. There was still one more thing left to do.

"What are you up to now?" Lisa's voice came from on top of the bed as Cathy hung halfway off it. "You'll end up with a big fat bump on your head if you're not careful."

"It's okay." Cathy wriggled back onto the bed, and sat crosslegged in front of Lisa. She presented a small box of black velvet. "For you."

The box was taken from Cathy's hands and the lid snapped open. Cathy smiled nervously as she read the surprise in Lisa's expression. She plucked one of the two gold rings from the case and slipped it onto Lisa's ring finger. "I love you Lisa."

Her heart soared when the words were repeated back to her. "I love you too."

Needless to say, sleep was still a long way away, as they were of course required to demonstrate these newly vocalized feelings. The first light of dawn was emerging as Cathy lay still, listening to the deep, even breathing of her sleeping lover. Cathy shifted so Lisa was in her line of vision. "I really, really love you," she whispered, intertwining her fingers with Lisa's and smiling as she felt the band of gold she had placed there. Finally her eyes closed and she slept the sleep of the truly contented.

The sense of contentment continued. Everything just seemed so right. It was like the pair of them fit together perfectly. *Made for each other* was a phrase that sprang to Cathy's mind.

They sailed through their studies. Although Lisa was not in the top percentiles as Cathy was, her grades were nothing to sneeze at. They studied hard but also left plenty of time for play.

It was not too long before Lisa admitted since most of her things had been carted in dribs and drabs to Cathy's apartment anyway, why not make it official? And despite being the one to coax their baby from the nest, Cathy was still a welcome and regular visitor to the Smith home, so much so that Lisa would often wonder aloud if Cathy were indeed the real daughter and she was just some blow-in from the street.

Lisa had not shared the same relationship with Cathy's parents. But then Cathy did not share the same sort of relationship with her folks as Lisa did with hers. Cathy was close to her brother, but apart from that, they weren't a tight-knit family, their emotional distance no doubt exacerbated by their geographical distance. Cathy had been sent to boarding school for her final two years of high school, so since age fifteen contact with her parents had been limited to school holidays and the occasional weekend visit.

Despite this, Cathy felt an overwhelming need to introduce Lisa to her parents. She was nervous about the visit, not only because she desperately wanted them to like her "good friend", but because she was unsure of Lisa's reaction to finally seeing the family home.

When it happened, Cathy heard an, "Oh . . . my . . . God." From the corner of her eye, she saw Lisa's eyes widen as they rounded the final bend of the road leading to the rambling Georgian mansion set deep in a valley a couple of kilometers from the Albany township. "Shit Cathy, I know you said your family was quite well off, but—" Lisa trailed away, attention back out the window, head shaking in disbelief.

"This doesn't change things between us does it?" Cathy asked hesitantly that night. It was past midnight and despite being in a separate wing to her parents, they kept their voices low. Cathy had finally told Lisa everything, including the extent of the trust she was to receive when she was twenty-one.

Lisa threw herself backward onto the bed, pulling Cathy with her. "Yes Cathy. It does. I hate you and I hate your money."

"Hey Cathy," Lisa whispered a short time later. She was at the bedroom door, ready to make her departure. "Do you think your folks like me?"

"Definitely." Cathy's mother, always of few words, had quietly appraised Lisa during the evening. Her father was more animated, although he did question the poor girl endlessly over her studies, which accounting firm was she aiming to work for once she graduated, and what were her career plans further down the track. Lisa had managed surprisingly well, even fending off the inevitable question about a man in her life with a disarming smile and an *I'm too busy with my studies for that* reply.

Cathy did a quick check of the hallway to make sure all was clear then kissed Lisa lightly on the lips. "I'll see you in the morning." She stood in the doorway until Lisa disappeared into the next bedroom. Cathy climbed into her lonely bed, wishing her parents would grasp the notion that girls are supposed to share a room on sleepovers so they can "natter" all night. She considered sneaking into Lisa's room but decided against it, imagining Maria, the longest serving member of the household staff, shrieking and frantically crossing herself as she discovered them in bed together. Better to be safe. A couple of nights without nattering weren't going to kill her.

Two days later there was a screech of brakes as Cathy pulled into the parking bay at their apartment. Luggage was forgotten, two car doors slammed and two bodies hurled themselves up the stairs. Cathy couldn't remember who kicked the front door shut, but she was glad someone did. Fabric tore in the haste to remove clothing.

"Oops." Cathy relinquished her hold on Lisa's shirt. "Sorry."

"You can buy me a new one tomorrow." Lisa's hands were everywhere, one skimming inside Cathy's top, the other busy with the buttons on Cathy's 501s. Her breath was ragged as she sought Cathy's mouth with her own and said, "Now stop talking and kiss me."

Lisa hopped around, one leg in and one leg nearly out of her jeans, determined to stay upright while she relieved Cathy of her clothes. The result saw them both crash to the ground, Lisa taking the brunt of the fall when Cathy fell on top of her. She gasped as all the air in her lungs escaped at once.

However, her winding did not prove a long-term disability. As soon as Lisa regained her breath she concentrated on taking Cathy's away. She was highly successful. Expert fingers sought and found the center of her desire. Cathy, who despite frequent exposure, never failed to be overcome by the extent of Lisa's ardor, clung desperately to her lover as she rose higher and higher. Tiny bursts of light exploded behind her eyelids and she cried out, no longer able to contain the bubble of pure energy that had blossomed within.

It was with this memory that Cathy drew a sharp intake of air into her lungs, her memories so vivid she had been holding her breath. She still held her pen in her hand and it was still poised over the freshly scratched out *Lisa and Joel*. If her latest trip down memory lane had done anything, it drove home the fact Toni *must* have made a mistake. The passion she and Lisa had shared was not one to be denied. No matter what had gone wrong between them further down the track, Cathy just couldn't see Lisa transferring those same emotions to the opposite sex.

Cathy grabbed for the phone, determined to get to the bottom of this. She got to the second to last digit before again changing her mind. Now was probably not the best time to give Lisa a call.

Not while erotic images still floated in her head. Goodness only knows what she'd end up saying.

Cathy flipped her diary back to the current date. The page was devoid of entries. It was a blissfully appointment-free day. Such days were rare and offered a chance to really knuckle down and get some work done. She'd been fairly steaming along until she decided to stretch her legs and ended up poring over tiling quotes in Toni's office.

A thick sheaf of papers was halfheartedly pulled toward the work area of Cathy's desk. She had been charged with the task of determining the viability of a new business venture for one of her clients, but somehow, analyzing the financial statements of a suburban garden center no longer held the appeal it had that morning.

The columns of figures blurred into meaningless nothings as Cathy stared blankly at the page that topped the pile. Numbers were her life. But while she got immense satisfaction from making a set of accounts balance, or even better, finding out why they didn't, the mere thought of such an activity was enough to send most of the population catatonic. Maybe, just as Lisa told her all those years ago, she really was boring.

The first time Lisa expressed the concept was during the week leading up to their second-year exams. She bounded into the kitchen, fresh from a phone call with Rachael, a friend from class.

Rachael and Chris had received word their accommodation on Rottnest Island had finally been confirmed. It would be ten days beginning the Monday after final exams, in a three-bedroom cottage overlooking the bay at the main settlement. Two other women, names Cathy didn't recognize, had already put dibs on one of the rooms. Did Cathy and Lisa want the other one?

Rottnest was one of Cathy's favorite places, she and Lisa having spent a week of their midyear break there the past winter. Days were spent riding bicycles around the island, discovering secluded bays and taking long walks along windswept beaches. Nights were spent in their room at the island's resort, doing what island nights had been invented for. Yes, Cathy loved Rottnest.

In winter.

Summer was a completely different story. The island population swelled, its proximity to the mainland making it a destination for boatloads of day-trippers. When Rachael and Co. were booked, the place would be crawling with schoolies, all seemingly intent on breaking alcohol consumption records.

"Come on Cathy, lighten up," Lisa argued when Cathy said she'd rather not accept the offer. "We're kind of schoolies ourselves."

"Maybe so," Cathy conceded. "But that doesn't mean I want to be stuck on an island with thousands of them."

The picture Cathy painted of crowded beaches, queues at the shops, food outlets and everywhere else on the island was also not enough to deter Lisa. When it became apparent this little trip was going to happen whether she liked it or not, she changed tack, suggesting they stay again at the island's resort. Two years of boarding school had put her off communal living forever; at least at the resort they could shower and toilet to their own schedule. And they could meet up with the others during the day.

"Jeez Cathy," Lisa's expression conveyed her disgust. "The whole idea is to all stay at the one place." She folded her arms and muttered, "Stop being such a bore and have a bit of fun for a change."

Hurt, but determined not to show it, Cathy faced off against Lisa across the kitchen bench. "And just what do you mean by that remark?"

Despite her best efforts, Cathy's eyes brimmed and Lisa noticed. She rounded the bench and hugged Cathy from behind. Her tone was also softer. "I'm sorry honey. I didn't mean that. It's just I'd like to do the whole end of exam party thing. I did miss out on it at school you know."

Mollified—Cathy often forgot Lisa's school days had been a stark contrast to her own—she nodded and said, "Better ring Rachael and tell her to keep a room for us."

Despite her reservations, Cathy really did enjoy the trip. They did all the beachy things—swimming, snorkeling and sunbathing. All hired bikes (apart from official island vehicles, bicycles were the only form of transport on the island) and Lisa and Cathy showed off some of the island treasures discovered on their previous trip. At night they avoided the teenage hot spots, instead spending evenings on the veranda of their accommodation, drinking cheap cask wine, playing cards and munching on mainly barbecue fare as no one wanted to heat up the already hot little cottage by using the oven.

Not glad their little holiday was over, but happy to be home, Cathy hefted her luggage across the threshold. She plopped onto the lounge, fanning her face with her hands. "Shit it's hot."

Ten minutes later Cathy was much more comfortable. Lisa had turned on the television and the air conditioning and presented her with a tall glass of ice water.

"Thank you honey." Cathy accepted the glass and patted the seat next to her. Lisa didn't sit, but lay with her head in Cathy's lap, legs dangling over the arm of the couch. Cathy absently stroked Lisa's hair, half watching the television as she sipped from her glass.

The fuzzy feeling of domestic harmony that enfolded Cathy quickly disintegrated. The telephone hollered for attention. Lisa was soon on her feet and across the room.

Annoyed but curious, Cathy mouthed, "Who is it?"

Lisa put her hand over the mouthpiece. "Jack."

Cathy raised her eyebrows in surprise. Jack, short for Jacqueline, had been one of their little party on the island. They'd only been home for five seconds—why would she be ringing already? From Lisa's half of the conversation, it was apparently to ask them out. Cathy shook her head and mouthed a firm, "No."

Lisa scowled at Cathy but talked into the phone, "I'll call you back in five." The receiver clicked as it was placed quite firmly back onto its cradle. Hands on hips and still scowling Lisa demanded, "Why not?"

Cathy couldn't believe she had to explain it. They'd just spent ten days with these people. Didn't Lisa want to spend a bit of time alone?

Apparently not.

Both firmly standing their ground, they launched headlong into their first full-blown argument. Cathy stormed down the hallway, slammed the bedroom door, and promptly burst into tears.

An unknown amount of time passed before the door handle turned. Lisa entered, looking suitably contrite. Cathy was lying on the bed and turned to face the other way, but Lisa caught her shoulders and tugged her back around.

"What are you still doing here?" Cathy asked sarcastically. "I thought you were going out."

"No." Lisa grabbed a tissue from the box on the bedside table. She dabbed just below Cathy's eyes, trying to catch the fresh tears before they fell. "I didn't mean that. I'm sorry."

"Okay." Cathy didn't feel things were very okay at all. She took the tissue from Lisa's hands and blew her nose, and studied Lisa's expression. There was a definite air that something was being left unsaid. Cathy pulled herself into a sitting position, grabbed another bunch of tissues and clutched them tightly. "Talk to me."

Finally she coaxed the truth from Lisa. It brought on a new wave of tears.

"But I thought you liked spending time with me," Cathy said.

"I do." Lisa enfolded Cathy's hands in hers. "You're my favorite person in the world to spend time with, but that doesn't mean I don't want to spend time with other people."

"But we do." Cathy protested. She thought they had a good social life. They went out at least once a week with friends to either the movies or a restaurant or the University tavern. On occasions they hit the nightclub district to go to the gay and lesbian bars and clubs. Not to mention the video and pizza nights held at their apartment.

"I know *we* do, but we need to do things separately too."

Cathy didn't sleep well that night. She tossed and turned as she mulled over Lisa's revelation. Her ego was bruised. It hurt to be told she wasn't the sun, moon and stars to her partner. But she knew Lisa was right—no one person could be everything to someone else. Come morning she felt brighter.

She greeted Lisa with a coffee in bed. "So what are you getting up to today?"

"Well," Lisa accepted the mug and blew away the steam. "We still haven't unpacked, and the salt from the parking at the ferry dock will rust out my car if it isn't washed. Plus we need to get some fresh food into the fridge."

"Sounds like you're going to have a busy day then." Cathy ruffled Lisa's hair as she stood. "I'm going to have a shower then I'm going to see if Rachael wants to go shopping." She smiled sweetly and said, "For clothes."

Cathy suppressed her laugh until she was under the shower. The look on Lisa's face had been priceless.

She did spend the day shopping with Rachael. And she modeled her new outfit for Lisa, who then helped her out of it and demonstrated how much she missed Cathy during the day. Cathy fell asleep thinking this independence caper wasn't half bad.

For a short while it was decidedly good. Until Jack and Evelyn began playing a much larger role in their lives. Cathy had liked the couple when she met them at Rottnest. Not students, Evelyn worked as a "paper shuffler" for the Department of Housing. Jack also "worked for the government," but in her case it was a polite way of saying she was unemployed. They were slightly older than the rest of their group, twenty-two to their nineteen years. They were also committed nightclubbers.

In retrospect, Cathy wondered how they survived the Rottnest expedition. Ten whole days without their beloved nightspots. How did they manage?

The "come out with us" phone call on their return from the island was just the first of many. The next one came less than a week later and the following only two days after that. Both times Cathy went along, and she enjoyed herself up to a point. Yes, the music was good and yes it was great to go to gay venues and kiss and cuddle in public without suffering the stares of the world, but wasn't three times in one week taking the exercise a bit far?

"Come out," Lisa implored for what felt like the fiftieth time.

"No." Cathy stamped her foot in frustration. "How many times do I have to tell you—I don't want to go out again."

"I'll just go without you then."

"Fine! Go!" Cathy threw herself onto the couch and stared at the program they had been watching before the phone rang.

Lisa stalked defiantly to the bedroom. When she re-emerged she was dressed for the club. She stood in front of the television. "I'm going now."

"Fine." Cathy refused to look at her, keeping her eyes firmly on the portion of screen she could make out between Lisa's legs. She sensed Lisa's hesitation, both before she moved out of Cathy's way and once she reached the front door.

"I'm going now," she repeated.

"Good."

The front door opened and closed. Lisa reappeared in the lounge room.

Cathy finally looked up at her. "I thought you were going out."

"It won't be the same without you." Lisa sat heavily at the very end of the couch. "I think I'll stay home."

Cathy instinctively knew not to treat this as a victory. Sure enough, less than a week later they were treading the same ground. Only this time Lisa did make it past the front door. It was nearly three a.m. when Lisa finally slid under the bedcovers.

"I missed you."

Cathy slapped Lisa's hands away. "Piss off. I'm not talking to you right now."

Indeed Cathy managed to maintain her anger for the rest of the night and most of the next day. Not that Lisa noticed. She spent the best part of the day in bed nursing a hangover. When she did finally emerge from the bedroom, she had the dejected air of a naughty child who knew she was about to get punished.

But Cathy had moved beyond the desire to wring Lisa's neck.

All she wanted was to get past this. It was making her miserable. She told Lisa as much.

"I really do love you." Lisa clasped Cathy's hands. "And I'm sorry for hurting you. I really didn't mean it."

Cathy searched Lisa's eyes for some sign of insincerity, but found none. "I love you, too."

The next day they discussed their plans for Christmas, which was only two weeks away. By the beginning of February, a week before classes were due to start for their final year, Lisa was gone.

Initially Cathy thought it was just another of their arguments, that Lisa would stew for a while and return home as normal. For that had become their way of late. Life was a rollercoaster of fights and making up, arguments and apologies.

To her mind, Cathy had tried everything she could think of to work through the problems they were having. Yelling was ineffectual, the silent treatment even more so. She sat Lisa down on numerous occasions to try to get her to talk, to find the real root of the obvious deep discontent she was feeling, and why she had this sudden and acute fascination with the nightlife. But the reasons she was given did not seem to hold water. There had to be more than just an ongoing need to live it up with her newly acquired club chums.

Cathy accused Lisa of having an affair. Lisa vehemently denied it.

"Honestly Cathy," Lisa said, her angry tone softening. She had initially flared at the mention she was doing anything untoward. "I am *not* having an affair. I would never do that to you."

Cathy still harbored doubts, but took Lisa at her word, deciding another change of tack was required. Instead of ranting and raving, she would just let Lisa go. Hopefully, with no more barriers, she would snap out of this crazy stage and they could get on with life again as normal.

Deciding on the plan of action was the easy part. Living it was quite another. She spent many lonely nights as Lisa took full advantage of the free rein she had been given, staying out later and later and more often than not returning home cock-eyed from beer or bourbon, or whatever drink she had imbibed that night.

It was the night Lisa didn't come home at all that tipped Cathy over the edge. No longer able to hold her tongue, she flew at Lisa from the moment the key turned in the lock at nearly midday. Accusations of affairs resurfaced, as did old hurts and old threats from many arguments prior.

"Jesus Cathy. Get a grip will you." Lisa stood in the entrance, not having made it past the front door. "I've already told you, Jack and Evelyn split up last night. I stayed with Jack because she was upset."

"Yeah, and I'm sure you well and truly consoled her."

"Think what you like." Lisa shouldered past Cathy and stalked down the hallway. "I'm sick of this."

Still steaming, Cathy followed Lisa into the bedroom. "Well I'm fucking well sick of this too Lisa. Either pull yourself together or get out. I've got better things to do than sit around and wait for you to come to your senses."

Lisa spun sharply on her heel. "You know what Cathy? That's the best idea I've heard in a long while."

Within an hour of walking in the front door, Lisa walked out of it again, armed only with her keys, her sunglasses and whatever she had thrown into her backpack. The last words she said before closing the door were, "Enjoy your boring little existence."

For two days Cathy clung desperately to the belief Lisa would return. By day three Cathy was on the phone to the hospitals, praying Lisa had not had an accident but thinking it was the only plausible reason she had not come home. That afternoon she called Lisa's mum. No, Lisa had not been in contact. Yes, she would ring as soon as she found out anything.

Genuine concern echoed through the phone line, "Are you okay Cathy?"

"Yes Mrs. Smith," Cathy lied, wiping her eyes with a shirt sleeve. "I'm fine."

That same evening Cathy was nibbling on the dry cracker she called dinner when the phone rang. It was Lisa's mum. Lisa had called and given a contact number. It was Jack's. Cathy knew it by heart from the number of times she stood over the phone, fingers ready to dial and words ready to tell Jack and her partner to get the hell out of their life.

But she never had.

To Cathy's complete surprise, it was Evelyn who answered her call. Either Lisa had lied about Evelyn and Jack splitting, or they had patched things up.

"I'm sorry," Evelyn's chirpy manner made Cathy want to reach through the phone and strangle her. "She's not here at the moment."

"Can you ask her to ring me please?"

"Will do."

Cathy waited. And she waited. She avoided leaving the house for anything more than a quick dash to the mailbox in case she missed Lisa's call. But it never came.

The first time she left the apartment for any period of time was for the start of classes. Hopeful Lisa might turn up, Cathy scanned the crowd milling outside the lecture theatre. But she didn't show at either the lecture or the tutorial immediately following.

When she returned home, she found all of Lisa's things gone. Cathy sank onto the bed and for the first time admitted to herself that it was truly over. The empty drawers and horrendously naked space in the wardrobe drove home the fact that the woman who Cathy still loved helplessly was not coming back.

Cathy was desolate in her loss. She retreated into herself, spending long hours alone, her only contact with the outside world when she occasionally dragged herself to class. In the dark hours before dawn she would lay awake reliving the time she spent with Lisa and analyzing why things had turned sour. Cathy swung on a pendulum of blame. At one extreme she was at fault, at the other the rift was caused entirely by Lisa.

It was not long before Easter Cathy made the conscious decision to get back on track. Standing in front of the bathroom mirror, she fingered hair that had lost its gloss, and noted the dark shadows under her eyes. She had shed a tremendous amount of weight, and not having carried an excess in the first place, the reflection that stared back at her was gaunt and pallid. Her pendulum was high in its self-blame arc. As Cathy critically assessed herself she came to the conclusion Lisa had left because she was ugly unlovable, and stupid. Cathy was also staring down the barrel of her first academic failure. A raft of assignments were due before the Easter break and she hadn't started any of them.

As Cathy continued to study herself, the pendulum did a sharp swing in the opposite direction. Lisa may have chosen to leave, but she was not to blame for how Cathy handled it. She could either continue wallowing in her grief forever and a day, or she could rejoin the land of the living and try to get on with things.

Cathy decided on the latter. First thing she did was force down some food. Then she threw herself into her studies, rising early and working late to catch up on all she had missed. It was a struggle and she just made the deadline for the last pre-Easter assignment with minutes to spare. But she did make it. She continued to make it for the rest of the year, her devotion to her study providing a welcome distraction from all the triggers that served to remind of Lisa. Each time Cathy was reminded—by a song on the radio, a similar laugh or even by something as small as a familiar turn of phrase—she would tune it out by concentrating harder on her books. By the time her studies drew to a close her results reflected her hard work. They also did not go unnoticed by the companies conducting on-campus graduate recruitment interviews. Cathy was left in the enviable position of having to choose between three accountancy firms vying for her services, all of them large reputable companies, one based in Sydney. The choice was not a hard one to make. A few days after New Year, Cathy handed the apartment key back to her father, hugged her mother good-bye and boarded a plane for the other side of the country.

Six years later, Cathy landed back in Perth. It was not her first trip back; she tried for at least two visits to her family each year. But this time, when she walked out to the arrival lounge, it was not for a three- or four-day stay, it was permanent. Cathy had enjoyed her time in Sydney. It was a vibrant, multicultural city where there was always something happening. But over time its luster dulled and Cathy found her return to the East a bit more difficult with each visit she made to her home state.

Despite her homesickness for Western Australia, the decision to relocate did not come easily. Cathy had risen through the ranks of her company at speed and would be leaving a hefty salary package behind, not to mention colleagues she both admired and whose company she enjoyed. She didn't have a job waiting in Perth; she instead made the decision to hang out her own shingle. Financially there was no problem, her trust would more than cover her needs. Professionally, Cathy knew she was well equipped for the task. Emotionally . . . well, Cathy was pretty sure she was ready to face Perth again.

She had been. Time had done what time did best. It had ironed out the creases, and smoothed out the kinks in her armor. Cathy set to building her practice and rebuilding her life in Perth with gusto. Her doors opened for trade within two months. Sue was hired as receptionist shortly after that and twelve months later Toni came on board. Cathy had bought a house, leased a car and joined a couple of women's groups. Everything was going along swimmingly.

But there was always a lingering thought that one day she may run into Lisa. For the most part it was kept locked away, but occasionally Cathy let the thought wander freely. It was at these times Cathy wondered what Lisa was up to, what direction her life had taken, whether or not she was still even in Perth. Once she checked the phone book, but with *Smith* for a surname it was like trying to find a needle in a haystack. She also toyed with the idea of calling Lisa's mum, but never acted on it. If she and Lisa were to meet, it would have to be either by Lisa's doing or by chance. Cathy was not going to orchestrate any moves. Still, it was an interesting exercise to imagine how she may react to such a meeting.

However, none of Cathy's theorizing prepared her for the reality, which struck with a force as real as a physical blow to the body. Cathy winced as she remembered. There actually had been a physical blow to the body. She'd walked around with a sore arse for days after her tumble off the fence. But the physical pain paled in comparison to the jolt to her psyche.

Successfully quashed memories re-emerged in a torrent, so fast she felt she could not grip onto any of them. It was only when Cathy bid her goodnight to Toni and was in the safety of her car that she allowed herself to begin sifting through her jumble of thoughts. The task had occupied her for the remainder of the weekend, and the results were unnerving. Even more so in light of the doubts Toni later placed in her mind.

Now, finally resolute, Cathy shunted the garden center accounts away and drew the phone closer. Her fingers thrummed on the desk as she waited impatiently for the call to connect to Lisa's mobile. Cathy cursed as a woman's voice cheerfully announced the call could not be connected. Lisa must have either turned her phone off or moved out of range since they had spoken earlier. Still determined, Cathy figured she could try the fixed line. It was mid-afternoon; maybe Lisa had already packed it in for the day. On the fifth ring it switched to an answering machine.

"Hi you have reached Hawthorn Tiling. We're currently unavailable to take your call—"

The deep timbre of Joel's voice caught Cathy completely off guard, and she quietly placed the receiver back in its cradle, not wanting to listen to the rest of the message.

Her mind raced. Lisa and Joel worked together. Maybe they also shared a house. Separate bedrooms. The whole platonic housemate thing. Or maybe . . .

No. Cathy refused to believe it.

She didn't know what the hell to believe. All she knew was she wished she had never clapped eyes on Lisa again. Then she wouldn't have to face the fact time hadn't really healed, it had only delayed. Eleven years, two cities and two lovers later, and one look from Lisa could still send Cathy into a tailspin. That must surely qualify for some world record in pathetic.

"Damn you Toni." Cathy folded her arms on the desk and rested her forehead on the cradle that they formed. "Of all the tilers in Perth, you had to choose Hawthorn Tiling."

"Damn cat." Virgil was next to take the verbal onslaught. "Should never be allowed out of the damn house."

Interior design trends, tax deductible capital works and the general state of the nation all took a thrashing. It made Cathy feel a bit better. Not much. But a little.

Chapter Seven

"I'm never going to get this done." Lisa hefted the washing basket full of freshly dried clothes onto her hip so she could pick up the phone. All morning she'd been fielding calls—so much for her bonus Friday off. Their last job finished a day earlier than expected and with no weekend work scheduled, three days of leisure stretched ahead. Hence this morning had been earmarked for a flurry of housework to get it out of the way.

Forgetting she'd set the answering machine after taking the last call, Lisa started as the machine kicked in. Oh well, she was here now. May as well pick up. She shifted the washing basket again so it sat more firmly on her hip. "Hello."

"People are going to start to talk if you don't change that thing."

"Hey Steph," Lisa broke into a smile. Steph had already had a go at the Joel message less than a week ago, just before she flew out to Melbourne. Lisa promised to change it, but never seemed to get round to the task. She hated talking into a machine. "When did you get back in?"

"Late last night. And Van left this morning for a weekend soccer camp—"

Lisa could almost see Steph pouting on the other end of the line. Van's job as a high school sport teacher rarely took her away for more than a day, so Steph was used to having a warm bed and a warm body in it when she returned from her own business trips. "So you're looking for a playmate," she cut in.

"Uh-huh."

"You can come over and watch me vacuum if you like."

"Now there's an offer I can't refuse. I'll be there in half an hour." The phone clicked and the line went dead.

Lisa hurried to the bedroom with her washing basket, delighted at the welcome interruption Steph would be making into her day. One of her closest friends, Steph was a buyer for a chain of clothing stores and subsequently was often away over East or in some exotic rag trade location. Combined with Lisa's own topsy-turvy work schedule, contact other than by phone was frequently a strategic nightmare. Despite the reins it placed on their get-togethers, Steph's career choice suited her perfectly. Even without the fringe benefit of a steady supply of the latest fashions, she was glamour to the core, her manner and confidence commanding attention wherever she went.

True to form, when Lisa answered the knock on the door, an impeccably attired Steph greeted Lisa with kisses on each cheek, gave a brief but firm squeeze around the waist, and swept down the hallway straight for the kitchen. "I hope the kettle's boiled, I'm in dire need of a caffeine fix."

As soon as Steph was furnished with a coffee, they began their usual argument over what they should do with themselves. Vacuuming was quickly discarded as a lousy spectator sport. Lisa didn't want to go shopping, and Steph didn't feel like going out to lunch—she'd just got back from foodie heaven in Melbourne and was all gourmet-ed out. Eventually, they decided daytime television was as good an activity as any. A quick trip to the local store to stock up on definitely non-gourmet goodies and they settled in for a dose of talk shows and B-grade movies.

"I don't believe we're supposed to be sucked into believing this is real." Lisa threw a green M&M at the screen. It bounced off the head of the talk show guest who had just announced he was having an affair with his fiancée's sister *and* her best friend. "What a load of crap."

"I can't watch this shit anymore," she announced a few moments later. The fiancée had stormed onto the stage with arms swinging. Yet another on-stage fight was about to erupt. But of course, no blows ever made contact. "Do you mind if I change the channel?"

Steph shrugged, alternately nibbling on her chocolate biscuit and sipping on her third coffee as Lisa flipped channels on the remote.

"Stop here," Steph pointed at the screen. "I like this one."

"Ah ha." Lisa teased. The program was a long running soap. "Now we know what you do on your days off."

"And what of it?" Steph huffed. She leaned forward and pointed again at the screen. "He's married to her, but she's pregnant to his youngest son."

Lisa rolled her eyes and focused her attention on trying to find the last of the red M&Ms in the packet, "Riveting."

"It is. Watch," Steph said as she poked Lisa in the side. "You see that stupid look she's giving behind his back as he gives her a hug? That's because even though she's married to him and pregnant to his youngest son, she's actually still in love with the oldest son."

"So why isn't she with the oldest son then?"

"Because he was in a plane crash at sea and everyone thought he was dead, but he wasn't, he was just missing, and when he came back she had already married the father."

"Oh." Lisa went back to her red M&M search, half thinking how stupid it was and half thinking about the parallels between the show and her life at the moment. Well, no fathers and sons were involved and no one was pregnant or married and no one had been in a plane crash, but *she* could see the similarities.

"Steph," she ventured.

She got a distracted, "Hmm."

"Have I ever told you about my first girlfriend?" Lisa knew full well she hadn't. She had never told anyone.

That got Steph's attention. A true romantic at heart, she thrived on all tales of human relationships. The television was immediately forgotten. "No."

"Well, do you want to hear about her?"

Steph's response was another foregone conclusion. "Of course I do." She pulled Lisa to her feet. "But let's get another coffee first."

They settled at the kitchen table armed with fresh brews. Lisa was a bit nervous, mainly because she had vowed to tell Steph the whole story, warts and all. She hoped Steph wouldn't think too badly of her by the finish. Steph was watching Lisa expectantly so she launched straight into it.

"Well we met on the first day of Uni . . ."

Lisa told how she'd quickly developed a blinding crush on Cathy. How her disastrous experience at school made her determined not to do or say anything to let Cathy know of her feelings. How the knowledge of the sleeping arrangements in Cathy's two-bedroom (but one had been converted to a study) apartment sent her reeling from the moment she dropped her overnight bag onto the bedroom floor. How the way she coped with the thought of lying next to Cathy that night had been to get blind drunk. How, had she known Cathy shared the same feelings she'd probably have gotten drunk anyhow because she'd have been so nervous.

"And so it was actually the next day that we, umm, got together. And then—"

"Whoa there girl," Steph held her hand up to halt Lisa mid-sentence. "So both of you liked each other?"

Lisa nodded.

"But neither of you had any idea the other was also lesbian?"

"Cathy later told me she was almost sure I was, but I was totally clueless about her."

"So, what happened? Did one of you do the big *there's something I want to tell you* thing?"

Lisa felt heat rise up her neck. "No, not quite."

"Ooh," Steph sensed Lisa's discomfiture and correctly interpreted it as owing to a juicy snippet of information. "Do tell."

"Come on," Steph coaxed when Lisa steadfastly refused. "You know I love all the *how we got together* tales."

Knowing she had to say something or they'd never move on, Lisa decided to be obscure. "Let's just say everything became obvious when I discovered Cathy was big on water conservation."

Steph frowned, "What?"

"Figure it out for yourself." Lisa reached for Steph's yet-again empty coffee cup and rose to turn the kettle on for a refill. "Now do you want to hear past day one or not?"

Settled back at the table Lisa continued. She told of her coming out to her folks, the decision to live together and an abridged version of the night Cathy presented her with her ring. That Cathy's family was what she could only describe as super rich was a detail Lisa omitted. Cathy had been reluctant to make that aspect of her life common knowledge and Lisa didn't feel it her business to spread the word.

It was while relating the interrogation given by Cathy's father on her first visit to the Braithwaite estate that Steph snapped her fingers and said, "A shower."

It was Lisa's turn to frown, "What?"

"A shower." Steph repeated, a triumphant grin spreading. "You and Cathy had a shower, or maybe it was a bath, together."

"Shit Steph," Lisa couldn't believe Steph was still back at the starting blocks. She wished she'd just been forthright instead of cryptic. "Have you heard a word I've said since then?"

"Of course." Steph treated Lisa to her most haughty look. "Let me summarize." Points were ticked off on her fingers, as she said, "You find a woman with looks, brains and personality who you adored and who obviously adored you right back. You shared the same goals, got on like a house on fire, and yet you break up with her—"

"Hang on a sec," Lisa interrupted. "I haven't told you who broke up with whom yet."

"But it *was* you who broke it off wasn't it?" Steph said confidently.

"Yes." Bewildered, Lisa asked, "How do you know?"

"Just call me an astute observer of the human condition." Steph held her cup up in a self-congratulatory salute. "So," cup back in its saucer, she leaned forward on the arms she folded across the table. "Tell me what happened."

Lisa sat silent, pulling the sugar bowl closer to give her something to fiddle with as she tried to find appropriate words. "I don't know Steph. It was as if one day I was madly in love and worshipped the ground Cathy walked on, then the next our perfect little world didn't seem so perfect anymore."

"The rose glasses came off?"

"No." Lisa said slowly. "It was more me that changed."

A vague feeling of discontent toward the end of the second academic year had been the first clue that all was not as it should be. Initially Lisa discarded the feeling as being jaded from the hard slog she put in all semester. She had to work that much harder than Cathy to get grades that weren't as high. She was tired and she just wanted the academic year to be to be over and done with. Come the contact-free week leading up to exams, she hit the books without enthusiasm.

It was while poring over a mock exam question for her auditing unit that the vague feeling finally crystallized, *I don't think I could do this every day for the rest of my life.* When Lisa told Cathy this, she received a consoling squeeze around the waist. "Honey, it's just a unit we have to get through," Cathy said, and launched into the inventory of what their practice would and wouldn't be specializing in, and auditing wasn't part of it. Usually this future accountancy practice planning brightened Lisa's spirits—it was the goal they were both working toward—but on this occasion it served to further dishearten.

"I felt I was being swept away by Cathy's plans."

"But they were your plans too."

"I know. But as I was coming to the realization that just because I was reasonably good at the accounting thing it didn't mean I wanted to do it for the rest of my life. Our shared plans suddenly became Cathy's. In my mind anyway. I felt like the future had been all mapped out for me and I didn't like it."

"Did you tell Cathy this?"

"No." Lisa squirmed uncomfortably. "I didn't. And things just sort of snowballed from there. I became enthralled with the lifestyle that Jack and Evelyn led and—"

"Hang on," Steph interrupted. "Back up a bit. Who were they?"

"Sorry." Lisa explained meeting Jack and Evelyn at Rottnest, how she had taken an immediate liking to them, and how they seemed to lead such exciting lives. From what they described they had a huge circle of friends and were out almost every night. When they weren't at a pub or a club, their one-bedroom unit was overflowing with people.

"Doesn't sound very exciting to me." Steph sniffed.

"I'd agree with you now," Lisa said, nodding. "But at the time it sounded like it was. And listening to them describe their lives just served to make me feel more like I was missing out on something. So when we got back to Perth and they asked us out I jumped at the chance."

"But Cathy didn't?"

"No. That was the night we had our first real argument." Lisa glanced from her sugar bowl to Steph. "I hated it. I felt so bad for making her cry." Unable to hold eye contact, she fidgeted more actively with her prop, watching the sugar crystals fall from the spoon she kept dipping into the contents. "But that was only the first time. I was such a bitch to her, Steph. I knew how much I was hurting her each time I walked out the door, but I still went."

Lisa fumbled her way through the days and weeks leading up to her leaving. What at the time seemed real and valid reasons for her actions now sounded like feeble excuses.

The hardest to admit was her growing obsession of what it would be like to sleep with another woman. Initially the thought never crossed her mind—she was out to have a good time, a few drinks, dance and meet people. But the attention she received—that every new face at the club received—got to her. Women bought her drinks, showed more than fleeting interest, flirted with her. She flirted back, shamelessly. But she never went beyond that.

"So although Cathy was convinced you were having an affair, you weren't?"

"No. I was faithful to her until the end."

Steph picked up on the clue immediately. "And after the end?"

"I was screwing someone else two days later."

Stealing a glance to see Steph's reaction, Lisa was surprised to find she wasn't registering either surprise or shock. Instead of some disparaging remark, Steph asked, "Was it everything you were looking for?"

Lisa shook her head. She could remember the night, although she couldn't remember the woman's name. It happened on the couch in Jack and Evelyn's lounge room. That was her temporary bed; she landed there straight after walking out on Cathy. It was late, a bevy of friends had not long left and Jack and Evelyn—their own breakup having lasted the sum total of one day—had retired to their room. But this woman stayed. Lisa remembered the episode as hot, sticky and excitingly physical. She also remembered being wracked with guilt afterward. The woman held her as she cried, telling her it was all right, she'd done nothing wrong. Lisa woke alone the next morning, which was just as well, as she probably couldn't have looked the woman in the eye anyway. She also avoided meeting the eyes of Jack and Evelyn. She was sure they had heard the whole thing. Lisa spent the day curled up in a corner of her bed/couch, chewing on her fingernails and quietly fretting. It was when Jack left to pick Evelyn up from work that Lisa reached for the phone. She only dialed three digits of Cathy's number before she pressed on the tabs to cancel the call.

"I just couldn't do it," Lisa replied when Steph asked why. "I felt so bad, and I knew she'd be able to tell what I'd done as soon as I spoke."

"So what did you do?"

Lisa gave a wan smile and said, "I called mum instead."

Steph knew how close Lisa and her mum were. "And she passed a message on for you?"

"Yeah. Mum told me Cathy had been asking if she knew where I was, so I gave her Jack's number."

"But Cathy didn't call?"

Lisa shook her head. "No. I waited for two days."

"And you didn't try calling her again?"

Again Lisa shook her head, eyes brimming as she recalled the moment she realized she had thrown away the best thing that had ever happened to her. She swiped her eyes with the back of her hand. "No. By then I was convinced she hated me. After all, she was the one to tell me to leave."

"Lisa," Steph passed a tissue dug from the depths of her handbag. "You were a bloody fool. You should have called."

"That's better." Returned from her trip to the bathroom, Steph headed straight for the kettle. "I thought I was going to pop."

Lisa declined the offer of another coffee. She watched as Steph mulled over their conversation, and agreed totally when Steph described her as a "fool." She wondered what adjectives Steph would add when she discovered Lisa had not only not telephoned, but had sneaked back to the apartment to retrieve her things when she knew Cathy would be in class.

"Oh Lisa. You didn't? Imagine how the poor woman felt when she got home."

"I know." Lisa cringed, recalling the snatch and grab, when she stuffed all her clothes and personal items into plastic garbage bags. She hefted them down to her car, then returned to the apartment one last time for a quick check. The quick check became extended,

Lisa stopping in each room, running hands over furniture, fingering items on the shelves and in the cupboards, remembering. She eventually left, leaving the key on the kitchen bench, softly closing the front door behind her.

"So I guess that was the time you dropped out of your course?"

Lisa nodded, Steph correctly making the assumption that her cowardice in facing Cathy helped ring the death knell on the studies she was already doubting she wanted to pursue. She hadn't even taken her texts from the apartment. "I officially became a Uni drop-out and joined the dole queue."

The switchover from student allowance to unemployment benefits was surprisingly easy. As was Lisa's new routine of doing next to nothing.

Totally lacking in motivation, Lisa made little to no effort to look for work. The only constructive activity she undertook in the first month was to find her rundown house. Despite Jack and Evelyn's open-door policy, their cramped one-bedroom apartment was closing in on her, and her back was aching from sleeping on the couch. The space her house afforded meant it was soon another hangout for her new set of friends, and along with the friends of her three newly acquired housemates, there was never a dull moment.

"This place used to rock." Lisa looked around her new kitchen and dining area, and although they no longer bore any resemblance to the original, she could still picture the near squalid conditions they existed in. "Poor old dear next door, I think we nearly sent her to an early grave. She called the police on us twice for excessive noise." Lisa smiled grimly, and said, "I reckon she must have nearly had a coronary when Janice appeared on the scene and started blowing the roof off the place again."

"Speaking of which," Steph interjected, "Have you heard from her lately?"

"Nope. Not for a while now. I reckon she's given up."

"Good," Steph muttered, closing the topic with a wave of her hand.

"Don't be so hard on her."

"Lisa!" Steph shot Lisa a withering look. "Please don't tell me you're going soft on her."

"I'm not." Lisa had recently come to the conclusion she was more like Janice than she cared to admit. With this realization came the feeling she was probably just as deserving of her friend's contempt.

"Oh please," Steph snorted derisively when Lisa tried to explain this. "Don't ever put yourself in the same basket as her. She's a using, manipulative little wench who flits through life not caring who she hurts in the process."

"But I—"

"Look Lisa," Steph interrupted. She was on a roll now, and waved away Lisa's attempt to further berate herself. "You were young and confused and you made a few stupid mistakes. But I challenge you to find anyone who hasn't done something in their past they regret. Besides, I choose my friends carefully." Steph tipped her head to one side, daring Lisa to disagree with her. "And as you know, I accept nothing less than the best."

Lisa hardly had time to appreciate Steph's display of loyal affection before she switched tracks. "Now, I take it from your sudden need to reveal the pearls of your past that you've either seen or heard from Cathy recently."

Steph phrased it as a statement as opposed to a question, but Lisa knew it was pointless asking how she had guessed. She'd just get the *astute observer of the human condition* explanation again. However, Lisa was glad Steph was so astute. She needed some sound advice as she'd been tying herself in knots over the past days, ever since taking the call from Cathy advising they had won the tiling contract.

Apart from a "you're bullshitting me" comment when Lisa described the circumstances of their initial meeting, Steph listened quietly as Lisa related all the contact she'd had with Cathy since then, which in sum total was the time spent measuring up for the tiling and the "you've got the job" phone call. Cathy had been all business on the phone so Lisa responded in kind. Nevertheless, she hadn't wanted the call to end. When it did, she turned her phone off, just to allow time to absorb the fact that Cathy actually chose them for the job. It was the last thing Lisa expected, even though her quote was fair. Cathy had been at the forefront of Lisa's thoughts ever since.

"So I've seen her twice and spoken to her once on the phone, and for the life of me I just can't stop thinking about her."

"Hmm." Steph rested her chin on her hands, regarding Lisa carefully. "Are these warm and fuzzy 'I'm so looking forward to doing the job because it's nice to see you again' thoughts, or are they 'I wish I'd quoted higher because I really don't want to deal with seeing you' thoughts?"

Lisa took a moment to reply as she tried to make some order of her feelings. Not overly successful, her words spilled out in a rush. "They're 'I didn't think you'd accept my quote but I'm glad you did because the look and smell and sound of you drives me crazy and I want to see you again although I'm scared shitless you hate me and only accepted because I quoted cheapest' thoughts."

"It's all a moot question anyway." Lisa sighed. "Since Cathy is seeing Toni."

"But you don't *know* that," Steph argued. "You're only assuming." She folded her arms. "I think you should call her."

"Yeah, right," Lisa answered sarcastically, forming a hand into a mock handset and speaking into it, "Hi Cathy. Lisa here. I was just wondering if you'd tell me, are you going out with Toni? You are? Okay, that's all I wanted to know. Bye."

Steph wasn't convinced. "I think you should call her."

"Come on Steph, have you forgotten what I just told you about how I treated her? Even if she isn't seeing Toni, what are the chances she'll even want to be friends with me?"

"Ring her and find out."

"But I'm going to see her in less than two weeks. After eleven years, what difference is another few days going to make?"

The answering look told Lisa a few days meant everything.

"I don't have her home number," she said lamely.

Steph's eyes darted to the kitchen clock. "It's only just gone five. Call her at the office. And if she's not there, try her mobile," she called as Lisa retreated down the hallway to stand in front of the phone. Lisa glared at it like it was the enemy. Diary open to the details Cathy relayed while they made the tiling arrangements, Lisa took a deep breath, *here goes nothing.*

Already tense, she jumped out of her skin when the phone rang just as she placed her hand on the receiver. The romantic notion that maybe Cathy had also been thinking of her and was on the other end of the line flashed through her mind. It made her smile. "Hello."

"Hey girlfriend."

Relief and disappointment fought with each other for brain space. "Hi Joel."

"You answered fast. What were you doing, sitting on top of the phone?"

"No, I just knew it would be you and fell over myself to get to your dulcet tones as fast as possible."

"I can go one better than that. How would you like to see me in person?"

"Don't you have a date with Scott tonight?"

"Yeah, but it's not until he gets off work. He's got the late shift again." There was a slight hesitation over the line. "I was sort of hoping I could come over and hang out for a while."

"Sure." Lisa sensed the neediness in Joel's tone. This was date number two between Joel and Scott the bottle shop attendant, and already she'd picked up little clues he was more serious about this guy than he had been with anyone for a long while. "You can get ready to go out here if you like, it's closer."

"Thanks Leese. I'll see you soon."

Lisa hung up the phone, closed her diary and went to face Steph, who was still waiting in the kitchen. Predictably, she was standing over the kettle, waiting for it to boil.

"So?"

"Well, we've got more company this evening."

"Really!" Steph's face exploded into a grin. "I told you so."

"Don't get too excited," Lisa said as she opened the fridge and scanned it. She was sure there were at least one or two cans of Coke hiding in there somewhere. "It's Joel."

The reproach in Steph's tone was unmistakable. "You *did* ring didn't you?"

"No." Lisa poked around. There they were, right behind the head of lettuce. "I'll do it tomorrow."

"You're the biggest coward I've ever met Lisa Smith." Steph let out a frustrated groan and hit Lisa on the back of the head with a wet dishcloth.

Toni swirled wine in her glass, watching the rich red fluid curtain down the sides. She was all but ready to call it a day. Friday drinks certainly were a somber affair this evening. So somber that Sue's half-full champagne flute sat unattended on its coaster, her having left a few minutes prior to "find someone who at least pretends to have a pulse."

"Well, here's to another Friday." In a last ditch effort to pull Cathy out of her reverie, Toni lifted her glass in a toast.

"Cheers." A glass appeared above the back of Cathy's chair. She had swiveled it to face the window only moments after Sue's departure. Toni wanted to assume something wildly exciting was happening beyond the plate glass. However, she guessed it was more a continuation of Cathy's mood.

It seemed a dark cloud had descended over the office of late, affecting all its inhabitants, with the exception of Sue of course, who rarely seemed to let anything get under her skin. Cathy had been irritable and waspish the last few days, brushing away Toni's attempts at striking up a conversation that had anything to do with anything other than work. She'd also been putting in longer than normal days—both this morning and the previous saw Toni greeted with e-mail sent in the wee hours. The e-mails were short and to the point, with no salutation at the beginning and just a single *C* at the bottom to signify the end of communication.

Cathy's mood rubbed off on Toni, and she too became irritable and moody. Just that afternoon she snapped at Julie for some minor discrepancy in the work presented for checking. To Toni's horror, Julie burst into tears.

Julie snuffled into the tissue Toni offered, and Toni apologized profusely, feeling incredibly guilty for taking out her frustrations on a co-worker. She quickly checked her watch. It was already late afternoon. "Let's pack this up for the week," she suggested as Julie blew her nose. "I brought in a good bottle of red today. We can get a head start on the others."

Julie managed a feeble smile but shook her head. "If it's okay, I'll pass on the offer."

Toni nodded and didn't push the issue. She apologized again and bid Julie a nice weekend. Julie didn't look at her as she mumbled a good-bye, but Toni felt eyes on her back as she turned and left her office. *Some mentor* she chided herself as she made her way down the corridor.

Now, as Toni sat watching the back of Cathy's chair, she tossed up telling her of the incident. Toni knew she should let Cathy know sooner rather than later—she was the boss after all—even though she was unsure of Cathy's reaction in her current frame of mind.

Cathy, having finally turned away from the window, listened quietly as Toni spoke, asked a few questions, and gave what was obviously her closing remark on the matter, "Just be a bit more aware in the future. You know how sensitive she is."

Toni blinked. Cathy's reaction wasn't as harsh as expected, which of course was good, but it stirred indignation. "Maybe we should all be a bit more aware," she muttered.

"Excuse me?" Cathy placed her glass quietly on the desk. "I didn't quite catch that."

Toni half wished she'd held her tongue, but then again she was glad she hadn't. Steeling her resolve, she defiantly met Cathy's stony look. "I said—maybe we should all be a bit more aware how we handle things. Julie's not the only sensitive one around here you know." Toni didn't let her eyes waver from Cathy's face but she held her breath for the return.

Again, Cathy did not react as expected. Her shoulders slumped and she was the one to break eye contact. There was suddenly some piece of unseen dirt under one of her fingernails that she seemed intent on extracting. "Point taken Toni. I know I've been in a mood lately. I've taken it out on everyone and I'm sorry."

Cathy looked so miserable, Toni's ire dissolved immediately. However, now that an opening had finally been offered, Toni wasn't going to let the opportunity slip away. "What exactly is wrong Cathy?" she asked gently. "You really aren't yourself lately."

Toni could almost see the walls come up. Cathy stopped her finger fidgeting and straightened from the slumped posture she had assumed. "Nothing's wrong." She shrugged. "Maybe I'm just extra pre-menstrual or something."

"Hey," she continued as Toni sat in frustrated silence. "Have you heard of the film *The Good Girl* showing down at the Luna? It's supposed to be good, and funny too. I sure could do with a good laugh. How about it?"

Again Toni sat in silence. At that moment Cathy seemed the most infuriating person she had ever come across, but before she knew it she heard herself agreeing to the offer.

Toni knew she hadn't just agreed to watch a movie, but to an hour and a half—maybe more—of sitting in the near dark in close proximity to the woman who was driving her to distraction. Hell, why not go for broke and draw out the frustration as long as possible, especially since the cinema was smack in the middle of Leederville's café and restaurant strip? "Let's make a night of it, grab something to eat and catch the late show."

"I'll just be a minute, okay?" Toni dropped her keys on the hall table and galloped into the bedroom.

"No need to rush," Cathy called as the bedroom door slammed.

"We've got plenty of time." She checked her watch and lied, "Ten minutes in fact."

They actually had at least fifteen minutes if they wanted to get to the theatre for the start of the session, closer to twenty-five if they missed the ads and new movie previews. But if Toni thought they only had ten minutes she may well be ready in twenty.

Cathy smiled at the expected curse that came from the bedroom. Toni was no doubt cursing her own embarrassment as opposed to the press for time, the unscheduled stop at home being so she could don a new outfit. She could be such a klutz sometimes. Dinner came to an abrupt halt halfway through the main course and halfway through another of Toni's tales. As usual, she'd been illustrating her story with expansive hand movements. One such demonstrative sweep brought her glass of wine straight into her lap, spilling the contents over both her blouse and her slacks. Cab-sav, too. The outfit was ruined.

Cathy had offered to feed Virgil while Toni made herself presentable. Virgil seemed to sense Cathy was the chef this evening, weaving in and out of her legs from the moment she walked through the front door. Cathy stepped into the kitchen and Virgil was at her food bowl, meowing expectantly.

"Yum, yum. Pilchards in aspic jelly." Cathy screwed up her nose as she forked a serving of the freshly opened tin into the ceramic dish. She popped a plastic can lid over the remains and placed it in the fridge.

Virgil's affections were obviously a display of cupboard love. She completely ignored Cathy from the moment the food hit the bowl. Cathy left her to her noisy munching, wandered from the kitchen to the sitting room, and did a quick check of the window from which Virgil had made her escape. True to Toni's word, the fly wire had been replaced and the window now kept securely closed. No more late night wanderings for this little feline.

Cathy was under no such restrictions. She glanced to the back door, thought better of it and took a step away. A moment later she had reconsidered and the key to the deadlock was in her hand.

Once outside she breathed in the night air. The night was cool but not cold. Very soon they would experience the annual "cool change" where the nighttime temperature suddenly seemed to plummet.

Indeed, a number of the neighbors were making the most of the weather before being forced indoors for the winter. The smell of barbeque sausages drifted from the yard immediately to the left and voices rose and fell from all directions. Cathy tuned into the individual voices, discarding them if they came from the wrong direction, or did not match what she was looking for. She was not really expecting to find the voice she was hoping to hear, and she didn't know what she would do if she did hear it, but suddenly, there it was. Another female voice took over when Lisa's trailed off, followed by the rising strains of joint laughter. Cathy listened more intently, but from her distance could not make out what was being said.

A quick time check revealed only five minutes had passed. Toni was probably still peering into her wardrobe. Before the ethics of her actions could be debated, Cathy was across the yard, up the back steps and plucking the gate key from the hook just inside the door. Careful not to let the back door lock behind her and praying the gate didn't squeak as she pushed it open, Cathy found herself in the laneway.

Congratulations Cathy. She was quite disgusted with herself as she carefully picked her way across the cobbles. *You have officially sunk to new depths. Eavesdropping on the neighbors—really.*

After their afternoon indoors, Lisa suggested that she and Steph sit outside while Joel spruced himself up for his date. The grass was quite dewy, so they settled in the chairs surrounding the large patio table. Conversation rolled from topic to topic. What was the plan for Lisa's upcoming birthday? Should they go as a non-couple to Dee and Rebecca's fourth anniversary party the following evening? Why do petrol prices always shoot up the morning after you couldn't be bothered filling up the tank the day before? Eventually, Steph steered the talk back to Cathy. She wanted to see for herself where Cathy "dropped in."

"Come on then." Lisa hauled Steph to her feet. They walked arm in arm, Lisa pointing out where her beloved amphora had been placed before it came to grief, and Steph making the appropriate sympathetic noises. They descended into companionable silence as they neared the rear of her garden.

Steph peered at the twiggy stump that had been a lavender bush. "This is where she fell?"

"Yep." Reading the *ouch* in Steph's voice, Lisa added, "It didn't look like that at the time though. I had to prune it right back because most of the stems were crushed. It would have given a much softer landing before I attacked it. Although," she admitted, "I bet it still hurt like hell."

Steph giggled. "I've heard of falling for someone Lisa, but this is ridiculous."

"Ha ha." Obviously this incident would provide Lisa's friends with fodder for months to come. "You can't say anything I haven't already heard from Joel."

"Don't worry. He'll forget about it soon enough and move onto something else." Steph turned to face Lisa in the poor light, and said, "Have you told him what you told me about her this afternoon?"

Knowing Steph was referring to Lisa's *I can't stop thinking about Cathy* revelation, she shook her head vehemently, "Can you imagine what he'd be like when we go to do the job? He wouldn't be able to keep his mouth shut. Anyhow," Lisa folded her arms and said firmly, "If I've told him once, I've told him a thousand times, I'm through with women."

Whatever Steph was going to say in reply was lost as Joel called loudly from the back door, "Hey Leese, where are you?" But the skyward roll of her eyes indicated she thought Lisa was full of it.

"We're down here," Lisa called back. "What do you want?"

"I can't find my mobile. Do you know where it is?"

Joel had changed in the spare bedroom. "Try the bedside table."

"I've already looked there."

"Stop yelling," Lisa yelled. "We're coming." She grabbed Steph by the arm and tugged her back toward the house. "Come on. Let's find the caveman his talking stick."

"I bet it *is* on the bedside table."

"Yeah," Lisa agreed. What was it with men that made them unable to see what was right in front of their face? "Me, too."

"How do I look?" Joel did a slow twirl in the middle of the kitchen.

Lisa's suspicions that Joel really liked Scott were confirmed. Joel looked resplendent in new black dress trousers and a black long-sleeved shirt. His black leather shoes were so highly polished they sparkled.

Lisa gave a low whistle. "Joel, you'll knock his socks off. You look great."

"Really?"

"Really." Lisa adjusted his collar and pointed him in the direction of the front door, "Go on Romeo. Better get your skates on if you don't want to be late."

She turned to Steph as the front door closed, "So, now big boy's gone, what are two good-looking gals supposed to do to amuse themselves on a Friday night?"

"It's getting late." Steph checked her watch. "What's to do?"

Lisa shrugged, out of inspiration. "We could always see if there's a decent movie on the telly."

A quick scan of the television guide revealed nothing of note. "Looks like they program around people who actually have a life."

"Well, you might have had a life if you'd picked up the bloody phone."

Lisa chose to ignore Steph's dig, snapping her fingers as an idea struck. "Hey, let's go see a movie. There's a new Jennifer Aniston film showing in Leederville. I can't think of the name—" Lisa grabbed the newspaper off the coffee table and thumbed through the pages. "Here we go," She stabbed a finger at the cinema schedule, "*The Good Girl.*"

"I read a review about that one. It's supposed to be good." Steph stretched to study the screening times. "We'll have to leave right now though. Or we'll miss the start."

"Give me one minute to throw on something half decent." Lisa leapt off the couch and was in the hallway before Steph made it from her seat. She grabbed Steph's keys from the hall stand and tossed them. "I'll be out before you even get the engine warmed up."

Toni fussed with a stray strand of hair as she brushed her teeth. After an extended gargle she studied her reflection in the mirror of her ensuite bathroom. Hair was in place, teeth were clean, deodorant and perfume reapplied. All she had to do now was get into the clothes she'd selected and she'd be ready.

"Shit." A glance to the clock on the bedside table revealed she had already used more than her allotted ten minutes. Most of that had been used to select her outfit.

"I'll be one more minute okay?" she called through the bedroom door, shrugging into the long-sleeved cotton shirt she'd laid out on the bed before retreating to the bathroom. She got no answer. Toni dismissed it, thinking Cathy had probably just taken a trip to the toilet. But, as she slipped a belt through the loops of her black slacks, it occurred to her how strange it was that Cathy hadn't already been banging on her door, telling her to hurry up. Cathy hated to be late.

I hope she hasn't descended into a mood again. Toni thought to herself as she tugged on ankle-high boots and reached for her suede jacket. After all, she'd worked so hard to lift Cathy's spirits. She'd been successful. Cathy had become more animated as their dinner progressed. She'd even laughed out loud when Toni came to grief with her glass of wine. Toni hadn't thought it particularly funny as she'd only bought her outfit the week before. The only consolation was that the most expensive part of her ensemble, the jacket, had been slung across the back of her chair so it avoided being hit by the spillage. Actually, that wasn't the only consolation. Cathy suggested soda water may help and called for a glass and a cloth. The subsequent dabbing had been ineffectual as far as the red wine was concerned, but Toni found Cathy's ministrations to her clothes highly effective in removing all traces of ire at her out of pocket loss. Hell, had Toni known Cathy would do the dabbing she would have tipped the bottle of wine over herself before they'd even ordered the entrées.

Toni blew into her hand and inhaled. Still minty fresh. Very important, especially if she was required to lean over and whisper something witty in Cathy's ear during the movie. She tugged open the bedroom door and called, "Okay, I'm ready."

She was speaking to thin air.

"Where's she gone Virg?" Toni asked of her feline friend, who she found on the kitchen table, attending to her post-dinner wash. Toni lifted the protesting Virgil from the table, admonishing her gently, "You know you're not supposed to be up here."

"I'm out here."

Toni turned to the source of Cathy's voice, frowning as she discovered the sitting room also empty. Then she noticed the back door was open, just a fraction.

"You'll get piles sitting out here," she said lightly as she joined Cathy at the bottom of the concrete steps. One glance at the hangdog expression told Toni it was as feared—Cathy had turned moody again. So she tread carefully, and said, "We're already running a little behind. Shall we get going?"

There was no snipe at Toni's protracted preparations, no lecture on time management. Instead, Cathy stood from the step, glanced at her watch, mumbled something about not realizing the time and headed inside.

Toni gave Virgil a quick cuddle then trotted to meet Cathy at the front door, snatching her keys from the hall stand as she passed. She got the sinking feeling Cathy was going to cancel on her, but again she was mistaken.

Cathy dangled the car keys. "Do you want to drive? I don't feel like it."

Never one to miss an opportunity to get behind the wheel of Cathy's BMW, Toni accepted the keys. A grin spread as she shut the front door behind her. The evening was now extended, the one-car deal meaning Cathy would have to drop her back home instead of leaving straight from the cinema. That left plenty of time for Toni to work her magic and cheer Cathy up again.

Despite the faulty start, it was going to be a good night. Toni was sure of it.

The appearance of an elongated shaft of light took Lisa's attention away from the screen. It was a signal the door to the cinema had been opened.

"Oh, for God's sake," she muttered as another light, that of an usher's torch, added to the distraction. It was already a good five minutes into the movie. Why couldn't people organize themselves better and be on time? By Lisa's way of thinking, walking in late to a movie was as serious a sin as leaving your mobile on and having it ring. First there would be the clumping as the latecomers picked their way down the aisle, followed by the shuffle and loudly whispered "sorry, excuse me, sorry" as they squeezed past other moviegoers to get to their seats. Just as well there were no vacant seats in the near back row she and Steph had chosen, she'd have happily poured her popcorn over them. Lisa turned to glower in the direction of the aisle, hoping the latecomers picked up on her none too pleased vibes.

She blinked as she found something familiar in one of the figures. Then her eyes widened as the figures swept in and out of dark and less dark in unison with the flickering of the screen. Steph received such a sharp poke in the side that she jumped. Lisa whispered urgently, "It's her!"

Lisa's poke was answered with a slap on the arm. "It's who?"

"Cathy!" Lisa indicated a point halfway down the length of the cinema. "Just there. In the aisle."

Steph craned to see, head bobbing from side to side as she strained for a better view. "Which one?"

Which one? Lisa couldn't believe Steph had to ask. *The goddess of course.* "The taller one."

"Is the other one Toni?"

Lisa nodded in the near darkness, after the woman sitting immediately behind them told them in no uncertain terms to shut up. Lisa hunched down in her seat, aware she had broken one of her other rules of cinema etiquette. She didn't even utter a word when yet another latecomer entered the cinema a few minutes later, mainly because the interruption didn't register; she was too busy staring at the back of Cathy's head.

She was still staring when the lights came up and people began the mad dash for the exit. It was a prod from Steph that brought her back to reality.

"Get moving or you'll miss her."

Lisa balked, "But Toni's here as well."

"That's all right." Steph pulled Lisa to her feet and gently pushed her so she had to start shunting past the quickly emptying seats. "A friendly hello is not going to hurt."

"But what am I supposed to say?"

"You could always try, *Hello. How about a coffee?*"

Lisa rolled her eyes. Trust Steph to work in a coffee somewhere along the line. "But . . ."

"But nothing." Steph gave another push, this time not so gentle.

"Hey watch it," Lisa turned to her friend, annoyance building at the constant prodding. "I don't think me falling headlong into the crowd is going to create a good impression."

"Do you promise you'll go and say hello?"

"I promise." Lisa crossed her heart and turned her attention back to the aisle just in time to see Cathy and Toni pass by their row. Neither was looking in her direction. Cathy was busy pressing buttons on her mobile phone. Toni was doing some *I'm dying to see what you're doing but I'm not really looking* glances at Cathy's mobile's display. Lisa waited for another few people to move past, then maneuvered into the crowd and let herself be herded toward the exit. She waited at the cinema doors for Steph to join her. There was safety in numbers.

Toni was leaning against a pillar at the perimeter of the lobby when she spied Lisa. She couldn't believe it. What was it with this woman? She stays out of sight for years then all of a sudden she's everywhere like the plague?

As Lisa headed her way, Toni was torn between telling Cathy, who was busy replying to a text message sent by her brother, or turning the other way and hoping they hadn't been seen.

Oblivious to the debate going on in Toni's head Cathy snapped her mobile shut and popped it into a jacket pocket. Her eyes sparkled as she said, "Mark's going to be a dad again."

"Really? That's great." Toni smiled back, pleased for Cathy, who already played the long distance but doting aunt to her brother's soon to be five-year-old son, and pleased to see the news served to cheer. Cathy had managed a few smiles during the movie, but it didn't take Einstein to realize something was still eating away at her.

From the edge of Toni's peripheral vision she could see Lisa almost upon them. Common sense prevailed. She couldn't just turn and flee, dragging Cathy along. Anyway, the woman would be playing a larger role in their existence in a few weeks time, so for the sake of harmony she needed to at least aim for civility. Toni nodded in Lisa's direction, watching Cathy as her eyes followed the nod. "Look who's here."

As had been the case all afternoon and evening, Cathy's reaction caused surprise. Toni watched Cathy set her jaw, straighten her shoulders and shift so her feet were planted slightly apart. The impression it gave was that Cathy was steeling herself. Very odd. A protective instinct kicked in and Toni sidestepped to stand closer.

"Hi." The smile Lisa gave was slightly nervous, as if she sensed the collective unease. "Fancy bumping into you two."

Hellos were passed all round. After a short silence Lisa touched the arm of her companion, and said, "This is Steph."

Toni couldn't help smiling as she accepted Steph's hand. From the way she was dressed, Steph could have just stepped out of the pages of *Vogue*, but without the vague, half-starved look. The woman positively oozed charisma, and from her confident stance she was well aware of it. "Pleased to meet you."

"Likewise." Steph flashed a set of perfectly straight teeth then turned her attention to Cathy. "Hi Cathy. Lisa's told me a lot about you." She winked, adding, "All good, I promise."

Toni noticed that Cathy seemed taken aback by that comment. When Cathy didn't reply, Toni filled the gap of silence, blurting out, "So what brings you here?"

As soon as the words were out of her mouth she realized it was a dumb thing to ask. Obviously they were here to watch the movie.

Lisa shrugged and smiled, "Girls' night out."

"That's right," Steph gave Lisa a friendly pat on the shoulder. "This one here is keeping me sane while my significant other is off kicking a leather bag of wind around a paddock."

It took Toni a moment to understand. *Ahh . . . football.* She wondered if Steph's significant other was a league player. From what she'd seen on television they tended to collect the glamorous ones as their girlfriends/trophies. Who cared? Toni didn't follow any of the football codes, and she certainly didn't want to get into a discussion about it.

But Steph had already moved onto a new topic. Again she turned to Cathy. "Lisa also tells me she'll be working for you in a few weeks."

"That's right." Cathy nodded, for the first time looking in Lisa's direction.

Lisa responded with a grin, also turning slightly more toward Cathy. "Joel said to tell you thanks by the way. He's really looking forward to it."

Toni prickled. Had she suddenly become invisible? "What's he up to tonight?" she asked, just to get herself back into the conversation.

Lisa gave her a decidedly odd look. "Boys' night out."

Again it took Toni a moment to register. Joel was probably

propping up a bar somewhere. Either that or he and his mates were ogling women at some strip club. Oh well, if Lisa was okay with that, it was her problem. But, along with football, the antics of the men in their lives wasn't something Toni wanted to dissect. She was frantically seeking an out to the conversation when Lisa said, "We're just going to the coffee shop next door. Would you like to join us?"

It happened Toni didn't need to find an excuse, Cathy piping up, "Thank you, but we'll have to decline, we've both got early starts tomorrow."

Toni shot a quick glance to Cathy. That was an utter lie. For her part anyhow, she was planning on nothing more strenuous than a late lie-in. But in the second their eyes met Toni picked up on the quiet desperation for escape. She didn't understand it, but she played along. "That's right. A big day."

"Okay," Lisa said lightly, obvious in her effort to mask her disappointment. "Some other time maybe."

"Sure." Toni felt a little twinge of guilt. "Some other time."

"And what do you make of that, *Ms. Astute Observer of the Human Condition*?" Lisa turned to Steph, who was watching the retreating figures of Cathy and Toni through the glassed entry to the cinema complex.

"I don't know." Steph sported a baffled expression, obviously frustrated at her inability to read the situation. "Something's off."

"Yeah," Lisa agreed glumly, "Any hopes of me and Cathy being . . . anything." She didn't need to be an astute observer of the human condition to read the road signs. It was quite obvious Cathy couldn't bear to be near her. For most of the conversation Cathy hadn't even looked at her, then when she did it was as if Lisa had suddenly sprouted horns and a tail.

"I wonder why Toni asked you what Joel was up to?"

"Who knows? Maybe she's got the hots for him or something."

Steph didn't even raise a smile at Lisa's poor attempt at humor. "No, I mean why would you know what Joel was doing anyway?"

"Who knows?" Lisa repeated. "Maybe she assumes that just because she's joined at the hip to her business partner that I am too." Feeling a pang of jealousy it wasn't her joined to Cathy's hip, Lisa pushed Steph in the direction of the café. "Let's get some caffeine into you. It's been nearly two hours, you must be going into withdrawal."

A few minutes later they were tucked into a cozy corner of the tiny premises. Lisa was sprinkling sugar onto the froth of her cappuccino, at pains to ensure she got an even coating. Steph was stirring her as yet untouched black coffee, lost in thought.

"You know," Steph said eventually, still stirring. "I don't think Cathy and Toni are together."

Lisa snorted. Obviously the lack of caffeine had addled Steph's brain. "Yeah right."

"True." Steph nodded away Lisa's sarcasm. "I think Toni's in love with Cathy, but from what I saw she didn't have that confidence of being loved back. She was trying too hard. I think Toni wants Cathy, but she hasn't got her." Steph's spoon was pointed toward Lisa. "I also think she's very much threatened by you."

"Oh come on Steph, why would she be threatened by me?" Lisa wanted to believe Steph was right, that the *astute observer* was picking up on something she wasn't. But the evidence was right before her eyes. "You saw Cathy tonight."

"Yes I did. And I still think there's something strange going on. Why would she want you to work for her if she hates you?"

"Because—"

"Yeah, yeah. Because you quoted cheapest." Steph finished Lisa's now common refrain.

Lisa sighed, nodding her assent as Steph again launched into her lecture about why Lisa should ring Cathy. But Lisa knew she wouldn't call. Rejection wasn't one of her strong points. As it was, it was going to be hard enough fronting up for work when the time came.

⁓⁓

The display on the clock radio changed from 4:03 to 4:04. Toni had been watching the display change since 2:16. She'd also been pondering yet another turn in the night's events, the one that saw her as she was now, lying on one side of Cathy's king-sized bed, Cathy curled up on the other, even breathing indicating at least she was able to get some sleep.

Despite the bed's dimensions, Toni was perched precariously on the very edge. Another inch or so and she'd fall off. But it seemed the safest option at the moment. Toni knew she couldn't trust herself. She'd nearly overstepped the mark earlier in the evening and she wasn't going to tempt fate again. Not when Cathy was relying on her as a friend.

Toni had known something was up all evening, but it became glaringly apparent once back in Cathy's car. Cathy hurried them to her vehicle, which was parked what seemed like miles away, their late arrival back in Leederville seeing the major car parks completely full. The walk was brisk and quiet, Cathy striding ahead with head down. Again Cathy dangled the car keys and Toni accepted the offer to drive. But she had hardly settled into the driver's seat when Cathy burst into tears.

"Oh Cathy, what's wrong?" Toni swiveled herself as far as the restrictions placed by the steering wheel would allow.

Cathy looked at her through tear-filled eyes, then her face crumpled and she reached for Toni, arms circling her into a half body hug as she buried her head into Toni's neck.

"It's okay," Toni soothed, rubbing a hand up and down Cathy's back, her other stroking her hair. "It's okay."

They stayed that way until the torrent of tears subsided to a whimper. Head still buried in Toni's neck Cathy mumbled, "Can you take me home please?"

"Sure." Toni halted her hair stroking, her other hand coming to rest in the small of Cathy's back.

"Umm Cathy," she said a short time later, neither of them having moved. "I can't quite drive like this."

"Sorry." Extricating herself from Toni's hold, Cathy sniffed and wiped her nose with a tissue dug from a jacket pocket. She dabbed a fresh corner of it at the lapel of Toni's suede jacket. "Sorry. I've made it all wet."

"It's okay." Toni made light of the potential damage to yet another piece of clothing, more concerned at how empty her arms felt now that Cathy was no longer in them. She brushed a stray strand of hair from Cathy's face, searching eyes that still shone with unshed tears. The urge to kiss them away was incredible. Instead she pushed the thought away, ashamed at how her body was stirring at such an inappropriate time. She wriggled back into a driving position, snapped her belt on and instructed Cathy to do the same.

They spent the journey home in silence, Cathy staring through the passenger window into the night, Toni concentrating on the road and getting her charge home safely. Toni knew it was pointless to push. Cathy would only talk when she was ready.

And indeed, once home and settled on the couch, Cathy had been ready. In between bouts of tears, the missing pieces of Cathy's life story fell into place. For once Toni listened without interruption, all the questions she had been collecting over the last four years finally being answered. The process took a couple of hours, and by the finish Toni was exhausted, and all she'd done was listen and pass tissues. Cathy herself looked totally wrung out, eyes puffy and red rimmed.

Toni was stifling a yawn when Cathy asked, "Will you stay with me tonight?"

The yawn was quickly swallowed. It was a good few months since Toni had shared Cathy's bed, invitations to stay coming to a halt around the time Toni's feelings toward Cathy moved to a higher level. "If you want me to."

Once in her bedroom, Cathy disappeared into the walk-in wardrobe, returning a few moments later, T-shirt in hand. Toni caught the tossed shirt and headed to the guest bathroom down the hall. Despite her quick clothes change and hurried teeth clean, Cathy had already crawled under the covers by the time Toni returned.

"Thank you for listening Toni."

"My pleasure." Toni slipped between the sheets, the linen cool against the bare skin of her legs. She settled on her side, facing Cathy, thinking, *I'd do anything for you.* "Sleep well."

"You, too."

They both reached to turn off their respective bedside lights.

Once Toni's eyes adjusted to the darkness she saw Cathy had turned to face the window. She watched her, hands forming into tight balls to stop them from reaching out. Finally unable to stand it anymore, Toni flipped over and screwed her eyes shut. But sleep wouldn't come. In an effort to take her mind off the flowering in her groin, she turned her thoughts to Cathy's revelations.

Initially Toni had been irked to discover Cathy harbored doubts about the *Lisa and Joel are more than just business partners* theory. She thought it was just another of Toni's exaggerations. Toni knew she embellished her stories (why tell a dull tale when a few enhancements could add the needed spice?) but in this case she'd only told it as she'd seen it.

That Cathy had been spending her time gathering a body of evidence to further disprove Toni's theory also came as a surprise, especially the confession she'd been listening in on Lisa's conversation from behind the fence. It was that overheard conversation which all but erased any final hope Toni was mistaken. A fresh paroxysm of tears emerged as Cathy said, "Lisa told Steph she'd told Joel she was through with women."

Once the rush of tears slowed, Cathy told how Lisa's pointed comments about girls' nights and boys' nights were the final straw. She felt she was being given a clear message of, "Stay away, I'm no longer interested."

There was no need for Toni to ask if Cathy was in fact interested. Of course she was, she wouldn't be in this state if she weren't.

Toni struggled to understand. It was obvious Cathy had been deeply in love with Lisa. In light of the circumstances in which their relationship ended, she just could not comprehend how Cathy could hold onto such feelings. Certainly Toni had never experienced a love like that. Her relationships either ended with the desire never to see the woman in question again, or they made the post breakup transition into friends. Indeed, the woman she left Melbourne over was now in the friend category. They spoke regularly on the phone and just the previous year, she and her new girlfriend had stayed with Toni for a week while on holiday.

Cathy's other relationships followed the same path. Her first lover, a fellow boarder, had been pulled out of school halfway through the final year, her diplomat father being offered a "safe" post in Europe and thinking a new country experience would be good for his daughter. Cathy bid her first love good-bye with a lot of tears, but the anguish faded to be replaced with a bank of pleasant memories and no great regret at the loss. The woman now lived in France with a longtime partner and she and Cathy were pen friends, exchanging letters/e-mail a couple of times a year, and phoning each other at Christmas. Similarly, Cathy's two lovers during her time in Sydney were now regarded as friends. As with Toni and her Melbourne ex, Cathy kept in phone contact and open offers to stay were in place should either be in town.

"But I don't know what it is about Lisa," Cathy cried. "I thought I was over it, but from the moment I saw her again I haven't been able to get her off my mind."

It was on the tip of Toni's tongue to suggest maybe it was a combination of the abrupt end to their relationship and the extended period before bumping into each other again that was causing such a spike in her feelings. But she didn't voice her thoughts. Cathy was coming to her own closure on the issue.

It seemed closure included clearing the decks. Toni mentally cheered when Cathy said maybe she should cancel the tiling job.

"If that's what you think is best," Toni said slowly, hoping her tone sounded casual. She knew she was being mean-minded, even irrational. The sense of competition she felt with Lisa didn't make sense, especially since they weren't even running in the same race, but she just couldn't help herself.

"I think so." Cathy wiped her eyes. "I'll ring Monday, let them know."

Monday was a long way away. Were it up to Toni she'd have rung first thing in the morning. But it wasn't her decision. "Okay."

Toni watched the clock's display change again: 4:05. Never mind Monday, even morning seemed an eternity away, especially when time was being marked on a minute-by-minute basis.

The bedclothes rustled. Toni listened to the movements, deciding they were too prolonged for just a shift during sleep. Cathy was waking. Sure enough, soon came the swoosh of a tissue being pulled from its box, another rustle of linen, then a quiet sob.

Toni rolled over, heart wrenching as she watched Cathy in her misery. Worries of her lack of self-trust were pushed aside and she shunted across the bed, imitating Cathy's posture so they lay curled up together like a couple of spoons.

Toni did a long arm stretch for the tissue box that sat on Cathy's bedside table. Once it was within easy reach she cuddled back in and wrapped an arm securely around Cathy's waist. Quite a few soggy tissues later the latest wave of tears subsided.

Another spent tissue was tossed onto the bedside table and Cathy let her arm flop over the side of the bed. "You must think I'm a real cry baby."

"Not at all." Toni assured. "If you think you're bad, you should see me once I get going. Last time they started loading up the ark again."

That raised a quiver of laughter. Toni smiled into Cathy's hair, pleased.

"Toni?"

"Yes?" Toni decided Cathy's hair smelled like spring.

"Do you think I'm attractive?"

The question was so unexpected it took a moment to respond. "Of course I do." She gave Cathy's waist a quick squeeze and said softly, "You know that."

Cathy's voice was small as she asked, "Why?"

Realization dawned. Cathy was feeling insecure. It was a side Toni had never seen before. In all the time she had known her, Cathy always presented as self-sufficient and strong. Toni found the vulnerability endearing. And she had no problem finding material to give the much needed ego boost.

"Well, let's see now, where do you want me to start?" Toni shifted so her elbow was propped on the pillow and her head rested on her hand. "I think you're about the smartest person I've ever met, you've got a great sense of humor, you're kind and generous and you're a great cook . . ." Toni carried on with her seemingly endless list, naming all the traits that made Cathy the person she adored. "And not to forget, Virgil gives you the stamp of approval." She gave Cathy another squeeze. "That's very important you know."

"Very," Cathy said with amusement in her tone.

Again Toni was much pleased. She rattled on, "And of course there's the fact you're the best looking and sexiest boss I've ever had."

Toni bit on her bottom lip. She hadn't meant for that to come out. She'd gone too far again. She was sure of it when Cathy shifted in her arms. Toni loosened her hold to allow Cathy to move away.

But she didn't, she only turned over so she faced Toni. "Really?"

"Yes." Toni tried for a lighthearted tone, "But you already know that too."

Cathy didn't answer and in the darkness of the room Toni could not define what she was thinking from her features. On impulse she moved so her head rested on the pillow instead of on her hand. She was now so close she could feel Cathy's breath warm on her face. Still Cathy didn't move away.

"Cathy—" Toni's voice cracked as her conscience battled with her physiology. Cathy was exposed and vulnerable and she was supposed to be providing the solace of a friend. Whatever happened now, Cathy would be sure to regret it in the morning.

Her conscience won. Toni gave Cathy a brief, light kiss on the corner of her mouth and wriggled so there was a little more distance between them. The taste of salt from dried tears told her she had done the right thing.

It was just a shame the rest of her body screamed in protest.

The protest continued when Cathy returned Toni's kiss with one of her own. It turned into outright mutiny as another lingered, slowly deepening as a soft tongue parted Toni's lips to explore her mouth. Toni gasped as an insistent knee also parted her thighs. Legs entwined in Cathy's, thoughts of rights and wrongs fled, worries of regrets in the morning disappeared and, at least for the time being, the universe outside the confines of their bed ceased to exist.

Chapter Eight

The full-length drapes shrouding the balcony from view were heavy, but they were not quite fully drawn. The resulting chink of light was bright enough to let Cathy know it was already late morning. She gingerly lifted the arm that lay over her stomach and slipped from under the covers. The movement made Toni stir.

"I'm just going to get us some coffee," Cathy said in response to the half-asleep, "Where are you going?"

She slipped her housecoat over her shoulders, tied it loosely around her waist and left the bedroom, pulling the door behind her, but not enough so it clicked shut. Her next stop was at the bathroom down the hall. She was surprised at her reflection. It was not difficult to see she had been crying. There was still telltale puffiness around the eyes, but it certainly wasn't the toad-like appearance she'd been expecting. Cathy splashed cool water over her face and neck. It relieved the sting of her eyes, also removed the traces of lovemaking leftover from the night before. What it didn't remove was the feeling of renewed vigor that came from long overdue physical release. Neither did it remove the feeling of guilt that came from the fact she had taken Toni's kindness and concern and used it for her own short-term gratification. She knew how Toni felt toward her, knew she would not turn down an advance. She had used that knowledge to fulfill her overwhelming need for reassurance that she was still okay.

The feeling of guilt endured as she made the trip from the bathroom to the kitchen. It stayed with her for the minutes that passed before she quietly pushed the bedroom door open again.

Cathy placed a tray laden with mugs, sugar, milk and a coffee plunger on the bedside table closest to Toni.

She sat on the edge of the bed. "Coffee's up."

In her absence Toni had moved so she lay sprawled out on her stomach. She squinted one eye open and closed it again. "What's the time?"

Cathy pushed the plunger down as far as it would go. "Nearly ten thirty."

Toni groaned, and Cathy smiled. She could imagine Toni did that every morning when her alarm sounded. She watched as Toni slowly came to life, stretching all limbs then turning and lifting into a sitting position. She yawned widely and raked fingers through tousled hair. As if suddenly realizing she was naked, Toni pulled at the sheet so it covered her breasts. Cathy smiled again. It was a bit late for such a display of modesty. But her amusement was short-lived; it occurred to her that Toni was as uncomfortable as she was. She now had her arms folded across her chest and was looking everywhere except at Cathy.

Long moments of silence stretched between them. Cathy busied herself pouring the coffee. She added sugar and milk to one of the mugs and held it out.

"Thanks." Toni held the mug to her mouth but did not drink. Cathy could tell she was hiding behind it.

"Toni," Cathy blurted, unable to stand the silence any longer. "About last night—"

She halted mid-sentence, aware at how awful that well-worn line sounded. "Toni," she began again. "Thank you for last night. For . . . everything."

Toni just nodded, blowing on the steam of her coffee. Cathy was not used to this. Usually she had trouble getting Toni to shut up. Her feelings of guilt grew. No matter what anyone said, sex changed everything. "I'm sorry Toni. I feel like I've taken advantage of you."

A flicker of surprise crossed Toni's face. "I'm the one who's sorry Cathy. I feel like I've taken advantage of you."

"But I was the one who started it."

"But I continued it."

"But I shouldn't have started it."

Toni cocked her head to one side. "Did you hear me complaining?"

"Well, no." Cathy agreed, her lips twitching up at the corners. She'd heard a lot of things last night, but nothing close to a protest.

"There you go then. We're equally guilty." Toni placed her mug back on the tray and folded her arms protectively across her chest again. "The big question is, where do we go from here?"

"Toni," Cathy said as she unfolded Toni's arms and took hold of her hands. Hard as it was she looked her square in the eye. "I love you dearly as a friend, but I'm just not ready for anything else right now." She dropped her gaze. "I just can't give you what you want."

"I know that Cathy." Toni pulled her hand from Cathy's grasp and used it to tilt her chin so she was back to eye level. "Despite what you may think, I didn't come down in the last shower. And after what you told me last night, I'd be very surprised if you suddenly saw me as the great love of your life."

Cathy opened her mouth to argue but was silenced with a finger over her lips.

"Shush. I'm not finished. I just want you to know that if you need me, in *any* way at all, I will be there for you. No strings attached."

"No Toni," Cathy shook her head, fully realizing the extent of the offer. "I couldn't do that."

"Oh." Toni's shoulders slumped. "Was I that bad?"

"Oh no," Cathy said quickly. "You were wonderful, it's just—" she trailed away, Toni's grin alerting she was being teased. Cathy poked her in the ribs, having discovered during the night that Toni was acutely ticklish. "You little rotter."

"Stop it!" Toni squirmed as Cathy continued to poke. She grabbed Cathy's wrists and wrestled her, eventually getting her pinned.

Cathy wriggled underneath Toni, feeling the unmistakable resurgence of lust. In the hours before dawn she had rediscovered the joys of having a woman on top of her, underneath her, within her. Cathy rephrased that in her mind. She had discovered the joys of having *Toni* on top of her, underneath her . . . Toni, her closest friend and also her employee. Cathy stopped her wriggling.

"Toni—"

"Yes?" Toni's fringe fell onto Cathy's face, tickling her lashes.

Words last spoken on Toni's lounge room floor reemerged. "I don't want to ruin our friendship."

Toni's lips brushed Cathy's. Her voice husky, she said, "You won't."

Cathy fitted words in between the soft kisses being rained down upon her. "I don't want you to ruin our friendship either."

"I won't." Toni released Cathy's wrists, using one hand to lift herself, the other to open the folds of Cathy's housecoat. She settled back down, stomach to stomach, breast to breast.

"I don't want—" Cathy's next sentence was cut short, her mouth encased by Toni's. She forgot what she was going to say anyway, Toni grinding her hips and her own responding in the instinctive lover's motion.

"Uh oh, I told you she wouldn't be happy with me."

Cathy completed the turn into Toni's driveway, at the same time following Toni's gaze to the window to the left of the front door, the main bedroom window. Virgil was on the windowsill, standing on her back legs, front paws against the glass. As if knowing it was her errant servant in the car that had just pulled into her driveway, Virgil's mouth opened in a long, very disgruntled meow.

Cathy glanced to the clock on her dashboard. "Well it is after one. She probably thinks her throat's been cut by now."

Toni half turned in the passenger seat. "Are you sure you won't come in and protect me?"

Cathy laughed, "I think you can handle Virgil by yourself."

Toni folded her arms. "You'll be sorry when you read tomorrow's headline, *Macedonian marvel mauled by famished ferocious feline.*"

Cathy laughed again, Toni well in form. "I'll call the body baggers if you don't appear at work on Monday."

Her expression sobered, sensing Toni's continued disappointment they would not be spending more of the weekend together. "I would come in and protect you," she said gently, "But I really do have a lot to get through today."

It wasn't a lie; she did have a pile of errands to run. And her plans for the evening weren't a fabrication either, they'd been in place for nearly two weeks. Her Sunday morning tennis match had only been arranged the day before, Jo calling her at work and suggesting since the forecast was for fine weather, maybe they should make the most of it. Regardless of the short notice, it was a date Cathy wanted to keep. Sunday afternoon was pegged for housework. Grazia, the woman who had been coming once a week for the last five years, was on a well-earned break in Sicily, so Cathy decided for the next six weeks she may as well do it herself. Of all her plans for the weekend, this was the sticking point, as Toni was unable to hide her offense that housework took a higher priority than she did. Cathy said it didn't, explaining what she really needed was some time alone to digest things. "I'll call you Sunday night," she promised.

"Okay," Toni nodded, brightening somewhat.

Cathy reiterated her promise to give Toni a call, then made one last attempt to convince her to hand over her suede jacket so she could get it dry-cleaned. An inspection of it while Toni was in the shower revealed a dark blotch on the lapel, testament to her tears.

"I'm taking a load of things in anyway," she indicated to the backseat where a fortnight's worth of dry-cleaning lay. "So it's really no trouble."

Toni acquiesced, shrugged out of her jacket and tossed it onto the pile.

A quick hug and kiss later and Toni was out of the car and walking up the driveway. Virgil disappeared from the window and was at Toni's feet as soon as the front door was opened. Cathy returned Toni's wave and watched until her beautiful friend closed the door behind her. For indeed she was a beautiful friend.

Cathy pulled out of the driveway, acknowledging that, despite the rush of affection she felt for Toni, it was still only the affection of a friend. A friend who had, for a short while anyway, managed to make her forget her current woes.

She was immediately reminded of them when she pulled up at the stop sign at the end of Toni's street. A right turn would put her enroute to the dry-cleaners. A left turn would take her to the start of Lisa's street. An opening in the traffic came and went as she pondered right or left. Her indicator blinked to the left, then left again. Within moments she was stopped outside Lisa's house. It wasn't some sixth sense that told Cathy she had the right residence, it was the tray-top utility parked in front of the garage that gave the visual clue she needed. The business name Hawthorn Tiling was emblazoned across the door.

Cathy let the engine idle in neutral as she considered her next move. During the short drive from the end of Toni's street Cathy visualized walking confidently to Lisa and Joel's front door and calmly announcing their tiling services would not be needed after all. Now, Cathy felt anything but confident and she reverted to her original plan of ringing on Monday to break the news. She set her car into gear and sped off, hoping neither Lisa nor Joel had been watching from one of the windows.

This time Cathy did aim for the dry-cleaners. She spent the

journey arguing with herself. By the time she arrived she had decided she was totally screwed up. Here she was, pining for a woman she could not have, while another—one she both trusted and adored—was offering herself to her. To top it off, her solution to dealing with the Lisa issue was to stick her head in the sand and hope it just went away. Which it wouldn't. Even if she did cancel the tiling contract, Lisa would still be around. After all, she did live right behind Toni.

Swag of dry-cleaning tickets in hand, Cathy walked back to her car, deciding it was high time she grew up. She hated having her plans put awry, and she didn't want to put the schedule of a small business awry either, so the tiling contract would stand. Who knew? Maybe she and Lisa could one day become friends. After all, it wasn't like Cathy didn't already have a number of straight people in her circle. And she'd already proved she could be friends with past lovers. She'd never had someone fall into both categories before, but anything was possible. As for Toni, well, she wouldn't be happy when Cathy told her she had changed her mind again, but she was sure to get over it. And as for a future between her and Toni, well, a strong foundation of friendship certainly seemed like a good springboard to greater things.

Cathy turned over the ignition, much happier now she had made some solid decisions instead of pussyfooting around being a pain to all and sundry.

Finally finding a parking spot at the popular suburban shopping center, Cathy made a beeline for the news agency, but veered when she spied a florist on the other side of the mall. Not long after, and sure Toni would get a kick out of the flowers that would land on her doorstep sometime that evening, Cathy stood in front of the racks of greeting cards. She needed two. The first, for her nephew's birthday, was easy to pick. Anything with a dinosaur on it was sure to be popular. She found one with not only a dinosaur print, but a microchip that made a dinosaur-like roar when the card was opened. Cathy checked the envelope was the right size for the card then set off in search of card number two.

This was harder. She didn't like any of the anniversary cards in the limited selection, most spouting sentiments aimed at male/female couples. The ones that didn't had words to the effect of *from all of us*, or *from your daughter* or some other category Cathy didn't fit into. Unfortunately there wasn't one that said *from your friend at the wine club*. Cathy sighed as she continued her scan. She had to pick something; Dee and Rebecca's anniversary party was tonight.

To be truthful, she was in two minds about attending. She had never even met Dee, and only knew Rebecca because she was a recent addition to the once-a-month wine club Cathy had been a member of for nearly as long as she had been back in Perth. Hence the invitation had been unexpected, and at the time she accepted it seemed like a good idea. But right now, the prospect of celebrating successful coupledom didn't hold much appeal.

I will go and I will have a good time, Cathy told herself as she plucked a homogenous card from the rack. And she probably would have a good time, so long as her invitation hadn't been with the intention of matching her up with one of their single friends. Couples often did that. Cathy couldn't count the number of times she'd been taken by the arm—*there's someone I'd like you to meet*—and had been thrust into conversation with a stranger, well aware of the covert *are they hitting it off* glances she and the other unfortunate single were then subjected to. As Cathy handed over the money to pay for her purchases, it occurred she could ask Toni if she wanted to go. It wasn't a sit-down dinner, so there should be no problem if one extra turned up. But, Cathy admitted as she pocketed her change, she wasn't yet ready for the message such a move would send to the world.

Cathy thrust the whole anniversary thing to the back of her mind. She still had to buy a birthday present for her nephew, plus there was the weekly grocery shop to do. If she stopped dawdling, maybe she could also get most of her housework cleared away before evening. Then her Sunday afternoon would be free to spend . . . however she liked.

Maybe with Toni. Between the sheets. The thought made

Cathy quicken her step. Yes, sex did change everything. But not necessarily for the worse.

Lisa pulled into a bay immediately outside the entrance to the liquor store located not far from Dee and Rebecca's house. Still playing the part of Steph's *you're not Van but you'll do* date, the part she'd assumed from the moment Steph opened the door to her home looking fabulous in heels and a slinky black dress, she trotted to the passenger side of her Ute and tugged on the handle.

"Stop trying to be butch." Steph slapped away the hand Lisa offered to help her out of the high cab of the utility. "It doesn't suit you."

"Fine, have it your way." Pretending to be offended, Lisa withdrew her offer of assistance and strode into the store.

It didn't take long for Lisa to spy the wine she wanted. Not having advanced far from her cask days, Lisa chose wine under two criteria. Firstly, it had to come from the wine region in the southwest of the state—apart from supporting local produce Lisa had yet to be disappointed with any of that region's wines. Secondly, she had to like the look of the label. Luckily, over Christmas she discovered one to her taste that fitted both categories. She grabbed a bottle from the fridge, then walked over to Steph who was still making her selection.

Lisa switched her weight from foot to foot as Steph took her time, picking up bottles and turning them over to read the descriptive label on the reverse.

"Come on Steph, hurry up," she urged impatiently. Lisa hated to be late.

"Keep your knickers on." Steph picked up yet another bottle. "We've got plenty of time."

"Hurry up," Lisa repeated a few minutes later. Steph had finally narrowed her choice to two quite pricey bottles, but she held one in each hand, unable to make up her mind. "What's the story, have you been taking lessons from Rebecca?"

Lisa found Rebecca's latest craze most amusing. Stocky by nature and pudgy by virtue of her love of Guinness, Rebecca made the switch to wine the summer just gone because she figured it was less fattening. Rebecca did nothing by halves, and two months ago joined a women's wine club. The last time Lisa had dinner at Rebecca and Dee's place, Rebecca was showing off her newly learned skills, waxing lyrical about the palate and bouquet of the wine she had selected to go with their meal. Lisa had hardly been able to hold in her laughter as wine was swished around in the glass, then around Rebecca's mouth. She was surprised Rebecca didn't have a spit bucket beside the table.

"Not quite." Steph grinned. "But I was speaking to Dee today and she said Rebecca's invited some of her new wino friends, so I'm looking for something a bit out of the ordinary."

"Oh." Lisa looked uncertainly to the bottle she had selected, no longer sure its funky label would stand up to scrutiny. She hadn't cared when it was just Rebecca, but now making the right wine choice took on a whole new import. She held the bottle out to Steph. "What do you think of this one?"

Steph shrugged, "I like it."

"So do I."

"Then get it. If they don't like it they don't have to drink it."

Lisa eyed her friend with suspicion. It wasn't in Steph's nature to care what others thought, so it occurred maybe Steph had also heard from Dee that one or more of the winos were single. She wouldn't put it past Steph to thrust an expensive bottle of wine into her hands and push Lisa off with instructions to play nice. "If that's your theory, then why are *you* making such a fuss?"

Steph's response shot that idea to pieces.

"You know," she said as she placed the bottles back on the shelf. "I really don't know."

Lisa followed Steph to a less-expensive rack where a bottle of her current favorite, a Merlot, also from the Southwest wine region, was quickly pulled.

"Finally," Lisa muttered as they aimed for the cashiering point. What a load of fuss for nothing.

Within minutes Lisa was driving up and down Dee and Rebecca's street, looking for a parking space. Cars lined both sides of the road and were double-parked on the front lawn. Most of the cars she recognized. She shared a lot of friends with Dee and Rebecca. The unknown vehicles served to remind her that new friends were there for the making. This in turn reminded her of Steph's penchant for playing Cupid.

"Now don't you even *think* about playing the matchmaker tonight," Lisa warned as she eased her utility into a narrow space between an old Jaguar and an even older Volkswagen.

The look she received was one of pure innocence. "I wouldn't dream of it." Steph flashed Lisa one of her most charismatic smiles, and said, "Besides, you're my date for tonight, remember?"

"Some date you turned out to be," Steph huffed as she climbed into the cab of Lisa's utility. She adjusted her dress, pulling at the hem so it at least reached the midpoint of her thighs. "Desert me while you go off chatting up the women."

Lisa grinned as she turned the key in the ignition. It was late and they were the last to leave, after staying behind to help Dee and Rebecca clear away at least some of the detritus that signaled their party had been an outstanding success. She aimed her Ute toward Steph's home. "I wasn't chatting her up. We were just having a conversation."

"Yeah right," Steph pulled a packet of mints from her bag and popped one into her mouth. She also popped one into Lisa's mouth. "I saw that little exchange of phone numbers."

Lisa screwed up her nose at the news that Steph had witnessed the swapping of business cards with Emma. Steph would of course jump to conclusions, when there were really none to jump to.

Lisa and Emma were both sitting on the couch for the dinner part of the evening so naturally they had gotten talking. That they were still on the couch two hours later was simply because they didn't seem to run out of things to say. Plus Lisa was getting her first lesson in wine, with Emma exploding all of her preconceptions about wine buffs by presenting the art in a lighthearted, totally non-pretentious manner.

"If you're interested you may like to come along to one of our meetings," Emma suggested when Lisa discovered she could actually taste the undertones of passion fruit in the wine she had brought. Up until that point she thought the description on the back of a wine bottle was a load of rubbish; to her most wine just tasted like fermented grapes. "It's really quite fun."

Emma did a good sell job on the wine club. No, it wasn't a serious affair where the members looked down their noses at anyone who couldn't pick the vintage in a blind test. It was quite the opposite. The club was designed to be a forum for women to share their appreciation of wine, but it was also a social gathering with the opportunity to meet some great people. Plus there was the added advantage of getting some good deals on bottles of plonk.

"Okay, okay." Lisa grinned, her thoughts immediately turning to Rebecca when Emma launched into a description of the twice-yearly dinners they held, multi-course feasts where each course is accompanied by specially selected wines. "You've convinced me. How do I join?"

"You just need to come along." Emma whisked a business card from her wallet and quickly found a pen on the telephone table next to the couch. She wrote details on the back of the card, the address and date of the next meeting. "It's two weeks on Tuesday." Emma handed Lisa the card, adding, "I've also put my home number on the back—in case you need any further info."

"Thanks." Lisa checked the front of the card. So, Emma was a vet. Useful if any of her rock doves ever took a turn. "I'm not sure if I can make it though. That day is supposed to be the finish of a tiling job I'll be doing. Sometimes we run behind and just have to keep going until it's done."

Emma raised her eyebrows. "Roof tiling?"

"No," Emma evidently found it hard to believe roof tilers would be working into the night. "Wall, floor. Indoor type tiling."

"Really," Emma exclaimed. "I have a friend who's looking to get her kitchen done. Have you got a card? I can pass it on to her."

"What do you find so amusing?" Lisa inquired of Steph, who seemed to find something intensely funny about her description of the business card swap with Emma.

"Oh Lisa," Steph patted her on the knee. "Are you blind? Do you really think she just happened to have a friend in need of some tiling?"

"Why not?" Lisa shrugged. It seemed perfectly acceptable to her.

"And you've got the date and place for the meeting. Why would you need further details?"

"I don't know." Lisa shrugged again, and said, "Maybe I'll think of something closer to the time."

"Honey, I think it was an invitation to call."

Lisa stole a quick look to Steph before turning her attention back to the road. "Do you think so?"

"I'd put money on it."

"Oh." Lisa hadn't picked up on that vibe at all.

"Poor woman," Steph intoned sadly. "She obviously doesn't realize you're allergic to the phone."

"Shut up Steph." Lisa slapped Steph on the arm. "If you're not careful you'll be walking the rest of the way home."

Chapter Nine

"My, my, you're in early for a Monday morning." Sue bustled into the staff room toting her oversized carry bag. She sidestepped Toni, who was leaning against the kitchen bench, sipping from her favorite mug.

Sue grinned cheekily as she pulled open the fridge door to transfer cartons of milk to the shelves. "Actually, you're in early for *any* morning. I don't think you've *ever* beaten me to work."

"First time for everything." Toni held her mug to her lips and smiled into it.

As promised, Cathy had called on Sunday. The call included an invitation to come over and Toni didn't need to be asked twice. She gave Virgil an early feed and a cuddle, gave the roses that arrived late Saturday afternoon a last sniff and nearly fell over herself in her hurry to get out the door.

Hoping for a repeat performance of the Friday night/Saturday morning activities, Toni was initially disappointed to discover

Cathy had started her period, but their resulting afternoon curled up together in front of the television watching DVDs was enjoyable in its own right. As was the rest of the night, Toni jumping at the offer to sleep over again.

Although they went to bed quite late, Cathy rose at some ungodly hour to shower and dress for a breakfast appointment.

"It's a potential new client," Cathy chided, as Toni tried to pull her back onto the bed when she bent to give a good-bye kiss. "I can't go looking like I dragged my clothes straight from the washing basket." Cathy smoothed down her jacket as she said, "You should get up anyway. Poor Virgil will think you've deserted her."

Cathy was right. When Toni arrived home, Virgil greeted her with disdain, gobbling down her food and avoiding all attempts to be pet. She ran straight out the cat door when Toni unlatched it for the day. Plans for a play destroyed, Toni showered and dressed, washed out the litter tray, and headed out the door to work. She beat Sue into the office in just enough time to turn on her computer and leave it to boot up while she made herself coffee.

Sue closed the fridge and turned her attention to the cupboards above the bench. Toni watched as packets of biscuits, a box of tea bags and a jar of coffee were pulled from Sue's bag.

"I always wondered why you carried that great big thing."

Sarcasm dripped as Sue strained to reach the top shelf and said, "I'm just the stand-in while the tea and biscuit fairy is on holiday." Task finished, she turned to find Toni grinning at her. Sue poked out her tongue, realizing she was being teased. "And my, aren't you in a good mood this morning too. What happened, did you get some on the weekend?"

Toni went scarlet and Sue squealed, "You did!" She whispered conspiratorially, "Anyone I know?"

"None of your business!" Toni fired back, her face flaming brightly. She avoided looking at Sue by turning to the sink, and emptying her coffee mug. "Don't you have mail to sort or something?"

"Not yet." Sue laughed out loud. "I've got plenty of time."

Toni cringed. Sue obviously wasn't going anywhere while there was the chance of extracting some juicy gossip. And Toni sure wasn't going to give her any. She mustered what she hoped was her best poker face and said, "Well I haven't."

Aware she was being watched, Toni walked stiffly out of the staff room to her office and closed the door. As she settled behind her desk she wondered how she could avoid Sue for the next decade or so, just long enough to get the Cathy-induced smile off her face.

Toni checked her schedule. No appointments until ten, then only one in the afternoon. She should get plenty done today. A few clicks of her mouse and the depreciation schedules she had been working on the Friday just gone appeared on her screen. She got down to work, humming to herself as she double-checked her calculations.

Half an hour later Toni was washing her hands when the outer door to the bathroom swung open. Damn. It was Sue. And Toni had been so careful to check the corridor before she made the dash to the toilet.

When Sue stepped into the cubicle, Toni took the opportunity to escape, hastily turning off the taps and grabbing a few sheets of paper towel. They were just being tossed into the waste bin when Sue's voice floated over the cubicle door.

"Julie's going to be heartbroken you know."

That got Toni's attention. "What?"

"Julie." The toilet flushed and Sue was still tightening her belt as she re-emerged. She took her attention from her waist to Toni. "Don't tell me you haven't noticed. She's got a crush on you."

"What?" Toni repeated, flabbergasted. She thought back for some clue, but found none, except maybe the continued eagerness to impress and the tears on Friday. Oh dear. She really had had no idea.

Sue rolled her eyes and wriggled her eyebrows knowingly. "Ahh, of course you haven't noticed, you've been too busy panting after the boss."

Toni felt heat rise on her cheeks again. "Don't you think that joke's wearing a bit thin?" she said hotly.

Sue grinned, but as she continued to watch Toni the smile fell from her face and was replaced with a look of astonishment. Her hand flew to her mouth. "It was Cathy!" Sue looked like her eyes were going to pop out of her head. "You made it with Cathy! And don't try to deny it," she warned, gleeful in the knowledge she was right. "It's written all over your face."

Knowing that protesting the truth was futile, Toni nodded. As soon as she did, a smile formed and spread. She just couldn't help it; she was fit to burst, she was so happy.

Sue, for her part, was shaking her head in wonder. "I don't know how you melted the ice queen, but girl, you must have something going on. I can't tell you the number of women who have tried and failed."

Toni flushed at the compliment of sorts, despite finding it unnerving that Sue seemed to know the status of Cathy's personal life. But then Sue always knew everything that was going on. Well, not quite everything it seemed.

"So," Sue asked, "What's the deal with Cathy and Lisa?"

Ah ha. Now the reason for Sue's compliment became clear. It was meant to butter her up and extract information. Sue obviously thought someone privy to Cathy's bed would also be privy to every detail about her. Toni feigned ignorance. "Lisa who?"

Sue snorted, seeing through Toni's fib in a second. "Lisa long legs. Tiler Lisa."

"Oh her," Toni hoped her tone conveyed nonchalance. "Nothing as far as I know."

"Oh come on," Sue scoffed. "Blind Freddie could tell you something was up. Cathy couldn't take her eyes off her when she came to do the quote and she nearly popped when you announced she was straight. And she's been downright odd ever since she made the announcement Lisa and what's-his-name would be doing the tiling." Sue folded her arms, "What's the deal?"

"If it's so important to you, why don't you go and ask Cathy yourself?"

"I may just do that." Sue became intent on washing and drying her hands, and was all of a sudden infuriatingly quiet.

Toni watched Sue turn to leave the bathroom, almost certain she wouldn't ask Cathy. After all, she would have already done so if she felt she'd get a response other than *you're fired*. "You wouldn't dare."

"Why not?" Sue stopped halfway out of the door. "Cathy doesn't bite." Her eyebrows wriggled suggestively as she said, "Or does she?"

Toni didn't grace Sue with a response. Instead she just glared at the door as it swung shut, then pulled it back open and stomped down the hallway. Sue's laughter echoed from the reception all the way to Toni's office. Toni wished she had hire and fire rights. She'd show the trumped up little gossip who could bite the hardest.

She was still bristling when a knock came on her door around nine thirty.

"What!" she barked.

"Well someone sure got out of bed on the wrong side."

Toni broke into a smile as Cathy entered and crossed the floor to settle into one of the chairs opposite her desk. "Hi. How was breakfast?"

"Filling." Cathy patted her tummy. "And fruitful. We've got another one to add to the books." She leaned forward in her seat. "Which is just as well it seems. Lucky it was me just then and not one of your clients. I reckon you could have scratched them off your list with that little welcome."

Toni waved Cathy's reprimand away; she had it covered. "I knew it wouldn't be a client. I don't have anyone due for another half hour."

Cathy folded her arms, her disapproval evident. "And of course you never have anyone pop in without an appointment?"

"Sue would have rung through," Toni said testily, upset Cathy was upset with her. "Stop making such a big deal out of it."

"I am not making a big deal," Cathy shot back. "And stop arguing the point."

Momentarily dumbstruck, Toni just stared when Cathy rose to leave. As the door closed behind her Toni sat wondering what the hell had just happened. Her answer came only a minute later, when another knock sounded on her door.

"Come in," Toni said in the most polite voice she could muster.

Cathy entered and sat back down again. "I'm sorry Toni. I shouldn't have snapped." She gave a little lopsided smile. "I guess I'm just having trouble changing all the hats I wear with you now."

"Huh?" What on earth was Cathy on about?

"You know, boss hat, friend hat . . . lover hat."

"Oh." Toni knew she took full advantage of the liberties Cathy allowed because of their friendship, but it hadn't occurred Cathy may now see the same liberties as taking advantage of the privilege that came with sleeping with the boss. Toni smiled sheepishly and said, "I'm sorry too."

With the forgiving nod that greeted her from across the desk, Toni decided to push her luck just a little more, "There's a reason why I was so grumpy before."

"Oh Toni," Cathy said, shaking her head in exasperation as Toni related details of her conversation with Sue earlier that morning.

"No wonder Sue had that silly grin when I was talking to her this morning. Well," she sighed, "We may as well publish it in the paper now."

"Are you embarrassed about it?" Toni asked in a small voice.

"Don't be such a silly." Cathy waved the question away as ridiculous. "I just would have liked to keep the information to ourselves for five minutes, that's all."

"Well," Toni continued with her confession. "There's something else—"

Cathy also waved away the news that Sue was sniffing around for information about Cathy and Lisa. "Good luck to her. No one knows except you, me, and of course, Lisa. So she can just dig away. Anyway, speaking of Lisa, there's something else I wanted to tell you."

"What's that?" Toni asked warily, wondering what news Cathy had to break now. The night before had seen Cathy announce she'd changed her mind about canceling the tiling. Toni had been unhappy at the news, but Cathy managed to convince her she was doing the right thing. After all, they'd cleared the days of appointments, the crafty Sue had already made arrangements for the break, and it was highly unlikely any other suitable tiler would be able to fit in with their plans at this stage.

"Well, it's not so much about Lisa, it's more about the rest of the renovations and how they'll fit in around her . . . and Joel."

Relieved the news was nothing more than renovation related, Toni leaned back in her chair and listened as Cathy explained what she'd decided on the drive between home and breakfast.

It seemed she suddenly realized they were all so caught up in the tiling that all else had fallen to the wayside. Painting was still to be arranged, office furniture ordered and—another item was tossed into the renovation pile—new carpet for the offices selected and installed.

As far as Toni could see, the furniture shouldn't be a problem, so long as the supplier had the pieces Cathy liked in stock. Similarly, choosing carpet wouldn't take long, but when would it be laid? Then there was the painting. First they'd have to get quotes, arrange a suitable time and . . . the whole exercise seemed too hard.

"Piece of cake." Cathy waved the potential problems away. "I've got a client who paints houses for a living. I'm sure she'll give me a good price. And I'm sure it can be fitted around the tiling somehow. Same with the carpet, except I don't have any contacts there. Do you?"

Toni shook her head.

"Oh well, what are you doing around one today?"

"Going looking for carpet," Toni said matter of factly.

"Great." Cathy flashed one of the smiles that made Toni want to melt. She stood. "I'm going to go make some phone calls."

"By the way," Toni said before Cathy could reach the door. "Did you have any idea Julie has a bit of a thing for me?"

There was no hesitation in Cathy's reply. "Yes, of course I did."

Toni's eyes widened. That wasn't the answer she expected. She'd just thrown it in to see how Cathy would react. "Really?"

Cathy grinned. "No not really. I just wanted to pretend for one minute I knew what was going on in my own practice." She tilted her head slightly and said, "What are you going to do about it?"

"I thought I'd just ignore it." Toni shrugged. "What else can I do?"

"Good idea Toni." Cathy gave a knowing smile, and said, "We've proved that theory works."

"We have haven't we?" Warmth spread throughout Toni's body. She squirmed in her seat, wishing Cathy would snap the lock on the office door and get her gorgeous behind onto Toni's desk.

But Cathy didn't. She reminded Toni of Julie's sensitive nature, told her to be careful, gave another of those melting smiles, and left.

"I love you," Toni said quietly in the direction of the closed door. She turned back to her computer, closing down the still unfinished depreciation schedules. They'd have to wait until later. Her 10:00 a.m. was due any minute.

Cathy emptied her briefcase of required contents before slipping it under her desk for the day. She placed her diary in its usual location at the top center of the desk. Next came a couple of files she had intended working on over the weekend, but had not gotten around to. Finally she pulled out the envelope containing the card she selected for Rebecca and Dee. She placed the card on the desk's work area. Cathy sat down, thumbing her diary to the page where their address details were recorded.

Despite her best intentions, Cathy hadn't made it to their anniversary celebration, one thing and another leaving her in a definite non-party frame of mind.

She had been flying through her Saturday afternoon, achieving everything planned, even making a good start on the housework. The whole place was dusted and vacuumed, and the kitchen now sparkled. But it was around the time she was stripping down the bed she suddenly felt all weepy again. She fought against the tears for the time it took to get the sheets into the washing machine, but it must have been the rush of water as the machine filled that set off her own waterworks. Feeling very alone and very sorry for herself, Cathy sunk to the laundry floor and wept. She missed her brother and his little family . . . she missed Lisa . . . she missed Toni. She missed her life before it suddenly got complicated.

The washing machine was in its first spin cycle by the time Cathy hauled herself to her feet. It was then she felt the familiar tug in her guts and the headache that was more than a post-tear thud. Cathy took herself to the bathroom and it was as suspected—her period had arrived. That was the last thing she wanted at the moment, but it provided an excuse to bow out of her evening engagement. She called Rebecca and gave her apologies, saying she was sorry but wasn't feeling well.

Still by the phone, Cathy tossed up ringing Lisa, but had no idea what she was to say. *Hi Lisa, I love you—are you sure you want to be with Joel?* Then she tossed up ringing Toni, *Hi Toni, come over, I need you again*, but she decided against that too, her conscience pricking. She did ring her brother, spending over an hour on the phone to him, his wife and her nephew. Another rush of tears came when she finally hung up. Why did they have to live so far away?

Having already failed miserably in her promise to stop pining, Cathy decided to go for broke, spending a good part of her evening sitting cross-legged on her bedroom floor, sifting through the shoebox kept right at the back of her wardrobe. It was the one already pulled from its home twice in the last few weeks. Once again she pored over the contents: cards, letters and photos, small trinkets and tokens, and all the little notes passed to her in lectures, left under her pillow or stuck to some item in the pantry or the fridge. Finally Cathy snapped open the lid of the small black velvet box, removed the single gold ring and slipped it on her finger. It still fit. Briefly she wondered what had happened to the other ring. Had it been kept, sold or maybe even thrown away?

Soon after, the shoebox was again stored out of sight, although the memories it conjured were not out of mind. She made up the bed but didn't put herself into it, instead choosing to occupy herself by cleaning the bathrooms. It was past eleven when she finished. Still not tired she turned to the bookshelves in her study and selected a novel she had already read twice. She fell asleep with the book in her hands and woke the next morning feeling groggy and cramping. Determined to keep her tennis appointment, she swallowed some painkillers, some juice and a banana, and headed out to smack the living daylights out of some fuzzy balls.

Each time Cathy had a spare moment, she filled it. She completed her housework after returning from tennis and lunch. As soon as the last item of washing was folded and put away she headed for the video store, selected a couple of DVDs, then kept her promise to ring Toni.

Toni reacted as predicted when Cathy announced she had changed her mind about the tiling. She also got a bit upset on discovering Cathy stayed home the night before but had not rung. But she did settle down. Once settled, she took Cathy's final piece of news—that physical activity was curtailed due to circumstances beyond Cathy's control—in unexpected good humor.

Disappointed sex was temporarily on hold, Cathy was surprised at just how much she enjoyed lying with her head in Toni's lap, having her hair stroked as they watched the movies. It was very soothing, so soothing she nodded off for a little while. On waking, Toni related all she had missed of the movie, then made them both dinner and kept Cathy happily amused as they settled into an evening of hot chocolate and chatter. Once in bed, it was time for cuddles and a tummy rub. Cathy fell asleep feeling safe and warm and very wanted.

The warm feeling washed over Cathy again as she copied Rebecca and Dee's address onto the envelope. She popped it into her outgoing mail tray and pulled her desk phone closer. But the moment Cathy began dialing the number already committed to memory her warmth and fuzzies disappeared and her heart began to thump.

It was answered on the third ring. "Hawthorn Tiling. Lisa speaking."

Cathy's heart thumped harder. Why did the woman still have such a damn fine voice? Not deep, but definitely heading toward the lower end of the scale, it assumed a delicious resonance over the phone. *Stop it!* Cathy gave herself a silent reminder friendship was now the aim of the game and launched straight into the call. "Hi Lisa, it's Cathy. I was just wondering if you had a minute to spare?"

Cathy concentrated on what was being said instead of the voice that conveyed the information. Unfortunately the news was not particularly good. Ideally, the tiling should be completed first, then the painting and finally the carpet. It all made sense really, for even with the best of care, tiling was a dusty, messy process, not something that should be done with either fresh carpet on the floor or wet paint on the wall.

"Of course, the carpet could be laid first," Lisa said. "After all it's only your office that has its own bathroom, so we can lay down dust covers and plastic over the carpet. It's not an insurmountable problem. And the painting of the offices could also be done while we're tiling, it's just the rest of the areas that would have to wait until we're finished laying. But as we estimated, that probably won't be until sometime on Tuesday."

Cathy voiced concern it was all a bit of tight squeeze, especially since the offices were to be put back together on the Wednesday to begin trade again on Thursday. Lisa hesitated, "Well, what if we commit to completing the job by midday on Tuesday? That will give you a definite half day for finishing off the painting."

"That's very good of you." Cathy appreciated the offer but sensed it was not the preferred option. Especially since it was Lisa's birthday on the Saturday. It was bad enough she was working all through the weekend, so she didn't want to ruin any plans Lisa may have for a celebration by setting an unrealistic deadline. "But I don't want you two to work yourselves into the grave because I didn't organize myself properly. Just let me make some phone calls and I'll get back to you."

"Okay. Thanks Cathy. And Cathy," Lisa continued, "Thanks for calling to ask. A lot of people assume it's okay to have everything happen at once and it just ends up slowing everyone down."

"No problem." Cathy smiled into the phone, pleased. Then Lisa asked if she had decided on a carpet supplier as yet. When Cathy said no, Lisa said Joel knew a guy in the business, would Cathy like the details?

"Sure would." Cathy waited, hearing muffled voices as Lisa placed her hand over the mouthpiece to speak to Joel.

"Sorry Cathy," Lisa sounded slightly agitated. "Caveman here forgot to bring his diary today. But he's heading out soon to get his morning tea and said he'd drop by home on the way. Is it okay if I call you back in say, an hour?"

"No problem, speak to you then." Cathy pressed the tabs on the phone and checked her watch to see what time it would be in an hour.

Cathy set about making moves for her other renovation arrangements, all the while keeping an eye on the time. She didn't want to miss Lisa's call. After all, she needed the details for her lunchtime carpet spree.

Lisa leaned up against the brick pillar of the front veranda and closed her eyes. The weak autumn sun was warm on her face, further improving a mood that had been steadily getting better throughout the day.

It was a wonder what a few phone calls could do. Three in fact, Lisa just hanging up from her third communication with Cathy that day. The latest call was to advise that carpet had been chosen, ordered and arrangements made for it to be laid on the Tuesday, the day Lisa and Joel were due to complete the job. Lisa knew the call was imminent, Cathy promising to let her know what was happening. What she hadn't been expecting was for the call to come so quickly, Lisa only passing on Joel's carpet supplier contact details in their second conversation a couple of hours prior. But, Lisa admitted, if she knew one thing about Cathy, it was how quickly she worked after having made a decision.

More than the calls themselves, it was their tone that served to cheer. As usual Cathy had been all business and efficiency, but her manner was completely different to the one Lisa experienced at the cinema on Friday night. Now Lisa thought she might have been wrong in her assumption that Cathy hated her. It was more likely she had just had a bad day at the office. Or maybe she was premenstrual. Lisa knew from experience Cathy could be a bit testy around that time. Whichever, the contrast was so dramatic Lisa no longer dreaded fronting up to Cathy's offices to do the tiling. If anything she was kind of looking forward to it. Maybe she and Cathy could even become friends.

That last thought brought her mood down a notch. Friends was good, but Lisa wanted more. She was sure of it. Even now, only moments after hanging up the phone, Lisa was racking her brains trying to think of some reason to get back in contact. Maybe there was something else she could help Cathy with? Like recommend a good surgeon to remove that annoying growth on her side called Toni.

Lisa frowned, wishing she knew once and for all if Cathy and Toni were together. She was nearly sure they were, but Steph's continued insistence Lisa was jumping to conclusions had put doubts in her mind.

For the millionth time Lisa tossed up just asking Cathy outright. And for the millionth time she decided against it, no longer trusting Steph's judgment. Steph had been wrong about Emma fabricating a story of a friend in need of tiling as an excuse to get Lisa's details. Just that morning Lisa received a call from the "pretend" friend, and this evening was going to quote on tiling the splashbacks of her kitchen. If Steph had been wrong about that, then who was to say any of her other so-called astute observations were correct?

Her latest observation, made on the return journey from Dee and Rebecca's party, was that Lisa lacked the ability to make the first move with women.

According to "Doctor Steph," it clearly stemmed from the trauma Lisa experienced when she put herself on the line with Simone all those years ago. The rejection from Simone and her school friends had programmed Lisa to avoid such situations, thus greatly reducing her chances of finding happiness, and ultimately leaving her a lonely old crone.

Lisa thought Steph's armchair psychology was a crock and told her so. Besides, what would Steph know about the perils of dating? She'd been happily teamed with Van for nearly a decade, and prior to that Van was relentless in her pursuit, so all Steph had to do was sit back and enjoy the ride.

"So I guess you want me to overcome this disability by going to my high school reunion and facing up to Simone?" Lisa said sarcastically. She made a mental note to keep Steph away from her mum for the weeks leading up to the reunion. If they joined forces she wouldn't have a hope.

"No." Steph shook her head impatiently. "I just think you should do *something*. Either ring Cathy or ring Emma."

Well, Lisa *had* rung Cathy. It was just to pass on carpet details, but that counted didn't it? And as for Emma, just what was she supposed to say? "Hi, do you remember me from the other night? I actually like someone else but I'm not sure if they're available, so since you seem to be all right would you like to go on my standby list and do something this weekend?"

Lisa smiled, imagining the reaction that would get. Maybe she could start writing a syndicated column, "How to pick up women."

She was still smiling as she headed back indoors.

"Well look at Little Miss Sunshine." Joel met her halfway down the hall, his wheelbarrow full of tiles and debris from the bathroom they were demolishing. He winked. "That must have been some phone call."

"Just enjoying the weather. It's nice out." Lisa edged past the wheelbarrow. "That was Cathy by the way. She said to say thanks for the tip. Neil gave her a great price on the carpet."

"Gee that was fast." Joel repeated Lisa's earlier thought. "She doesn't muck about does she?"

"Nope," Lisa said.

And Lisa was through mucking about too. She was going to speak to Cathy. The very next time she called.

Lisa pulled her mobile from her pocket, just to make sure she had not inadvertently turned it off. After all, she didn't want to miss any calls. It wasn't good for business.

Chapter Ten

Lisa knelt on the floor of the reception, making sweeping motions with her trowel as she applied a layer of adhesive to the bare concrete. Once an area large enough for about a dozen tiles was covered she set the trowel aside and reached into the box sitting close to her thigh. She quickly ran a practiced eye over the tile then ran fingers around its edges to check for any imperfections. Satisfied, she pressed it into the adhesive, careful to ensure the spacing in between each tile was uniform. She repeated the steps until the layer of adhesive was covered. Lisa sat back and surveyed her handiwork. Happy all was as it should be, she reached for her trowel and began the process again.

Lisa half wished she had chosen one of the bathrooms or the staff room as her starting point. Any of those rooms would have provided her with a more mind consuming task, their smaller size requiring more intricate tile work and hence more concentration. As it was she worked quickly, almost robotically, moving across the floor without the need to stand. Each time a box of tiles was empty she tossed it to the corner of the room temporarily designated for rubbish. A new box was always within easy reach, Lisa having spaced them accordingly on the floor before she began working from the center of the room.

Despite the mind-numbing monotony of her current task, she had to admit she liked making such quick progress. Each time she sat back to check her handiwork she got immense satisfaction from seeing what had just that morning been a bare floor, begin to transform. Already Cathy's premises looked entirely different from the previous morning, day one on the job. To Lisa and Joel's delight, Cathy had arranged with a local charity for the removal of the carpet. If they lifted it, they could have it. A couple of charity representatives arrived and busied themselves with the still in good condition carpet, leaving Lisa and Joel free for the joyfully destructive task of smashing and removing the existing tile work from the bathrooms and the staff room. To their added delight, there were no nasty little surprises once the carpet was gone, just a bare concrete floor requiring little in the way of surface preparation. There had been no glitches in the previously tiled areas either, no signs of damp and no super-tough adhesives that took half the wall or floor with the tile. So, at least from their perspective, everything was running smoothly.

It was a shame the same could not be said from Cathy's point of view.

Lisa frowned as she worked, recalling the last phone call received from Cathy, one where she advised the painters would not be starting until Wednesday. It seemed they would also need all day Thursday, the day the offices were due to reopen. Cathy's irritation was evident, especially since she had to extend the office downtime until the following Monday, rearranging the delivery of the new office furniture to Friday. Saturday was now pegged for putting the offices back together and getting the computer network re-established.

"It's my own stupid fault," Cathy complained. "I should have arranged this ages before now. As it is, I'm lucky to have gotten the painters in at all. Gail had to do some serious shuffling to fit me in."

Lisa listened to Cathy gripe, sympathetic to her troubles but unable to offer a solution. She had no painter contacts and neither did Joel. Even if they did, it would be unlikely they could do any better at this late stage. Lisa hung up from the call thinking how unlike Cathy it was to be so disorganized; usually she had everything planned to the nth degree. She decided it must be Toni's bad influence, just as it would have been Toni who made Cathy late to the cinema. That too was very unlike the Cathy Lisa had known.

Lisa found Toni a convenient scapegoat ever since. Obviously, since Cathy's disorganization was Toni's fault, it was also Toni's fault Cathy was in a bad mood over her thwarted plans. Logic followed it was Toni's fault Lisa did not keep her promise to herself and ask Cathy then and there about her status with Toni. After all, Cathy was already in a dark mood. She wasn't going to darken it further by prying. Of course, it also had to be Toni's fault Cathy had not called Lisa again, their next contact not occurring until she and Joel rolled up the previous day to start work. Finally, it was Toni's fault Lisa still hadn't asked her question, primarily because Toni was again glued to Cathy's side for the half-hour they spent at the office before leaving Lisa and Joel to get started. After all, there was no way Lisa could ask about Cathy and Toni's status with Toni present. Could she?

Lisa scowled. This was why she should have chosen a more intricate starting point; she had too much thinking time on her hands. She pushed her thoughts aside, instead tuning into the much more cheerful noises coming from the other end of the premises.

Joel was whistling away as he worked on the main bathroom. Lisa had to smile when she heard the tune, one that had been repeated many times over the last days. It was Elton's "Blue Eyes". Lisa was under no illusion Joel was whistling the tune in her honor. No, Joel was in love with his blue-eyed bottle shop boy. He had been floating around on his little love-cloud for a good couple of weeks now. These days, apart from work hours, Lisa hardly saw Joel any more, unless of course Scott was on the late shift.

Far from being jealous she now took second place, Lisa was genuinely happy Joel had finally found love. She approved of his choice, Joel having brought Scott to her place for dinner and a once-over.

"I have to say I think you've chosen well," Lisa whispered when Scott took a trip to the bathroom.

Obviously pleased Scott passed inspection, Joel grinned. "You're not just saying that because he brought you a carton of your favorite beer?"

"Well, that helped." Scott had obviously quizzed Joel in what it would take to score a few points. "But honestly Joel, all bribery aside, I think he's great."

Lisa shunted across the floor again, tossing yet another spent box of tiles onto her rubbish pile. She rolled her eyes as Joel stopped his whistling, breaking instead into song. She would normally tell him to shut up—Joel wasn't renowned for his singing ability—but who was she to burst his little bubble of bliss?

Lisa even found herself humming along to his off-tune vocalizing, but stopped when she heard the lift ping. Cathy's offices were currently only accessible by those holding a lift key, a measure taken to ensure safety as much as security during the renovation work, so Lisa knew it had to be Cathy and Toni. Lisa quickly checked her watch and secretly smiled. It was not yet midmorning on day two, and already curiosity brought them for a site visit.

Her private smile became public when she discovered Cathy was alone. It occurred to her that this was the first time Lisa had seen Cathy without Toni being present. She also realized she was taking full advantage of the opportunity, openly taking Cathy in from head to foot. Lisa's heart jumped around in her chest. My God, she was gorgeous! It also occurred to her that now was her opportunity to ask *the question*, there finally being no barriers or excuses. Well, there was one. She was at least required to get through the civilities first. Lisa's smile widened, as she said, "Hi Cathy."

"Hi Lisa." Cathy's eyes darted around the reception, her steps measured as she approached. Her hesitation was not only to avoid the freshly laid tiles but also to avoid the boxes and tools Lisa had spread out over the room. She stopped a few meters from Lisa, just shy of the point where the hallway leading to the offices could be seen.

"It already looks so different, just without the carpet." Cathy cast her eyes over the area Lisa had covered since arriving that morning. "And you've certainly made fast progress."

Lisa watched Cathy's survey, pleased there was no evidence of displeasure at the quality of her work. To be honest, she would have been surprised if there had been. Lisa took pride in the results she produced and was very particular about maintaining a high standard. If anything, she was taking even more care than usual in this job. "This is the easy bit. The progress will be a bit slower once I reach the edges."

"You know, it never occurred to me you'd start at the middle."

Lisa nodded as she continued laying tiles. The lift had arrived just as she spread more adhesive, so she needed to get the tiles down before it became too tacky and unworkable. "It means you won't have whole tiles at one end of the room and odd sized bits at the other. It adds to the symmetry."

"It's going to look good, don't you think?"

Lisa nodded again. "It'll be great, and I love these tiles." She hefted one in her hand. They were reasonably large, heavy-duty commercial quality tiles in terra cotta tones. They had all the aesthetics of real terra cotta, but without the maintenance of their counterparts. These would look as good in twenty years as they did now. Real terra cotta, if the painful sealing and resealing process was not maintained, could end up looking grubby and worn. So it wasn't just Lisa's predilection toward anything terra cotta that made her say, "You made a good choice."

"Well, you and Joel steered us in the right direction." Cathy turned her attention toward the hallway. Joel rounded the corner, still singing away, only now he was wrecking a recent hit of Madonna's. "Hi Joel."

"Hi Cathy." Joel dropped a couple of empty tile boxes onto the increasing pile, winked at Lisa and retreated. Mercifully, he ceased his singing and resumed whistling. But Lisa still cringed. Enough was enough. If she heard "Blue Eyes" one more time she thought she'd throw up.

Cathy looked from Joel to Lisa. "He's certainly cheerful."

"He is isn't he?" Lisa smiled fondly in Joel's direction as she pressed a tile into the bed of adhesive. She reached for another tile and did her visual and tactile check for imperfections. Her fingers found a slight ridge on one edge. The tile was put aside for use in the offset border and another selected. Lisa glanced up, all of a sudden acutely aware she was being watched.

Cathy shifted her gaze from Lisa to the floor. "How long have you two been together?"

Attention back to pressing another tile into place, Lisa did a mental count. "Nearly seven years now. But we've known each other for about ten. We went to Tech together."

Lisa glanced up again when her peripheral vision caught Cathy take a quick step backward. "Hey, watch out for the—"

Her warning came too late. Cathy's heel had already clipped the box of tiles that lay immediately behind her. She didn't fall but Lisa saw her ankle roll. That it had rolled the wrong way was confirmed when Cathy yelped in pain and sat down heavily on the offending box to clutch at her foot.

Lisa forgot all about making sure her last tile was evenly spaced and was at Cathy's side in an instant.

"I'm okay."

"No you're not." The pained grimace when Cathy tried to put the slightest pressure on her foot was evidence enough, but an injury was confirmed when Lisa lifted the leg of Cathy's jeans to find her ankle already beginning to swell. Lisa called out to Joel as she undid the lace on Cathy's runner.

"Sorry." Lisa apologized at the additional pain she was inflicting but she continued to delicately maneuver the shoe from Cathy's foot. "Better now than later."

Joel joined them and they all peered at Cathy's ankle. All three also had a poke at it. It definitely wasn't broken but Cathy insisted it was just a roll and not a sprain.

"Honestly, this has happened before. It'll be fine in a few hours."

Lisa frowned at Cathy's ankle, at the same time thinking she certainly seemed to be clumsy these days. "I think we should get you to a doctor."

"You're still as stubborn as ever," Lisa scolded. Cathy flatly refused the notion she needed medical attention, instead giving directions to the first aid box that hung on the wall in the staff room. Lisa gently pulled the toothed tag to secure the bandage that now bound Cathy's ankle. "There we go. It isn't pretty but it's the best I can do at short notice."

"Now," she continued, brushing the grit off her knees as she stood. "We need to get you home so you can get some ice to it." The fridge that usually sat in the staff room had disappeared into temporary storage along with all the other furniture, so not even a cold carton of milk was close to hand.

"It's okay. I can manage." Cathy shifted on the tile box, making moves as if to stand.

"Like hell you can." Lisa saw the pain flash across Cathy's face. Not the first time in the minutes since Cathy's injury, Lisa felt an incredible rush of tenderness, and an even more incredible urge to kiss the pain away.

She also could have kissed Joel when he suggested Lisa drive Cathy's car home and he follow behind. What a good idea.

Cathy obviously didn't think so, suggesting she could just get a taxi, or, even worse, that she could give Toni a call. Toni could pick her up once she was through with her dental appointment. Lisa sagged, as it became apparent Cathy didn't want to share the intimate space of a car with her.

But Joel crashed on, seemingly oblivious to the tensions that hung in the air. "Cathy, if Toni's dentist is anything like mine, you'll have a hell of a long wait. They seem to run an hour behind even before the first appointment." He encompassed the entire premises with a sweep of his arm. "And the place is completely gutted, you can't sit on a tile box all day."

"But—"

"But nothing." Joel checked his watch. "I was going to go and get my morning tea in a few minutes anyhow. Let Lisa drive you home. At least then you won't have to worry about picking up your car later."

Not long after, Lisa was back on the floor, setting a cracking pace with her tiling, the adhesive she spread before Cathy tripped already drying. Joel was back in the bathroom, finishing his own section of tiles. Cathy remained on the tile box, foot propped on another box. Apart from tiling type noises, all was silent.

"Okay. All done." Lisa dusted herself down, wiping her hands on the rag she pulled from her back shorts pocket. "Let's go."

She helped Cathy to her good foot and half carried, half supported her on the short journey to the lift.

"I'll see you soon," she called out to Joel when the lift arrived. She pressed the button for the garage level of the building and the lift doors closed. Lisa kept her eyes firmly on the digital display. Despite there being a railing Cathy could grip onto, Lisa continued to be Cathy's support. After all, the lift was fast and the journey short, so there was no real point in releasing her hold. At such close range Lisa could not help but notice Cathy again wore her Yves Saint Laurent perfume. It, combined with Cathy's arm around her shoulder, served to make the journey down all the longer, but also far too fast.

Lisa didn't need to be told which car was Cathy's. The dark blue BMW had to be it. It was one of the larger ones, and from the look of it, it was almost new. "I see you got your Beemer."

"Uh-huh." Cathy nodded. "Although it's not really mine. The business leases it."

"Oh. How come?"

Cathy launched into the reasons, primarily the tax advantages and the ability to upgrade to newer models on a regular basis. Not that Lisa was really listening. She was too busy fretting over the prospect of driving such an expensive piece of machinery.

As they approached Cathy's car, Lisa was hoping it was an automatic. Adjusting to different gearboxes and clutches was definitely not one of her strengths. The first time she'd driven Cathy's car she'd stalled it three times, and that was before she'd even got it out of the University car park. From the address Cathy related to Joel, her home was in one of the much sought after suburbs on the Sunset Coast so they had at least twenty minutes drive ahead of them. It had not escaped Lisa's attention that, unless she took some convoluted route, at least part of the journey would be along the freeway. So she was hoping and praying the car was a point and shoot model.

Shit. Lisa silently cursed as she stole a glance to the gear shift while she helped Cathy hop in. It was a manual. *Oh well, at least the car's reversed into the bay,* Lisa talked herself up as she rounded the car to the driver's side, *I can just drive straight out.*

A few minutes later Lisa was in the driver's seat, the engine was on, seat and mirrors were adjusted and she was doing a trial of the clutch, brakes and gears. *Oh shit,* she thought as the gear stick slipped into an unexpected area. *I've broken it.*

"It's okay," Cathy smiled with Lisa's look of horror. "It's got six gears."

Oh great. Lisa inwardly cringed. *Six gears.* Wasn't the usual five enough?

Here goes nothing. She switched into first gear and eased her foot off the clutch.

"Sorry." Embarrassed, she gave Cathy a little lopsided smile. It helped to take the handbrake off. She turned the key in the ignition again. Take two.

This time she managed to get a few meters before losing second gear. Again she gave Cathy an embarrassed smile. Cathy's foot must have been hurting as the expression Lisa received in return was wan. Cathy said, "It's good to know at least some things never change."

"It is, isn't it?" Lisa relaxed slightly as take three proved far more successful. She even managed to coordinate herself enough to follow Cathy's instructions to pull down the windscreen visor and press the appropriate button from the three remotes that were revealed. She also managed to stop the car before it hit the still opening garage door, then successfully drive out of the building without stalling.

By the time Lisa was on The Boulevard heading toward the ocean she had decided anyone who chose an auto BMW was missing out on a real driving experience. Cathy's car drove like a dream, handling turns like it was glued to the road. Even the slightest increase in pressure on the accelerator made the car surge forward with power.

Cathy noticed Lisa's building confidence, and she leaned forward to turn on the stereo. She fiddled with the CD changer. "Tell me when you hear something you like."

Now that Lisa's entire concentration was not focused on driving, she was hoping to engage a bit of conversation. She chose the easy listening sounds of Moby, glad Cathy held the volume at a point where talk was still possible. Not that her chosen topic was going to be easy, but at least she wouldn't have to yell her questions.

"How long have you known Toni?"

"Since she started working for me. Around four years now."

Lisa's heart was in her throat. There was not point beating around the bush. She may as well just come straight out and ask. "Are you two . . . ?" She couldn't bring herself to say it.

"You mean are we more than colleagues?" Cathy responded.

Lisa kept her eyes on the road. Her bit of bitumen was ending, as they quickly came to the T intersection of West Coast Highway. She eased her foot off the throttle. "Yes."

"Yes Lisa. We are."

Lisa's heart fell from her throat down to the pit of her stomach, and it had nothing to do with the rapid deceleration of the vehicle as she braked to turn into the slip lane leading onto the highway. "Oh. Have you been together long?"

From the corner of her eye Lisa could see Cathy was watching her. "No, not really. Around two weeks."

Shit. Lisa felt like crying. That would have been around the time they had met up at the cinema. If only she'd listened to Steph's advice and phoned, maybe . . . But maybe not. They'd no doubt been leading up to a relationship for ages. Lingering looks over the ledgers, stolen kisses behind the stationery cupboard. Lisa swallowed hard. The thought and resultant imagery was just too awful to contemplate.

"Two weeks—really." Lisa turned to meet Cathy's eyes for a nanosecond before she looked back to the road and lied, "Toni seems nice. I'm happy for you."

"Thank you." Cathy turned her attention to whatever lay outside the passenger window.

They continued in silence until Cathy indicated the need to change lanes to make the right turn off the highway. The street had houses on one side and dunes on the other. The dunes commanded the residences be at least two stories high if they were to make the most of the ocean view.

Cathy nodded to the windscreen visor again. "If you press the left button on the middle remote," she paused a moment, and added, "Now. The gate will be open by the time you reach it."

True to Cathy's word, when Lisa turned into the driveway an electric gate was just disappearing behind a rendered brick wall. Lisa hardly had time to take in the residence, which was dominated by great expanses of glass and two enormous balconies, before she was given another instruction, this time to a button on the third remote, the one that opened the garage door.

The garage was large enough to hold three cars, but it was devoid of any other vehicles, so Lisa aimed for the space closest to the interior door, figuring it was an alternative to the formal front entrance. She hurried to the passenger side and helped Cathy out of the car, feeling quite depressed as Cathy's arm again circled her shoulders.

"There's a remote on the key ring. Press the larger button."

Lisa did as instructed and two short electronic blips came from inside the house.

"Disarmed the alarm," Cathy said in explanation.

"Jeez Cathy," Lisa had to laugh. "Is your home an annex to Fort Knox or something?"

"The house came with it all." Cathy shrugged, and said, "I may as well use it. It keeps out the unwanted."

"Aren't you going to close everything?" Lisa asked as they reached the door leading into the house. The front gate and the garage door were still open.

"What's the point? Joel should be here soon enough. He can just drive straight in."

"Okay." Lisa knew that was logical, but a little voice told her it was actually so Cathy could get the unwanted out of her house that bit quicker. The unwanted being her. She pushed open the door. "Let's get you inside."

She stopped short when confronted with a staircase on the other side.

"All this level is just the garage," Cathy explained. "The living areas are up there."

"Oh." Lisa looked uncertainly at the stairs. "Are you going to be able to manage?"

"Of course."

Three steps into their climb it was obvious Cathy was not managing very well, even though Lisa was taking most of her weight. Lisa quickly weighed her options. The last time she had carried Cathy it was across a flat floor and not up a set of stairs, but she was now a lot stronger than she had been all those years ago. Although not really sure she could pull off a warrior princess impersonation, Lisa scooped Cathy into her arms. Immediately, memories of holding Cathy flooded back. It had been their first anniversary and they were headed for the bed. Lisa quickly blocked the thought from her mind, concentrating instead on finding a firm foothold with each upward step.

"Will this do?" Once they'd made it to the first landing, Lisa let Cathy slide from her arms. Despite her strength, and although Cathy was still as trim as during her student days, Lisa's thigh muscles burned in protest. If Cathy wanted to get up to the next floor she'd have to do it by herself.

"This is good." Cathy had initially protested at being unceremoniously picked up, but soon halted when Lisa told her to stop complaining as every second she wasted was one second closer to being dropped. "I'll just settle on the couch."

Later, Cathy accepted a glass of water. "Thank you Lisa."

"Is there anything else I can get you?" Lisa squatted next to Cathy, who sat with her foot resting on the chaise section of the large modular couch. A makeshift icepack comprised of ice cubes wrapped in a tea towel was on Cathy's ankle and the bandage sat rolled up next to her thigh, ready for reapplication once the ice treatment was completed. Remote controls for the stereo, television and DVD player sat within reach on the coffee table, as did the receiver of a cordless phone.

"Actually there is." Cathy shifted slightly. "Can you get my briefcase? It's in the office upstairs. First door on the right after you get to the top."

Lisa bounded up the stairs. She was initially tempted to check out the other rooms, this obviously being the bedroom level of the house, but she didn't, having no real desire to see where Cathy and Toni . . . slept. She scanned the office, finding the briefcase on the floor underneath the large desk that faced the window. Briefcase in hand, Lisa bounded back down the stairs.

"Thank you."

Lisa admired the view from the expanse of floor to ceiling windows as Cathy snapped open the clips. From this elevation the dunes were visible, but did not obscure a panorama of ocean and sky. She turned from the seascape when Cathy said, "This is for you."

"What's this?" Lisa accepted the proffered envelope. It certainly shouldn't be another part payment, Cathy already handing over the first installment the day prior. No further payments were now due until completion.

"Open it and find out."

Lisa slid a finger under the flap and removed a birthday card. There were no flowery sentiments on either the cover or inside, just a short message wishing Lisa all the best for the day, but still she swelled, more pleased than she cared to admit that Cathy had, after all this time, remembered. Once again Lisa changed her mind about Cathy hating her. Obviously she didn't. Such a gesture was not likely from someone who harbored ill-feeling.

"Thanks Cathy." It was tempting to bend over and give a thank-you kiss, but Lisa resisted. She also knew it was not likely she would be able to stop at a peck on the cheek.

Cathy indicated to her ankle. "I was going to wait until the actual day to give it to you, but I figured I may not make it into the offices tomorrow."

Lisa made a split-second decision. Since Cathy was obviously willing to extend the olive branch then she could do the same. "Cathy, Joel's arranged a barbeque for tomorrow night. It'll just be a few people and, since we have to work the next day, it won't go late. If you're feeling better it would be great if you'd come along. Toni too of course," she added, somewhat halfheartedly.

Cathy must have sensed Toni's half of the invitation was more of an afterthought than genuine. She gave Lisa a sidelong look, but recovered quickly, flashing what appeared to be a genuine smile. "Thank you Lisa. I'll check with Toni, I'm not sure if she has any plans for tomorrow night yet."

Lisa nodded. Of course Cathy had to check with Toni. That's what couples did. She swallowed her jealousy, instead concentrating on passing on the needed details. She told how Joel had appointed himself chief cook and bottle washer so there was no need to bring anything except what they wanted to drink, and to roll up anytime between seven and eight.

Cathy shook her head when Lisa began reciting her address. "I don't need it."

"Why not?" Lisa realized Cathy just had to aim for the house immediately behind Toni's, but she continued with her thought anyway. She giggled, "Are you going to drop in over the back fence?"

She wasn't expecting the glare she received. Obviously it was a sore point.

Sore point. That thought made her laugh out loud.

Lisa stopped short, Cathy folding her arms and giving *the look*, the one that told her she was pushing her luck. Cathy's look may not have changed in all the years, but obviously her sense of humor had. Shame, in the past they had both shared the same sense of the ridiculous, often ending up with tears running down their cheeks they had laughed so hard. "Sorry."

Cathy nodded, but Lisa got the sinking feeling she had just sealed the fact Cathy would be a no-show the following evening. She felt like an insensitive clod. However, there was little time to undo any damage she had caused, Joel's horn sounding from outside. Jeez, he was a clod too. He could have at least knocked on the front door. What did he think he was, some jock come to pick up his chickie-babe for a date?

"Are you sure I can't get you anything before I go?" Lisa felt bad she had to leave Cathy to look after herself when she could hardly walk.

"I'm fine," Cathy assured. "The ice is already helping, so I'll be up and around soon enough. Although, if you could make sure the garage door and gate are closed, that would be good."

"Sure." Lisa made a note of the locations of the controls for both, laid her hand on Cathy's shoulder and gave it a slight squeeze, "Take care Cathy."

Once outside, Lisa slid into the Ute beside Joel. He had his arms resting on the steering wheel, attention focused on Cathy's house. "Nice place."

"Hum." Lisa snapped her seatbelt on, not particularly interested in the architecture. Her interest lay inside the structure. "What took you so long? Did you drive here backward?"

"Nope. I thought I'd give you two time to get settled so I had my morning tea overlooking the ocean." He dangled a brown bakery bag. "I saved you some of my bun."

The bag was placed on the dashboard when Lisa shook her head at the offer. Joel slid his Ute into gear. "How's hop-a-long?"

"She's okay." Lisa pointed out the bollard that sat a few meters inside the property perimeter and the weatherproof button Joel needed to press to make the electric gate slide closed. "I invited her to the barbeque tomorrow night."

Joel gave Lisa a sideways grin. "I guess I'd better buy another sausage then."

"Better make that two," Lisa said glumly. "Her girlfriend is coming along too."

"I thought you weren't sure anymore about Cathy and Toni."

"I am now. I asked Cathy today." Lisa slouched down in her seat and propped her elbow on the window frame so she could rest her chin on her fist. "Anyhow, I don't think they'll come."

"Why not?"

"I think I kind of upset Cathy when I laughed about her falling into my garden."

"Oh Leese. I'm sure you're just overreacting again. From what I've seen of Cathy she doesn't seem the type to get all shitty over something like that."

"Hmm." Lisa turned her attention to the dunes. "Whatever you reckon."

Joel picked up on the message that conversation was not wanted. He turned on the stereo, keeping the volume low and humming along to the music.

They were only minutes from Cathy's South Perth offices when Lisa spoke again. "Joel—" she ventured.

Joel stopped his quiet humming. "Yes?"

"I think I love her."

Joel applied the brakes as he neared the traffic lights. Once at a complete stop he turned his attention to Lisa, patting her consolingly on the knee. "I know honey."

That revelation made Lisa sit up straighter. How had Joel already come to that conclusion? She'd been very careful not to say anything to him.

"Come on Leese," Joel rolled his eyes skyward when asked how he had guessed. "How long have we known each other now?"

"Too long," Lisa quipped.

"Far too long," Joel agreed. "Long enough to know I've never seen you in such a tizz over a woman before."

"I am not in a tizz," Lisa said defensively.

"Oh, no?" The lights changed to green and Joel accelerated quickly, beating the next set of traffic lights, located only a short distance ahead. "So the fact you're Little Miss Sunshine when Cathy calls and Little Miss Misery most of the time in between is just a coincidence?"

"Yes, it is." Lisa folded her arms, fully aware Joel had read her correctly. "It's pure coincidence."

"Whatever." Joel grabbed the remote from the dashboard and aimed it in the general direction of the garage door. "Just as well you're through with women. Things could get messy otherwise."

"Shut up Joel." Lisa scowled, not in the mood for his humor. "You know I won't go there."

"Go where Leese?"

Okay, so Joel was going to make her say it. "I won't make a move on another woman's woman."

"That's my Leese, beyond corruption." Joel laughed, then sobered as he caught the steely glare coming from the other side of the cab. "So, I guess you and Cathy are just going to be friends then?"

"That's the plan." The moment the Ute was at a standstill, Lisa slid out of the cab, slammed the door, and stalked toward the lift.

Chapter Eleven

Lisa held her empty stubbie in the air. "Anyone need a refill?"

"Shit, I wish I'd never asked." She headed inside to the kitchen, armed with requests from five of the twelve people already clustered around her thankfully very large patio table. The kitchen table and chairs had also been temporarily moved outside, so there was still space for a few more guests. Which was just as well, Rebecca and Dee had not yet arrived, neither had Cathy and Toni. But they still might. After all it was only twenty past seven.

Steph jumped from Van's knee. "I'll give you a hand."

Lisa smiled as Steph followed her into the kitchen. Joel was playing doorman when Van and Steph arrived, so Steph had stepped outside to find Lisa and Emma sitting next to each other at one end of the long table. She knew Steph had been bursting to speak to her alone from the moment she spied the two of them together.

Lisa rummaged in the fridge. Steph stood behind her.

"You've obviously been busy since we last spoke," Steph said as she accepted the two bottles of wine Lisa passed.

"Uh-huh." Lisa juggled a bottle of vodka and lemon, a stubbie of beer, and a can of bourbon and coke. She closed the fridge door with her knee. "But it's not what you think."

Lisa twisted the cap off the stubbie and took a long draught. "We're friends, that's all." The mouth of the stubbie was pointed accusingly in Steph's direction. "Although it's no thanks to you. You're lucky you didn't bring your handbag with you Steph, 'cause I'd happily use it to hit you over the head."

Steph placed the bottles of wine onto the kitchen bench, eyes opened wide in the innocent manner she was so good at. "Why, what have I done?"

"Oh, just filled my head with stupid ideas I then acted on." Lisa placed her stubbie next to the bottles of wine, leaned against the bench and folded her arms. She wasn't really angry with Steph, she was more annoyed at herself for ignoring her own instincts and acting instead on Steph's theories.

It was Steph's theories that caused Lisa's suspicions to be raised when she was at Emma's friend's place to do the quote for the kitchen splashbacks. Not five minutes into her visit, who should arrive on the doorstep but Emma. However, Lisa soon laid her suspicions to rest. Apparently Emma lived only a few doors down and, seeing Lisa's Ute, decided to pop in to say hello to both of them. But the "Emma's interested in you theory" seemed proven the following evening, after Emma phoned Lisa at home. Lisa found talk easy with Emma. They just seemed to rattle on as if they'd known each other for years. But she was at a momentary loss for words when Emma asked if she'd like to join her for dinner and a movie. "I'm sorry," Lisa raced to find the right words to let her down gently, "I've just recently broken up with someone and I'm not ready for anything just now." It wasn't really a lie, it just wasn't quite the truth either. Lisa thought she'd been too harsh when there was an extended silence on the other end of the line. But her lack of tact wasn't the issue. Emma coughed and said,

"Umm Lisa, I'm sorry but I didn't mean it that way. I mean, I like you and all, but not you know—"

Lisa felt like a big twit. She also felt Emma would now think Lisa assumed every woman who spoke to her, wanted her. Luckily Emma wasn't thinking along the same lines. She blamed herself for her delivery; obviously she was sending out the wrong signals. Lisa said it wasn't that at all, it was one of her hopelessly romantic friends who had planted the idea in her head.

With that misunderstanding sorted out, Lisa agreed that dinner and a movie sounded good. After the movie, she'd agreed to the offer of coffee, spending the rest of the evening in Emma's lounge room with Emma's golden retriever at her feet, and Emma's black cat on her lap. They'd been in regular contact ever since.

"Sounds like you're already pretty good friends."

"We are." Lisa hugged Steph, sensing the touch of envy, especially at the announcement Emma and Lisa had taken up running together. To date, they'd only managed twice, because one or the other worked later than scheduled most evenings. However, the frequency was not the issue, it was the fact Steph had been Lisa's running partner before Steph's job made the organizing of that activity a strategic nightmare. "But you're still my very best friend. Even though you do get me into all sorts of trouble." Lisa added, not yet finished with all her news. "Now listen Steph, Cathy and Toni may also be coming tonight."

Lisa quickly related all that had transpired between Cathy and her, including the fact she now knew for certain Cathy and Toni were together.

"But if it's only been two weeks—"

"Don't even think about it." Lisa held up her hand in warning, repeating what she had told Joel just the previous day, "You know I won't go there."

"Please Steph, even if I did miss the boat with Cathy by no more than a minute it doesn't matter. I'm just going to have to live with the fact she's with Toni. So please, please, *please*, don't say anything."

"I promise."

"And please, whatever you do, don't mention the fence thing either. It went down like a ton of bricks when I did."

"I won't." Steph hugged Lisa. "Stop getting your knickers in a twist honey. I'll be good."

"Good." Lisa picked up her stubbie and the drinks for her lazy friends. She decided this was her last drink run for the night. From this point on, everyone could find their own way to the fridge. "I don't want any dramas."

Steph picked up the bottles of wine. "No dramas, I promise."

Cathy sat on the edge of the bed, arms folded as she watched Toni flick through her wardrobe. "It's a barbie Toni," she reminded. "Not the Academy Awards. Just throw on jeans and a jacket."

Cathy knew Toni was only dawdling over her outfit because she really didn't want to go to Lisa's barbeque. That was obvious from the moment Cathy mentioned it the previous day. Toni had phoned not long after she returned home from the dentist and on hearing of Cathy's injury came rushing over to play nurse.

The news Lisa had chauffeured Cathy home went down like a lead balloon, as did the fact Cathy was entertaining the idea of accepting Lisa's invitation.

Cathy flared, tiring of the green-eyed monster that appeared whenever Lisa's name was mentioned. "For God's sake Toni, get over it. She's been with Joel for seven frigging years. I don't think you have anything to worry about."

"Seven years?" Toni sat down heavily. "Shit, that's a long time."

"I know." Cathy dropped her gaze to her hands, feeling again the emptiness that gnawed in the pit of her stomach. She'd been feeling it ever since Lisa's casual announcement she and Joel were longtime partners. But she was trying to rise above it, and if she could, then surely Toni could as well. "So please, can we just move past this?" Cathy shifted in her seat, wincing at the stab of pain in her ankle, but pleased to find it was not as acute as before. By tomorrow she should be on her feet again. "I really would like to go Toni. And I'd like you to come with me."

They'd settled after that. Toni agreeing to accompany Cathy, and Cathy pleased that Toni seemed willing to get over her needless jealousy.

However, Toni appeared to have had a change of heart somewhere between then and now. Cathy's ankle was already sufficiently healed that she could drive, so as arranged, she arrived at Toni's shortly after seven. She was immediately irked to find Toni still in track pants and a sweatshirt. "Come on Toni," she urged. "You've got fifteen minutes."

Fifteen minutes up, and Toni still wasn't ready. Annoyance built. In Cathy's world, an invitation to arrive between seven and eight meant she'd turn up at seven thirty. By her time scale, unless she left this second, Cathy was now officially late. She stood from the bed. "That's it Toni. You've got one minute to get changed. If you're not ready I'm leaving without you."

"Okay, okay." Toni scowled in Cathy's direction but nevertheless pulled a pair of jeans off its hanger. "Although I've no idea why you'd want to spend an evening with a bunch of blokes standing around a barbeque, swilling beer and scratching their balls while the women sit in the kitchen and swap scone recipes."

"Antonia Ljanjovich!" Cathy didn't think she'd ever heard such a string of stereotypes. "I never would have picked you as a heterophobe."

Toni cocked her head to one side, frowning, and said, "Is there even such a word?"

"I don't know and I don't care." Cathy limped to the wardrobe and pulled out the first jacket she could get her hands on. "Here. Get this on and let's go."

Minutes later Toni was dressed, Virgil had been cuddled and it appeared there would be no more delays, except for Toni's apparent fixation with finding out if heterophobe was a word.

"Toni!" Hands on hips, Cathy glared at Toni as she loped down the hallway toward her home office. "Now is *not* the time to check your dictionary. You can do that when we get back."

Toni seemed to sense Cathy was reaching the limits of her temper. She stopped, turned, and within a few moments they were on their way to Lisa's house.

"I still don't think heterophobe is a word." Toni helped Cathy up the three steps leading onto Lisa's front veranda. "Although we could make it one. Wouldn't that be good," Toni grinned, "If we invented a word."

Cathy smiled, a lot happier now they had made it to Lisa's front door. Despite Toni's dawdling and Cathy's slow progress during the walk around the block, they arrived less than fifteen minutes after Cathy's self-imposed deadline. She took the weight off her ankle by leaning against Toni as they waited for their knock to be answered. "You're a dag Toni."

"Yeah I know." Toni slipped an arm around Cathy's waist, "But it takes one to know one."

A gravelly female voice called from the direction of the front garden, "Cathy?"

Both Cathy and Toni turned. Two women ascended the steps and joined them on the veranda. Cathy blinked. One of the women, the one with the gravelly voice, was Rebecca from the wine club. The other she guessed was Dee, their hand holding indicating they were a couple. *What on earth are they doing here?* Cathy wondered.

Rebecca broke into a grin. "I thought it was you." She quickly flicked her eyes over Toni but settled her gaze on Cathy. "I hope you're feeling better. We missed you the other week."

Cathy again gave her apologies for missing the anniversary dinner. She said she was much better; it was just a passing bug. They were in the middle of their introductions when the front door opened.

"Welcome ladies." Joel bowed formally, and said, "Everyone's out the back."

They all followed Joel down the hallway, Rebecca's heavy boots loud against the polished floorboards. "I didn't know you knew Lisa."

Curious, Cathy was disappointed that the doors they passed all seemed to be closed. The first set were double doors, dark wood framing opaque glass. Cathy supposed they led to the lounge room. "We went to Uni together. It's just lately we've caught up again."

Even more curious about Rebecca and Dee's association with Lisa than she was with the decor, Cathy asked, "How do you know Lisa?"

Rebecca thought for a moment then laughed. "You know, it's been so long I really can't remember." She shrugged at Dee, "What was it, some party or something?"

"No silly." Dee shook her head. "It was that picnic out in the Swan Valley. For Shorty's birthday. Remember?"

Cathy tuned out of their ensuing banter about who was at the picnic and whatever had happened to so-and-so, realizing Lisa must have known them from the days prior to Joel. It was good to know Lisa still had some ties with the lesbian community, and that Joel was seemingly okay with it. From comments overheard behind Lisa's fence, Cathy had feared he may put up barriers, feeling some threat to his manhood or something. But then again, he didn't seem the type of guy to be ruled by his testosterone. From the little Cathy had seen of Joel, she liked him. She stopped short of the thought he was good for Lisa, but still, he seemed okay.

Cathy halted her analysis as they reached the French doors leading out to the back. She wasn't going to make much of an impression on Lisa's friends if she was staring off into space, lost in her own thoughts.

Less than two minutes later, Cathy was again lost in thought. This time as she tried to assimilate the visual evidence with her preconceived notions, for the two did not coincide.

From the moment Cathy stepped onto the patio it was apparent the number of women far outweighed the men. In fact, Cathy could see only Joel and one other male in the entire group. Body language evidenced that most of the women were paired up—with each other. Her eyes opened in wide surprise as she spied Steph. The woman whose lap she sat on was quite mannish, but definitely a female and definitely not the male footballer she had been expecting. And from the affectionate looks they exchanged as Steph held court, laughing and joking with those around them, Cathy assumed she hadn't placed herself on the woman's knee because of a lack of seats. Emma was also present, seated beside Lisa. Cathy knew Emma was a lesbian. They'd known each other for a good three years, both longstanding members of the wine club. What Cathy hadn't known was that Emma knew Lisa.

Any shred left of her preconceived notions quickly disappeared as Cathy watched Joel interact with the other fellow—Scott, she remembered from Lisa's introduction.

The men were standing around the barbeque, but that was the only part of Toni's stereotypical prediction to come to light. Joel and Scott certainly weren't swilling beer and scratching their balls. They were sipping Chardonnay and looking lovingly into each other's eyes. Cathy watched the pair, very much doubting Lisa had changed so much she would condone her partner playing with another man's butt. There was only one conclusion to draw.

Toni had obviously come to the same conclusion. The quick glance they managed to exchange before Toni was drawn into a hug by a woman she introduced as one of her newer clients, revealed her similar astonishment.

Cathy desperately needed some space. As was reasonably typical, Toni's client took the opportunity of a social function to extract some free tax advice, so Cathy took the opportunity to escape. "Will you please excuse me?"

Ignoring the *don't go* look from Toni, Cathy stood and headed back inside.

She limped down the hallway, stopping at the double doors she had passed earlier. Once open the doors presented, as suspected, a lounge room. Cathy plopped herself onto the couch, feeling quite lightheaded as she absorbed her new surroundings. Three framed commemorative posters from the Sydney Gay and Lesbian Mardi Gras, one from only the year prior, dominated one wall. A corner bookshelf revealed a couple of shelves devoted to women's literature, many titles matching those in Cathy's own collection. Cathy picked up a stone sculpture from the center of the coffee table. The piece was finely crafted and pleasing to the eye, an abstract study of two women in what could only be described as an erotic embrace. Cathy ran her fingertips over the statue's curves, trying to ground herself with the cold stone.

She wasn't overly successful.

Lisa was in high spirits, having experienced an upswing in mood that, predictably, occurred at the exact moment Cathy appeared at her back door. Prior to that, Lisa had been making a real effort not to let her disappointment break through. She had been clock watching, and with each minute that passed she became more convinced Cathy wouldn't show. After all, history told Lisa if she was going to turn up it would be at seven thirty. Cathy's actual arrival had not been until nearly seven forty-five, and from the glance between Cathy and Toni only moments after they took their seats at the table, Lisa figured Toni was to blame for the tardiness.

Tardy or not, Lisa was thrilled Cathy had come. Reminding herself Toni was there as Cathy's partner, Lisa swallowed her first impulse, the one that told her to rush over to Cathy and give her a big hug. Instead she grinned a hello, quickly introduced everyone, and set herself ten minutes before she'd go and have a proper chat. She quickly changed her mind. Ten minutes was far too long. Five minutes was better.

Two minutes before her five minutes was up Lisa stole a glance to the far end of the table. She immediately noticed Cathy had gone pale. Then she watched her stand and limp back into the house.

Lisa paled at the thought that crossed her mind as her eyes followed Cathy's retreat, the thought that said maybe Cathy had some illness, one that affected her balance and made her fall down a lot. *Oh shit.* Maybe that's why she got upset when Lisa had laughed at her. Lisa touched Emma lightly on the arm and nodded her apologies to Lee and Fleur, who were busy telling of their recent holiday in the south of the state. "Can you just excuse me for a minute?"

"Will you get me another wine on your way back?"

"Sure." Her promise not to be fridge runner forgotten, Lisa took Lee's glass and headed inside.

Cathy wasn't in the kitchen or the dining area. A quick check of the bathroom also revealed it empty. Lisa glanced down the length of the hallway. The doors to the lounge room were open. Lisa quickened her step.

"It's a nice piece isn't it?" Lisa stood at the entrance to the lounge room, her voice soft so as not to startle Cathy at the interruption. Cathy was intent on the statue that lived on Lisa's coffee table, running her fingers over and around its form. "I picked it up at the last Fair Day."

Cathy took one last look at the sculpture before placing it back in the middle of the table. Lisa crossed the floor, now even more concerned at the state of Cathy's health. She looked like she was going to faint. "Cathy—are you okay?"

"I—" Cathy began, then stopped, not seeming to know what to say. "You—"

"Cathy." The look Lisa received was stricken. "Cathy, what's wrong?"

"I thought—"

"You thought what?" Lisa coaxed, Cathy again trailing away before finishing her sentence.

A minute later—when Cathy had told her what she had thought—Lisa burst out laughing. "You are kidding aren't you?"

All mirth vanished when it became clear Cathy was deadly serious. Lisa sank onto the couch, unable to believe what she was hearing. Her attention was momentarily diverted as another figure appeared at the entrance to the lounge room. It was Toni. Lisa ignored her and focused on Cathy.

"Can you please tell me what on earth gave you the idea I had turned straight?"

Cathy said in a small voice, "Someone told me you were."

"What!" Lisa's eyes opened wide, incredulous. Why would anyone be spreading that sort of rumor about her? "Who told you that?"

Cathy just shook her head, but Lisa didn't need to be told, quickly figuring who was the culprit. Toni had moved into the lounge room and was standing with hands in pockets, looking guiltily at her feet as she scuffed a shoe against the edge of the rug. Lisa swallowed the urge to throttle her, instead returning her attention to the figure perched next to her on the edge of the couch. "How could you take something like that on board Cathy? You, of all people, should know me better than that."

Lisa shook her head, trying to gather how she'd ended up in her lounge room with an ex-lover, being forced to defend her sexuality. "What have I *ever* said or done to make you believe something so stupid?"

She soon found she had apparently said and done quite a lot.

Of course she casually announced she and Joel had been together for seven years. She was a lesbian for goodness sake, why would she have thought Cathy was talking about anything but their business relationship? No, she and Joel did not share a house, and definitely not a bed. What an awful thought. Joel's damn phone message was only there because she hated talking into a machine and had not gotten around to changing it. Lisa made a mental note never to doubt Steph again. She'd been spot on about the phone message, also spot on something weird had been going on at the cinema. No wonder Cathy had looked at her so oddly. And she'd been right about Toni too. Obviously the woman was so threatened she had to make up some ridiculous story to keep Cathy away from her.

As if on cue, Steph's head appeared around the door frame.

"Hey Leese, we're waiting for you to—" Lisa glanced in her direction and Steph immediately understood something was going down, gave an almost imperceptible nod and disappeared again.

Lisa continued to provide answers to all the so-called evidence presented, all the while her eyes growing larger as it became clear how many innocent comments and actions had been interpreted altogether incorrectly.

"Yes," Lisa agreed, "I did say I was through with women." She frowned, unable to recall ever saying that in Cathy's presence. But, of late she'd been spouting that line to anyone who'd listen, so maybe she had said it in front of Cathy after all. "I've been saying that ever since I broke up with my last *girl*friend." The emphasis she placed on *girl* was intentional. "But no one who knows me believed a word of it."

There was a sudden silence. It seemed Cathy and Toni had come to the end of their material. Both of them looked utterly miserable.

"I'm sorry Lisa," Cathy said at length. Color had returned to her cheeks, but they were red and splotchy, advertising her embarrassment.

"Me, too." Toni said in a small voice. She was still scuffing her shoes against the rug. Lisa felt inclined to tell her to quit it before she ruined the edge, but she didn't. She almost felt sorry for Toni, knowing there was likely to be an argument once they went home.

"That's okay." Lisa forced a smile and nodded in the direction of the backyard. Barbeque smells drifted into the lounge. "I think dinner's ready."

"Come on you two." Lisa urged when Toni said maybe it was better if they left. "There's no reason why you should go."

Sensing the worry coming from across the room, Lisa crossed her heart and said, "I promise this will stay just between us, okay?"

Cathy and Toni finally acquiesced and the three of them headed to the rear of the house, Lisa stopping at the kitchen to get Lee her wine. The glass she left on the bench was gone, Lee obviously finding the wait too long and helping herself.

Steph shot a questioning look as Lisa resumed her seat next to Emma but Lisa shook her head slightly. Steph raised her eyebrows but didn't press the issue. Lisa knew there would be questions once they were alone.

"I wonder who that could be?" Lisa frowned as Joel resumed doorman status, a knock sounding not two minutes after she had returned to the patio. Everyone who should have arrived, had arrived.

Joel beckoned her from the back door.

"Don't you touch my sausage," Lisa jokingly warned Emma as she stood. Maybe this was Joel's way of getting her out of the backyard so her birthday surprise could be arranged. There had to be a birthday surprise, there had been every year prior.

She wondered what it was as she wandered back along the hallway. Last year it had been the four-burner gas barbeque they were using tonight.

"I tried to get her to go, but she insisted on staying until she saw you," Joel whispered as he pulled open the door.

Oh crap. Lisa's eyes narrowed when she saw the woman standing on her veranda. She was sporting a very petulant look and a very large bunch of flowers.

Lisa decided she must have done something very, very bad in a previous life. So much for no drama this evening. She folded her arms. "Hello Janice. What do you want?"

It was nearly midnight when all but the last of Lisa's guests left. Lisa sat on the front steps, waving to Van and Steph as their car passed her front gate. She yawned, tired.

Emma emerged from the house, keys jangling in her hand. "All done."

"Thanks Emma." Lisa had protested Emma's offer to help clear up, but not enough to prevent her from running a sink full of water and begin stacking dishes. Steph also pitched in, grabbing a tea towel. Lisa and Van busied themselves outside, stacking chairs and moving the kitchen table back indoors. Once the lifting was over,

Van made sure the two braziers that had kept everyone warm while outside were not smoldering. Lisa sat at the kitchen table and did nothing. After all, it was her birthday, she had every right to be idle.

Emma settled on the step next to Lisa. "It was a good night."

"It was wasn't it?" Lisa rested her chin on her hands. Despite being mistaken for a heterosexual by the ex she wanted and begged for a second chance by one she didn't, the night had turned out surprisingly well. Lisa was impressed by her own diplomacy. She had successfully maneuvered through two potential disasters without anyone, apart from the main players, being aware of what was going on.

Actually, she hadn't really displayed much diplomacy in her dealing with Janice.

Still reeling from what had been revealed in the lounge room only minutes beforehand, she answered Janice's request for forgiveness by telling her to piss off and shove her flowers "where the sun don't shine." Always a sucker for tears, however she retracted her remark when Janice's face crumpled. Still, she had been firm, refusing to let Janice past the threshold and reiterating that it was over between them. For good.

Realizing further protest was futile, Janice threw the flowers into a garden bed and left. Once Janice's car had sped off, Lisa retrieved the flowers and crept up the path to her next door neighbor's house, thinking old Mrs. Trimble would get a nice surprise when she opened her front door the next morning. Moments later, Lisa dashed up the garden path again. Given her luck at present, old Mrs. Trimble wouldn't see the bouquet on her doorstep, trip over it and break her hip. Lisa tossed the flowers into her wheelie bin. As she did so she wondered if tossing out perfectly good flowers was a lesbianly thing to do or if it would be seen as another piece of evidence she was obviously heterosexual. Shaking her head at the thought, *How on earth could Cathy have . . .* Lisa wiped her hands on her jeans and headed back inside, hoping Cathy and Toni had settled a bit.

However, it appeared she was worrying over nothing. In actual fact, Lisa was astounded at how well Cathy and Toni fared. She had seen them have a very quiet but earnest exchange as they resumed their seats. However, they were soon participating in the conversations around them, by all accounts seemingly having a grand old time. They stayed well into the evening, not leaving until the major exodus began soon after eleven.

"Lisa?"

Still thinking about the strangeness of the night, Lisa's reply was a distracted, "Hmm."

"Is Cathy the ex you recently broke up with?"

"No." Lisa raised her eyebrows. Why would Emma think that? She tossed up telling of the unscheduled visit from the actual recent ex but decided against it. It was late and she had an early start, so epic tales of her woeful love life could wait. "Cathy's an ex, but from a long, long time ago."

It seemed to take a while for that to sink in. Emma stared out into the night in silence. Eventually she spoke, "You still like her don't you?"

Lisa turned wide eyes to Emma. Having Joel pick up the vibes was understandable, they knew each other inside out. But for Emma to have also caught on . . . even though she and Emma had clicked they'd only known each other for a blip in time. "Am I that transparent?"

Emma nodded. "To me you are." She smiled gently, adding, "I can see myself in you."

Lisa returned Emma's smile, remembering she was involved in her own exercise of futility. A post-run heart-to-heart on a bench overlooking the lake they had just circled revealed Emma's long-term devotion to Justine, her neighbor from a few doors down. It seemed Emma had fallen head over heels for the woman from the moment she moved into the neighborhood a few months before Christmas. Only problem was, Justine liked men. Despite this, Emma continued to do anything and everything to ensure she had as much contact with her neighbor as possible. Hence the request for Lisa's business card. Knowing Justine was in the market for a tiler, it provided a valid excuse to pop over for a visit. Plus the possibility of a thank-you hug for the tip.

Lisa hooked her arm into Emma's. "We're both pathetic aren't we?"

"Totally."

It suddenly occurred that Emma should already know Cathy was not a recent ex of Lisa's. After all, they had been friends for years, both attending the same wine club. "Shouldn't you know who Cathy is and isn't seeing?" Lisa asked.

"Not really. She's not one to reveal much. I didn't even know she was seeing anyone until tonight."

"They haven't been together for long." Lisa sighed heavily. "Not long at all."

"Obviously long enough for you to develop a great dislike for Toni," Emma scolded. "She's really quite a funny woman you know. I like her."

"You're a fine one to talk!" Lisa retorted. During their heart-to-heart, Emma shot Justine's current boyfriend down in flames. Lisa met him while she worked on Justine's kitchen the weekend just gone. She found him okay. Nothing to write home about, but okay. "Paul's only crime is he has Justine and you don't."

"And Toni's only crime is she has Cathy and you don't."

It was on the tip of Lisa's tongue to point out that wasn't Toni's only crime. She was also guilty of spreading wildly inaccurate rumors. But she didn't spill the beans. She had promised to keep that little fact a secret and she would. "I know. I told you, we're both pathetic."

Lisa yawned and checked her watch. It had now gone past midnight. Luckily she and Joel had agreed to a late start in the morning, eight instead of seven. Even so, if she went to bed right this minute she'd still only get seven hours sleep and Lisa needed at least eight to run on full power. "I think I'd better go to bed."

"Oh shit. Sorry." Emma stood, pulling Lisa with her. "I forgot you had to work tomorrow."

"Well, you know. No rest for the wicked." Lisa drew Emma in

for their usual parting hug and kiss on the cheek. That Emma turned her head so they kissed instead on the lips was totally unexpected. Lisa pulled away.

But Emma was not to be swayed. "Kiss me," she said.

Lisa made sure this time she made contact with Emma's cheek. "There you go."

"Kiss me properly."

"No." Lisa lowered her eyes to stare at her feet. "I don't want to."

"Come on Lisa, humor me."

"Why?"

Emma shrugged, "It just seems stupid we both want what we can't have, but we get on so well I just thought, you know, maybe we can't see the woods for the trees."

Hands on hips, Lisa considered her friend. She thought it was a stupid idea. She knew she didn't need to kiss Emma to be certain of her feelings. But, well, what the hell. After all, it was only a kiss.

"So?" Lisa asked a few moments later.

Emma shook her head sadly. "Nothing."

"Me, either." Emma kissed nicely, technically perfect actually. But technique did not rouse passion. Lisa's grin was cheeky as she said, "Although I think I may have to go and have one of those chicken and pine nut sausages. They taste nice."

"They were good." Emma laughed as she hugged Lisa. "Well, goodnight then."

"Goodnight." Lisa watched Emma head down the path.

Emma didn't get far, turning back after only a few steps. "Can we try one more thing?"

"You're starting to freak me out Emma." Her suggestion they try another kiss, but this time Lisa was to pretend Emma was Cathy, and Emma was to pretend Lisa was Justine, seemed totally absurd. And what would it achieve anyway? "It's too late to be playing let's pretend on my doorstep."

"Humor me," Emma said again.

"You're lucky I don't run inside and call the men in the white wagon." Lisa warned as she again acquiesced and drew Emma into her arms. She closed her eyes and did as instructed, her mind filling with images of Cathy. Lips were warm and yielding as she mumbled into them, "Because you're totally off this planet."

"Shit Lisa," Emma opened her eyes long moments later. Her face was flushed and her breathing heavy. "You've got it really bad for Cathy."

"And you for Justine." Lisa pulled at the collar of her sports shirt feeling, literally, hot under the collar. And like Emma, her breath was labored. She knew this had been a bad idea. Now she was no longer tired and her body was crying out for more attention.

So too, it seemed, was Emma's. "Do you want to take this inside?"

"I do." Lisa admitted, easing Emma's hands from her butt and holding them by her side. Living out a fantasy for the length of a kiss was one thing, but Lisa doubted she could suspend reality for the duration of a lovemaking session. Besides, it wouldn't be making love, it would just be sex. And just sex, especially just sex with friends, was something Lisa had discarded years ago, along with her party-hard days. None of the women she casually bedded in the days before starting her tiling career were now in her life, and she didn't want Emma to disappear down the same track. "But I don't—if you know what I mean."

"Yeah." Emma lightly squeezed Lisa's hands before releasing them. "I think I do."

Chapter Twelve

The stairway was well lit, but the steps were steep, so Lisa picked her way carefully to the venue for the evening's meeting. The cellar.

It all sounded rather surreal, having a meeting in a cellar. Lisa imagined it as dank and cold, with a constant drip from an unseen water source sounding in the background. It wasn't like that at all. The cellar was cool but not cold, it was clean and roomy, large enough for the twenty or so women present. And there was no evidence of a drip. If there was one it was drowned out by the chatter of the crowd.

Lisa scanned the area. It took but a moment for her to spy the two people she most wanted to see and she headed straight for them.

"Hi Emma. Hi Cathy."

"Hey Lisa." Emma grinned, "You made it."

"Yeah finally." Lisa gave Emma a hello kiss on the cheek and tossed up also giving one to Cathy. She decided she would. Steph would have been proud of her. Glowing from the contact, Lisa diverted her attention to the large table that dominated the cellar floor. It was strewn with bottles, most empty, some with remnants of wine, a few uncorked but untouched. "Looks like you lot have been getting stuck into it."

"Mmm," Emma reached for a fresh glass. "We've been trying the latest offerings from some little country on the other side of the planet."

"And?" Lisa accepted the glass of white offered to her.

"Pretty crap really." Emma whispered.

Cathy nodded. "Crap."

"Crap," Lisa repeated, holding the glass up to the light as per Emma's instruction. "Is that a technical wino term?"

"It's a shame you had to arrive so late," Emma said as she walked with Lisa to her Ute. It had just gone ten and the night was already over. Apparently the evenings didn't usually wind up so early but since the wine was *crap*, most women had taken their leave, begging the excuse of having to work the next day. The patron for the night, the owner of the bottle shop, was not overly happy. None of the women were pushovers and couldn't be swayed into placing an order.

"Yeah. But it couldn't be helped." Lisa's late arrival was due to the need to get the tiling finished in time for the painters to begin work the next morning. It was Lisa's fault they were running behind, she'd slept badly on her birthday night and her progress the next day was slow and clumsy. So while Joel told Lisa she could pack it in and he'd finish it off—he knew how she was looking forward to the wine club—she refused the offer. Although she trusted Joel to do it right, she wanted to make doubly sure everything was just so. When they finished she dashed home, had a cursory wash, threw on some clean clothes and headed straight out the door. "I'm glad I did make it though. It was fun."

It had been fun. Made even more so by the company. Lisa half-expected Cathy to wander off and socialize with all her friends, but apart from a few short bursts of conversation as women entered their fray, Cathy seemed content to stay with her and Emma. Which suited Lisa just fine. The hour slipped by in a flash, and before Lisa knew it, the three of them were heading up the stairs and out to their cars. They reached Cathy's car first.

The temptation to kiss Cathy a second time was overwhelming. Again she gave in. Her lips brushed Cathy's cheek. "Goodnight Cathy."

Her kiss was returned. "Goodnight Lisa."

Lisa watched Cathy's car disappear into the night. She raised her hand to her cheek, which was still pulsating warmth from Cathy's lips. The time until Lisa would see her again seemed interminable, even though it was only nine hours away. As agreed, they were to meet at the offices at seven the next morning, half an hour before the painters were scheduled to arrive. All being well, Cathy would hand over the balance of payment. The knowledge the meeting would be her last regular contact with Cathy, apart from the wine club, was a fact that had been playing on Lisa's mind all day and all evening. She'd almost done the unthinkable a couple of times over the past hour, she'd almost made the first move and asked Cathy if she'd like to meet up one day soon for a coffee. But, as usual, she'd chickened out.

Having reached her utility, Lisa twisted the key in the lock and opened the door.

"Goodnight Emma."

"Goodnight Lisa."

Emma turned and walked a few steps, then stopped and turned back around. "Lisa?"

"Hmm?" Lisa eyed her friend with suspicion. She hoped Emma wasn't going to request another kissing session.

"I think you should ring Cathy."

Oh God. This was worse than a request for a kiss. Emma had turned into a clone of Steph.

"I'm going to see her tomorrow morning." Lisa folded her

arms, wondering just what Emma and Cathy had talked about before she arrived. "Why would I want to ring her?"

"Just humor me Lisa."

What exactly was it about Emma that made Lisa pander to her every wish? Before she knew it, her phone was out and Cathy's mobile number selected from the memory.

"Emma," Lisa pocketed her phone a few minutes later, "I love you."

"As you should." Emma grinned and headed for her car.

Lisa climbed into the cab of her utility. Life was suddenly much brighter. Toni may well be hanging around for tomorrow's final inspection of the tiling, but Sunday morning was to be just Cathy and Lisa. Coffee and a chat, that's what they'd agreed to. A chance to catch up on all the news of the past eleven years.

Lisa turned on the radio, channel surfed until she found something boppy, and happily sang along as she drove down the near-deserted Tuesday night in Perth streets.

Cathy pressed the button on her mobile to disconnect the call. It was lucky she had a hands-free kit installed. As it was, even with two hands on the steering wheel, she veered halfway into the next lane when Lisa suggested they meet. If she'd been driving with one hand, mobile glued to her ear with the other, she would probably have driven right off the road.

Unexpected as the invitation was, Cathy knew the thump in her chest was much more than a register of surprise. It was a combination of nerves, excitement, relief . . . guilt.

The final emotion overrode all others. It was the one that made Cathy reach back to her phone. She swapped attention from road to phone display until the name she wanted appeared on the screen. Her call was picked up on the seventh ring.

"Toni speaking."

Cathy's mouth went dry. "Hi Toni. I was hoping I could come over."

The surprise in Toni's tone was unmistakable, as was the slight inflection that indicated she was wary of the reason for the requested late-night visit. The plan had been to spend the evening doing their own thing and meet at the offices the next morning. "Okay, I'll see you soon."

Cathy did a U-turn at the next break in the median strip, already mentally rehearsing what she would say. She struggled to find the appropriate words. But there weren't any. The closer she got to Toni's house, the more she felt like a first-class heel.

She'd known from the start that getting involved with a friend, her *best* friend, was a big mistake. Especially since lust, and the fact the woman she really wanted was seemingly unavailable, were her prime motivators. That Toni walked into the relationship knowing all this was little consolation. Cathy nurtured their relationship despite knowing, deep inside, she would never really love Toni. Yes, there was a distinct possibility her platonic love could grow into romantic love, but she would never be *in love* with her.

The distinction was significant.

The closer Cathy got to Toni's place, the more her guilt spread. Her timing sucked. She should have done this days ago, the moment they limped back from Lisa's barbeque. But she hadn't wanted to make it look like Toni was immaterial as soon as Cathy discovered Lisa was, by all accounts, available. So she'd put it off. And put it off. Just to make things worse, she'd even had sex with Toni when they got back from Lisa's. Now, she was going to make her announcement hot on the heels of Lisa's invitation. Knowing the invitation was only for a coffee (despite a few obtuse hints from Emma earlier in the evening, she had no real idea if Lisa wanted anything more than to be friends) was beside the point. Her timing alone would make it look like she'd been biding her time, waiting to see if Lisa was interested before she made a move in either direction.

However, bad as it appeared, and bad as Cathy felt, she knew Toni deserved the truth. She just hoped they could salvage something of their friendship afterward.

I'm sorry Toni. Cathy played the line in her mind as she made the turn into Toni's street. *But I just can't be with you anymore.*

Toni stood in the kitchen, concentrating on the kettle. She was hoping the old adage "a watched pot never boils" was true. For if she kept watching the pot and it never boiled, then she'd never have to complete her coffee preparations, or make her way back to the formal lounge where Cathy was waiting. If she never made it back there, then she would never find out what Cathy wanted to say. Which, if her instincts were correct, would not be good news.

Toni had experienced a sense of foreboding from the moment Cathy called. The call was unexpected, so unexpected she'd nearly missed it. Out with friends for dinner, she'd only just put her key in the front door when the phone rang.

Actually, if she were honest with herself, Toni would admit that while the call was unexpected, it did not herald her sense of apprehension. That had begun on Saturday night, right about the time she discovered she had been very, very wrong in her assumption about Lisa. Ever since then, Toni felt like she was walking a tightrope between hope and despair.

Despair had been the first to take hold. Cathy wouldn't even look at her as they made their way from Lisa's lounge room to the back patio. "We'll talk about this when we get home," Cathy said under her breath as they resumed their seats. "Can't we just go now?" Toni asked, also under her breath. "No Toni we can't. I already feel like a fool. I don't want a scene out here." Toni's reply that there was no need for a scene, they'd just say something had come up, was not greeted warmly. "You can leave if you want. I'm staying."

Thankfully, the whole night had not been so strained. As if sensing the tension, Steph wandered to their end of the table and engaged them both in conversation. Toni's initial opinion of Steph, the one formed at the cinema, was confirmed. She was charismatic and charming. Within a short while, five others joined their little circle. To Toni's great relief, Cathy eventually relaxed and broke into laughter.

Hopes at putting the whole nasty episode behind them were raised as Toni watched Lisa interact with Emma. They had been sitting together when Cathy and Toni arrived, and Lisa headed straight back to Emma's side on the return from the lounge room. Lisa touched Emma frequently, little squeezes on the arm, a hand on the shoulder, a ruffle of her hair. Maybe they were an item?

Her hopes were dashed. As the evening progressed, Toni realized Lisa was by nature a touchy, feely sort of person, and her contact not limited to Emma. She hugged everyone, gave and received kisses freely, and generally seemed to be in some sort of physical contact with someone at any given point in time. Jealousy reared its head as the contact included Cathy. Lisa had been making her rounds and eventually landed in their group. The contact was minimal, just a brief squeeze as Lisa placed her hand on Cathy's shoulder. But she saw Cathy's lashes flutter at the touch.

She also saw the seeming inability for the two of them to keep their eyes off each other. Wherever Lisa moved around the table, Cathy seemed to point her body in the same direction. Whenever Toni looked at Lisa, it seemed Lisa's gaze was just leaving Cathy. Toni felt her heart slide to the floor. Whatever tenuous hold she had on Cathy, she could almost see it slipping away before her eyes.

That miserable thought was still top of mind when yet another blow came. The entire party was led by Joel to the rear of the garden for the presentation of Lisa's birthday present. Toni felt sick as she watched Lisa excitedly examine the large amphora, a heavy duty terra cotta affair supposedly to replace the more fragile one that met an untimely end a month or so prior. For the second time that night Toni felt like an idiot, this time because she'd presumed her twenty dollar offering would more than cover the damage Virgil had caused. The only positive to come out of the event was when Cathy snaked her arm around Toni's waist and whispered in her ear, "You weren't to know Toni."

It was a shame that same sentiment wasn't repeated once they made it back to Toni's place. However, contrary to Toni's fears, their arrival home did not signal the start of World War III. Their exchange was heated, but brief.

Cathy called Toni a fucking idiot for not only seeing exactly what she wanted to see, but spreading the fucking rumor around afterward. Toni pointed out she just planted the seed, it was Cathy who nurtured it until it sprang into life. Cathy then called herself a fucking idiot for even considering that any of Toni's tales held a grain of truth. Then she blamed Toni for causing her to descend to the language of a fucking fisher's wife.

That last comment made Toni smile.

Cathy didn't see the humor. "Fuck off. It's not fucking funny."

Toni plopped herself on the lounge next to Cathy. "Fuck no."

"Fuck off," Cathy repeated.

"You fuck off. It's my fucking house."

The look Toni received indicated that it was probably the first time Cathy had ever been told to fuck off. "Come here and say that," she challenged.

Already sitting next to Cathy, Toni had little maneuvering room. She brought her face right up to Cathy's, and started, "I said . . ."

"I know. It's your fucking house." Cathy finished for her, capturing Toni's face in her hands.

The kiss was so unexpected Toni was not ready for it. She was given a brief reprieve to come up for air before her mouth was again encased. Within minutes they slid from the lounge onto the floor, the coffee table unceremoniously kicked away by Toni's booted foot.

Reluctantly acknowledging that the kettle had indeed boiled, Toni poured water over the instant coffee already spooned into two mugs. Still thinking about the activity that took place on her lounge room floor, Toni felt her apprehension deepen. For, although initially elated Cathy still wanted to make love to her,

Toni found the act itself only further cemented her belief she was slipping away. For that night Cathy had been different. Very different.

From the beginning, Toni found Cathy to be a gentle, quietly responsive lover. She expertly took Toni to the brink and back again, whispering encouragement and frequent in her assurances of Toni's own skills. Toni would sink into sated sleep feeling languid and relaxed, like water lapping against powdery white shores. But this night Cathy was aflame, taking Toni on a ride that left her spent, even her bones feeling they no longer held any structure. Throughout the journey, Cathy kept her eyes closed, shuttering Toni from whatever private world she had entered. That Toni was physically present was never in any doubt. What was doubtful was exactly who Cathy was making love to.

Even that was not really in doubt. Toni guessed it was probably Lisa.

Toni didn't bother with the niceties of setting a tray with sugar and milk. She added the coffee accompaniments at the bench and headed down the hallway, a mug in each hand.

Quietly she approached the lounge room. She found Cathy exactly as she had left her, except now Virgil sat in her lap. Cathy was stroking Virgil, head bent as she softly spoke to her feline friend. Toni took the opportunity to watch the pair. How Virgil loved Cathy. She leapt onto her at every opportunity, nuzzling into the crook of her arm, or whatever other comfy spot presented itself, complaining loudly when Cathy decided it was time to move.

Like mother like daughter.

How Toni loved Cathy. She too, would leap onto her at any chance, nuzzling into the comfy spots and complaining loudly when it came time for her to leave.

Toni had kidded herself as much as Cathy had when Toni announced she was willing to have a no-strings relationship. Even as she'd said it, Toni knew she was already tightly bound in her devotion. She'd held onto the hope that, given enough time, Cathy could reciprocate her feelings. Unfortunately, Toni had not been given the luxury of time, and she doubted their two weeks together could compete with the eleven years Cathy had spent elevating Lisa to the status of demi-deity.

Toni lingered in her study of Cathy. Then, steeling herself over whatever was to come, she entered the lounge. "Coffee's up."

"Thank you Toni." Cathy accepted the mug but placed it straight onto a coaster on the coffee table. She patted the seat next to her and said, "Come sit with me."

"I think I'll sit here." Toni sank into the single-seater. She placed her mug onto the coffee table. She nervously raked fingers through her hair. "Okay Cathy. What's up?"

Twenty minutes later, the two mugs remained untouched, their contents gone cold.

Cathy sat forward in her seat, elbows resting on her knees. Toni also sat forward, her head in her hands. No tears had yet come, but the sting behind her eyes indicated they were not far away. "I think I'd like you to leave now."

"Toni." Cathy reached across to her but Toni shied away. "Toni. I'm so sorry."

"I know Cathy. Now please, I really don't want to see you at the moment."

When Cathy stood, the finality of it dawned on Toni. Once Cathy walked out that door, she would never be back, not as her lover. Grief burst forth. "She'll just end up hurting you again you know."

"Maybe so." Cathy rounded the table and squatted next to Toni's legs. "But I have to take that chance."

"I'd never hurt you like that."

"I know Toni." This time Toni didn't pull away, letting Cathy take hold of her hands. "You're the best friend I could ever have asked for."

"I don't want to be your friend."

"I'm sorry."

"I want you."

"I'm sorry Toni. I just can't be what you want me to be."

It was not too much later that Cathy left, softly closing the front door behind her. As soon as she was gone the whole house seemed to sigh, as if it too was mourning the loss.

"Oh Virg." Toni scooped up the ball curled at the far end of the lounge and held her tightly to her chest. She carried Virgil down the hallway and into her home office. Virgil settled into her lap as Toni waited for the computer to boot up. Used to the sound of the modem dialing the remote server, Virgil rumbled away, unperturbed by the electronic noises.

"Where shall we go Virg?" Toni asked as she browsed the airline's online booking system. Not willing to accept Toni's resignation, Cathy granted Toni immediate leave, telling her to take as much time as she needed. When she was ready, there would be a job and an office waiting for her. Toni couldn't see herself ever being ready to go back to those offices. Especially since they now had Lisa stamped all over them. "It has to be somewhere in Australia or you'll have to go into quarantine."

Toni decided on Melbourne. When all else fails, run home.

"You'll like Melbourne Virg." Toni logged off the computer and headed down the hallway to pack for the flight that would leave just before ten the next morning. "It's the city of style. You'll fit right in."

Logistics of leaving her house for any period of time were pushed aside. She could deal with that in the morning, sure one of her friends would be willing to pop in to water the garden and clear any fuzzy stuff from the fridge. For the moment, all she cared about was putting some distance between herself and the house over the lane. Given the hour, Toni doubted Cathy would go straight there, but come tomorrow, who knew.

Chapter Thirteen

The outlook over the ocean was bleak. Black clouds threatened and the wind churned the ocean into choppy, gray peaks. It was a shame. On a clear day Lisa imagined the view would be spectacular, a vista of ocean and sky with the horizon broken only by the land mass of Rottnest Island. However, unless already in the know, a visitor to the café in which Lisa sat today would be clueless that an island lay just twelve or so miles off the coast.

Lisa toyed with the glass of water she had poured. She wondered if the café would reduce their prices on such a day, the quick glance she had given the menu board before rushing inside to escape the weather, indicating the patrons were paying as much for the view as the food. Actually, view or no view, Lisa was appalled at the prices. How anyone would even entertain paying that much for a cup of coffee was beyond her. Oh well, she had agreed to Cathy's suggestion of the venue, and since the café was located only ten or so minutes drive from Cathy's house, she figured Cathy was probably a regular and could vouch for the quality. Still, the coffee had better be bloody good.

Despite knowing there was no need to check her watch, Lisa did so anyway. Five to eleven. Still five minutes to wait. Lisa had not meant to arrive so early, but that morning she'd taken one look from her window and decided it better to be safe than sorry. A storm had been threatening overnight, and the radio announced a road weather alert, so Lisa left home far earlier than necessary, just in case there was a delay of some sort. There hadn't been and she arrived just after a quarter to eleven.

It turned out her early arrival was fortuitous; Lisa had her choice of tables. On entering, the place was almost deserted (it crossed Lisa's mind no one was willing to pay such inflated prices), but within minutes the tables began to fill. Lisa watched patrons umming and erring over where to sit, smug in her prime window position. The floor was terraced so every table had a view, but that was beside the point. A window table was still a window table.

Lisa was relieved to find the dress of the other patrons little different than that of the coffee crowd in more realistically priced venues. There was the usual Sunday mix of casual and less casual, so she didn't feel out of place in her usual Sunday attire of jeans, T-shirt and, on this day, a lightweight jumper.

Sensing Cathy had arrived, Lisa turned her attention from the window. Cathy was indeed at the entrance. She did a quick scan, spied where Lisa was sitting and headed toward her.

Lisa watched Cathy approach, pleased to note she appeared relaxed. The last time Lisa saw Cathy, on the morning she did the final inspection, Cathy had seemed tense and . . . almost sad. Cathy was effusive in her praise of the tiling, but apart from that she had been of few words. The only item of a personal nature they discussed was the venue for today's coffee. Lisa was quite disappointed, Cathy was so up and down in her moods she didn't know which way to turn. So self-involved was Lisa, it wasn't until she left the offices she realized Toni had not been there. On the ride down in the lift, Lisa wondered if maybe they'd had an argument. Maybe

Toni hadn't been able to drag her arse out of bed in time for the early morning appointment and Cathy left without her. The thought was pleasing. She hated the idea of Toni dragging her arse out of any bed Cathy was in, but she liked the idea of them arguing over it. Immediately Lisa was disgusted with herself.

"Honey, there's nothing unusual about feeling that way." Steph reassured as Lisa confessed her thoughts in a phone call that night. "You're just adjusting to the fact they're together."

"Yeah I know." Glum, Lisa stabbed at her phone pad with a pen, and said, "But that doesn't stop me from wishing they weren't."

"Maybe you shouldn't be seeing Cathy then," Steph suggested gently.

Lisa frowned. Up until now, Steph had actively encouraged her to contact Cathy. "You've changed your tune."

"I know honey. But I had no idea just how strongly you felt until I saw you the other night." There was a pause over the phone line. "Maybe it's better if you just stay away. For your own good I mean."

"But I really do want to be friends," Lisa argued. It was the truth. She wanted Cathy in her life in some way, shape or form. And if friendship was the form, then so be it.

"Okay honey." Steph didn't sound very convinced. Again she paused and Lisa knew this time it was because she was still bursting to find out what had happened in Lisa's lounge room on the night of her birthday. But she didn't ask and Lisa didn't offer. "You just be careful Leese."

"I will," Lisa promised and they ended the call.

Lisa reiterated that promise to herself as she continued to watch Cathy approach. As with every time she saw Cathy, her heart began to thump. She let it thunder in her chest for the time it took her eyes to wander up and down the length of Cathy's frame. Lisa noted Cathy was dressed as casually as herself. Her jeans were dark denim, exposed button hipsters with—as was the fashion—legs that flared toward the ankle. They looked like favorites, frequently washed, comfortable and lived in. A form fitting T-shirt with a plunging neckline drew the eyes to . . . Lisa looked instead to Cathy's cardigan, a light-knit affair just visible under the wet weather jacket she still sported. She had no sign of a limp. Instead, the "Cathy walk" was back. The confident stride with just a slight, ever so sexy roll of the hips. The roll was perfect, a roll so many women practiced but few could master. It was the roll that had seen Lisa drag behind Cathy on their way to class, just to indulge in the pleasure of seeing her walk. Aware she was no longer just looking, but outright staring, Lisa gave her heart firm instructions to slow down, closed her mouth, set it into a smile and rehearsed a casual greeting. Lisa also noted it was bang on eleven o'clock.

"Looks like your ankle is all better."

"Uh-huh." Cathy gave her windswept hair a shake and shrugged out of her jacket. It was draped over the back of her chair before she sat down. "Like I said, I've done it before," she said, smiling, "An old tennis injury that keeps coming back to haunt me."

"Oh." This hobby was news to Lisa. "I didn't know you played."

"Very badly I'm afraid," Cathy glanced at the waiter who appeared and shook her head, indicating she was not yet ready to order. She turned her attention back to Lisa. "I got a bit too enthusiastic one day and overreached for a passing shot at the net. I should just have let it go as I usually do."

Lisa didn't believe a word of it. She imagined Cathy as a terrier on the court, running down everything and refusing to let even an obvious winning shot get the better of her. "How long have you played?"

"Let's see," Lisa could see Cathy thinking back. "It must be a good eight years now. I took it up when I lived in Sydney."

"You lived in Sydney?" This was another bit of news.

"For six years."

"Really." Lisa's eyebrows shot up and she leaned forward,

ignoring the coffee menu. Obviously they had a lot of catching up to do. "What made you move there?"

Cathy settled her eyes on her own menu. "I got a job offer and decided I may as well take it." The menu was pushed to the middle of the table. Almost immediately the waiter returned, pen poised over his pad. "I'll have a latte please."

Lisa ordered a cappuccino. They were both silent until he left. Then, more than a little interested, Lisa launched back into her questions, eager to discover what Cathy had been up to in the last eleven years.

"Wow Cathy." Lisa was also more than a little impressed with what she heard. "You've done really well."

Cathy shrugged away the compliment. "I did have a bigger kick-start than most, you know."

"Maybe so," Lisa conceded. "But I still think it's kudos to you. A lot of people would be content to take that amount of money and do bugger-all." Lisa wasn't exaggerating. Cathy's trust would be enough to see the average person in good stead for life, so long as they invested wisely and didn't fritter it away. Lisa could imagine, had she been given that amount of money at Cathy's age, it would have slipped easily through her fingers. Especially with no lack of "friends" to help her spend it. "But you chose to start your own business. And you go there every day, even though you could get someone to run it for you."

"Well, I have to do something to keep myself occupied." Cathy smiled. "Anyhow, I love what I do."

Lisa smiled back, and said, "You were born to be an accountant Cathy." She reached for a sugar sachet, their second coffees arriving at the table.

"Boring, you mean?"

Lisa glanced up from her studied sugar sprinkle. "No. Not boring. I just meant . . ." She trailed away, realizing what Cathy was driving at. If there was one thing Lisa remembered it was her parting shot at the door of Cathy's apartment. She wanted to say she had been so wrong, that she found Cathy anything but boring.

That she found her exciting, in every way. Instead she said lamely, "I meant you are good with figures and things."

Cathy just nodded, slowly stirring her latte so the milk swirled into the layer of coffee at the bottom. She pointed her spoon in the direction of Lisa's cappuccino, and said, "I see you still do that thing with the sugar."

"Old habits die hard." Completing her ritual, Lisa stirred the froth with its even coat of sugar and ate it with her spoon. "Besides, I've never managed to get into the lattes. They're too milky for me."

"Speaking of the accounting thing—"

"Yes?" Lisa interjected warily, Cathy's quick topic changes making her nervous.

"How did you make the leap from that to tiling?"

Lisa relaxed. It was her turn to tell her story. She licked the last of the froth from her spoon and set it onto the saucer. "Well, it wasn't planned. I saw this program on television—you know the ones where they do all the house renovation type stuff . . ."

After hearing Lisa's story, Cathy smiled, and said, "You should be proud of what you've achieved as well Lisa. You and Joel have built a great business, and I must say, it's no wonder. Not if what you did for me is anything to go by."

"Thanks Cathy." Glowing, Lisa took advantage of the time afforded by finishing her second coffee. "But it's just because I love what I do, too."

Cathy rested an elbow on the table, chin in hand. "You know, I should have listened when you started hinting you weren't sure about wanting to be an accountant. Looking at you now, it's quite obvious it wasn't meant for you."

Uncomfortable under the thoughtful gaze coming from across the table, Lisa picked up a sugar sachet and began playing with it. The mutual admiration session they had indulged in each other's achievements was all well and good, but it was time. Time for a long overdue apology.

"Cathy," Lisa placed the sugar sachet back in its bowl, determined not to be fiddling with anything. She clasped her hands in her lap. "Cathy, I'm so sorry for how I treated you back then." The temptation to dilute her statement with excuses to explain her behavior was strong, but she didn't. "I wish I could take it all back and do it differently."

The silence between them was long and drawn, Lisa waiting nervously for Cathy to give some sort of response. Cathy, for her part, seemed taken aback by the apology. Lisa could almost see her mind whirring, looking for something appropriate to say.

"How could you Lisa?" she said eventually, eyes glistening. "Do you have any idea how it felt when I got back and found all your things were gone?"

"I know." Ashamed, Lisa looked down past the table to her hands. "I'm sorry. It was an awful thing to do."

"Why didn't you at least call me?"

"I did."

Cathy folded her arms and glared. "Don't lie Lisa, you did not."

"I'm not lying, really. I didn't call you but I called mum, she said she'd passed my message on."

"I know," Cathy said impatiently. "I got your message. I meant why didn't you return my call?"

Lisa looked up sharply. "What call? I never got a call."

Cathy's eyes narrowed, "The call I made the very night your mum called me. I spoke to Evelyn."

Lisa shook her head, bewildered, "Honestly Cathy, I never got your message."

Cathy considered Lisa for long moments. Her eyes softened. "You're telling the truth."

"Yes."

They looked at each other, wondering what could have been. All the time that may have been different had Evelyn chosen to pass on the message.

Cathy was the first to speak. "It doesn't matter now anyway." She reached for the sugar sachet Lisa had played with before, pressing the contents from one end of the packet to the other. "If you think about it she probably did us a favor."

"How do you figure that?"

"I don't think it was our time Lisa." Cathy shrugged her shoulders, adding, "Do you think if she passed on the message it would really have made a difference?"

Lisa wanted to believe it would. But she knew, while there may have been a reconciliation, the same problems would have cropped up again. She and Cathy were in two very different headspaces at the time. "Probably not."

"And if she'd passed on the message maybe you would never have found your calling."

Since Cathy was being philosophical Lisa could too. "And you may never have accepted that job offer in Sydney." She imagined Cathy would still have received the offer, but Lisa's own grades were never going to be good enough for a similar opportunity. And she couldn't see Cathy flying to the other side of the country while she was in Perth working out her own professional year.

"Yes I would have," Cathy said confidently. "You'd have followed me."

Lisa really couldn't say what she would have done back then. But she knew if it were in question now, she'd already have her bags packed. "No I wouldn't."

"Yes you would."

"No I wouldn't." Lisa stood, also knowing if they continued this train of conversation she'd end up blurting something about a willingness to follow Cathy to the ends of the earth. "Where's the bathroom?"

"I don't know. I've never been here before."

"Oh." Lisa scanned the premises, looking for a sign. Spying one, she headed toward it, wondering that Cathy had never visited here, pleased purely because it meant it wasn't a hangout for Cathy and Toni. Lisa decided this was now officially her and Cathy's hangout. The coffee was good, too, she admitted. Well worth the outrageous prices. Well, almost.

"You should go check out the bathroom," Lisa said on her return. "It's really quite something. Although," she whispered conspiratorially, "The tiling leaves a lot to be desired."

Lisa watched Cathy rise from her seat. She watched her again as she sat back down a few minutes later, checking her watch as she did so. Lisa's mood flattened. Obviously it was time to end their date . . . their . . . meeting. Lisa wondered if she would be pushing her luck suggesting a third cup of coffee. She wouldn't sleep all night, but she was willing to live with that.

"Shit Lisa." Cathy exclaimed. "We've been here over two hours."

"Yeah I know." During Cathy's absence Lisa noticed the coffee and cake crowd had departed, to be replaced with the lunch crowd. The clang of cooking utensils came from the open kitchen and plates of food were being carried to expectant diners. "Time flies huh."

"I'm hungry. Do you want to stay and have lunch?"

"Unless of course you have somewhere you need to be?" Cathy continued, when Lisa didn't answer immediately.

"No. Lunch sounds good." The only official invite she had for the afternoon was the one arriving in the post at her parents' place a few weeks ago. The one inviting her to the school reunion her mum had pre-warned her about. An early cocktail affair, it would be starting in a few hours, at some yacht club along the river. Hell would freeze over before Lisa would entertain the thought of attending that one. However, elated at this invitation, Lisa grinned, "I've got no plans for the afternoon."

"Great." Cathy called to the waiter for the lunch and drinks menus. "Do you feel like wine or would you rather a beer?"

Already on a natural high, Lisa didn't really feel the need for anything alcoholic. Sitting on a glass of wine would be much easier than sipping on a warm, flat beer. "Wine's good."

The drink menu was passed across the table. "Do you want to choose?"

Lisa shook her head. "I need a few goes at the wine club thing before you can trust me with a wine list."

"Come on Lisa." Cathy planted the menu between them. "We'll decide together."

Within minutes, a bottle of dry white wine had been delivered to their table. Lisa studied the lunch menu, deciding just to ignore the prices and have whatever she felt like. She quickly scanned the offerings. One caught her eye: pan-fried barramundi served atop herbed potato rosti and accompanied by the chef's own mesclun selection with fresh garden vegetables and a lemon vinaigrette.

Fish and chips with salad. That sounded all right.

"I think I'll go for the fish."

Cathy's eyes darted to Lisa's selection. "That sounds good. But I think I'll go for the pasta."

Once their meals were placed in front of them, Lisa looked from her plate to Cathy's. As usual, as soon as she was served, Lisa got buyer's remorse. Why did whatever anyone else ordered always look more appealing than her own dish?

The food envy was noted. "Have you got grass is greener syndrome again?"

"No." Lisa picked up her cutlery.

"Do you want to swap?"

"No." Lisa thought the pumpkin pasta filled with pesto looked really good.

"Do you want to share?"

"Maybe." Lisa took one last envious look to Cathy's plate. "Can I just have a taste?"

Instead of being handed the fork, Lisa was offered just the pasta end.

"What are you laughing at?" Cathy looked bemused as Lisa chewed.

Lisa swallowed before answering. "You. You still open your own mouth whenever you feed someone."

"I do not!"

Lisa took a little sip of her wine. It was very nice. She congratulated herself on her choice. And it had been her choice, sort of. She'd put her finger on a couple of wines in the list and Cathy had either screwed up her nose or shaken her head. Lisa had chosen the first one that got the nod. She grinned at Cathy from behind her glass. "Yes you do."

Cathy's insistence that she didn't open her mouth while feeding someone was a longstanding debate. Cathy conceded that if she did, it was just because it was a natural human reflex. Many times, in cafés, restaurants, fast-food joints or the University cafeteria, they had been caught watching intently as diners fed each other. "See!" Cathy would say gleefully. "He's doing it too."

"Well if I do, it's just because it's a natural human reflex."

Lisa laughed at Cathy's continued stubbornness. Natural human reflex or Cathy-specific, Lisa found it adorable. Just as she found everything else about Cathy adorable. She cut that thought short, instead cutting off a small section of her fish and offering it to Cathy. Just to prove her point she kept her mouth clamped shut, despite experiencing the natural reflex to open it as Cathy opened hers.

When they were almost through their meal, conversation turned to the renovations Lisa had undertaken on her house.

"I still think you're very clever." Cathy was most impressed to discover Lisa had done a lot of the work herself. "Everything I've ever done to my place I've called in the experts. You must be very handy."

From what I remember you're pretty skilled with your hands yourself.

Unsure if she had voiced that thought out loud, Lisa stole a quick glance to the other side of the table. Cathy registered no outrage, so obviously she hadn't. But inwardly she cringed. For Lisa was failing miserably at this friend thing. If anything, she was acting more like a love-struck adolescent. Steph was right again. She should just have stayed away.

Lisa had fought against her urges from the moment Cathy fed her the first mouthful of pasta. She'd almost succeeded in cooling her blood, until about three minutes into their meal, when they both reached for the wine bottle at the same time. Their hands brushed. Lisa was the first to pull away, but by then the contact had been extended enough to make Lisa feel like Cathy's fingers were impressed into her skin. She'd been looking for ways to "accidentally" touch ever since.

Nothing had come to bear. Cathy didn't take salt so there was no reason to lunge for the saltshaker. Pepper was offered by one of those staff who seemed to do nothing but wander around wielding an oversized pepper mill, and the damn table had a sturdy four-way crossbar at its base so Lisa would have to stretch her foot and twist it in an awkward manner to make contact. Inadvertent footsies were subsequently out of the question.

Lisa decided to concentrate harder on the conversation, appalled at herself for even entertaining the thought of physical contact with someone who was with someone else. She focused on what Cathy was saying, which unfortunately meant she had to focus on Cathy. Nowhere seemed safe. She looked at her eyes but felt she would fall into their dark brown depths, never to be retrieved. She tried watching her mouth, but that, for obvious reasons, was even more dangerous. She stared for a while at the point just above her eyes, but that was also a bad idea, Cathy soon scratching her forehead and asking if she had something odd stuck there. Lisa lowered her gaze to Cathy's neck. But the T-shirt had done what its designer intended—it made the eyes follow all the way down the plunging neckline. Lisa nearly choked on her fish, her memory providing visuals of exactly what lay underneath the material.

Things were getting desperate. She had to do something to stop from launching herself across the table.

An idea struck. Bring up the girlfriend. Nothing had been said of partners, either past or present, throughout the whole date . . . meeting . . . whatever it was. Maybe it was time to do so. After all, talk of the girlfriend would be the psychological equivalent of having a cold shower.

"So, what does Toni think of the new-look offices?"

Cathy placed her fork quietly on her plate. "I don't know. She hasn't seen them."

"Oh." Lisa's head spun. Why on earth not? For all she'd known, Cathy and Toni spent the whole of yesterday putting the offices back together, even completing the restacking of bookshelves this very morning. That's what Cathy said *she'd* been doing anyhow. "I thought she'd been helping you with the computers and stuff."

"No Lisa. Toni and I have . . . parted company."

"Oh." Lisa said again, now totally unable to look at Cathy for fear her expression would convey her thoughts. The ones that were already mentally sifting through the dating possibilities. Lisa studied the remains of her meal. Just a bit of salad remained. She toyed with it, rolling a cherry tomato around the plate with her fork. As she did so, Lisa's mind was playing a scene of her walking along a beach with Cathy (in much better weather of course), Lisa surprising her with her favorite flowers, taking her to her favorite restaurant, sitting next to her in a theater. A movie, a concert, a play, it didn't matter. They'd court for a while, Cathy would realize Lisa was in fact the woman for her and then . . . the cherry tomato came to a stop, braked by her fork. "I'm sorry to hear that."

"Yes, well," From the corner of Lisa's eye she saw Cathy shift in her seat. "I had a couple of issues I needed to sort out."

"Oh." Lisa repeated for the third time. She rolled her tomato around again, but stopped, memories of her parents saying "don't play with your food" echoing through her mind. Unable to stop fidgeting, Lisa soon began poking with her cutlery once more, dipping and prodding with her fork until the tomato lay on its upturned prongs. She lifted her head to glance quickly at Cathy, knowing she shouldn't ask, shouldn't pry. She lowered her gaze to her plate again. Such a fine looking tomato, all ripe and red. "What issues?"

"Well." Cathy took a quick sip of her wine. "There's the fact that I still love you."

It was just as well Lisa hadn't a mouthful of wine, it would have blown all across the table. As it was there was a sudden crash of cutlery against crockery as Lisa shot a shocked look in Cathy's direction, at the same time her arms coming down hard against the tabletop. Her mouth opened although no words would come out. But her heart was doing happy little flip-flops. *She loves me. She loves me! SHE LOVES ME!*

"Umm, Lisa?"

Still dumbstruck, Lisa just stared gape-jawed at Cathy. Then it occurred Cathy was trying to tell her something. She turned her head in the direction of Cathy's nod.

"I don't think this belongs to me." The middle-aged man sitting at the table diagonally opposite them held out his glass of wine. There was a cherry tomato bobbing in it. Lisa took a quick look at her plate. Sure enough, her tomato was gone.

Crimson, she turned back to the man. "That's okay. You can have it if you like."

A matter of minutes later he had been furnished with not just a glass, but a new bottle of wine. The replacement had been courtesy of Cathy; she called a waiter over even before Lisa had time to absorb the fact she had launched a tomato torpedo with her fork. Mortified, Lisa just wanted to slide under the table and hide. But she couldn't. Cathy was watching her expectantly. Her initial amusement at Lisa's vegetable toss had long dissipated. Now she just looked worried.

Lisa knew she had to say something. If she were in Cathy's position, she'd be dying by now. What could she say? How could she express what she had been feeling since the night Cathy dropped back into her life? The yearning, the craving, the highs and lows, the desire just to see Cathy, be near Cathy, hear her voice, bask in her smile. The petty jealousies, the emptiness when Cathy left a room or hung up from a call, the euphoria when she arrived or was on the end of a phone line. All could be explained to Cathy in detail later. But for now it could be summed up in the same few words Cathy had just spoken. Lisa reached across the table and took hold of Cathy's hands.

"I love you too, Cathy."

Lisa saw Cathy's expression morph from worry to elation. She smiled softly and Lisa smiled back, warmth spreading as Cathy's thumbs stroked hers. They both leaned forward, Lisa blissfully aware they were going to kiss. But she was also acutely aware they were being watched.

Lisa glanced back to the table diagonally opposite. As suspected, Mr. Tomato Head was regarding her, and Cathy, with renewed interest. Jeez, what did he want—her to toss him a whole salad?

Not wishing an audience, she turned back to Cathy. "Do you think we could go now?"

Cathy nodded and they scraped their chairs away from the table. Lisa, having no jacket to retrieve, beat Cathy to the bill, plucking it from its holder and rushing to the counter. The total, especially with the added bottle of wine, meant no extra would be going onto the mortgage this month, but too bad, it was worth it.

They argued over it all the way outside.

"You can get the next one, okay?" Cold wind hit Lisa with a blast, despite the portico they stood under being on the street side of the building. Thankfully, it was not yet raining.

"Okay." Cathy gazed out past the portico, glancing up to the sky. "Let's make a run for it."

They reached Lisa's vehicle first. Lisa could see Cathy's car not ten bays down from her own. She also saw the sheet of rain fast coming in off the ocean. It would reach them within seconds. Lisa twisted the lock on the passenger door and ushered Cathy inside.

"Shove over," she instructed, climbing in after Cathy. The door was hardly closed before the front hit. Heavy drops thundered on the metal roof, echoing loudly in the cabin.

"Just made it," Lisa said, grinning. "A few more seconds and we'd have been soaked."

Cathy shifted slightly, her lips giving just the merest hint of a smile. Her expression conveyed an unspoken *too late*.

Lisa hardly dared to look at Cathy as she tugged at the neck of her jumper. The air in the cabin all of a sudden seemed very close, humid and steamy. Lisa also shifted in her seat, her thigh lightly brushing against Cathy's.

That slight touch was enough to unravel the both of them.

The look they exchanged was brief, but charged. Cathy hurled herself at Lisa. Lisa hurled herself at Cathy. Neither was at all gentle, their kisses fierce and their hands grasping, clutching desperately at material that got in the way of skin.

"Oh God, Cathy—" Lisa pressed her palm against Cathy's groin and her head swam at the heat that met her hand, radiating through the denim.

"Lie down." A sure hand guided Lisa downward until her head rested on the bench seat. At the same a time a knee parted Lisa's thighs so she had no choice but to rest one foot on the floor, one on the seat. Cathy lay half over her, her other leg jostling for position with Lisa's in the cramped space under the steering wheel.

Lisa groaned as the knee between her thighs slid higher. She could feel her own heat, it trapped by the double layer of denim that separated her skin from Cathy's. As if parting her legs further would suddenly make the offending material disappear, Lisa lifted her foot off the floor. It found the dashboard, coming to rest on the top of the steering wheel. Cathy's knee was insistent; it grazed over Lisa, was momentarily gone, grazed again. Lisa arched into Cathy, the point between her legs throbbing in her need. She drew Cathy down to greet her lips, kisses gaining urgency in time with the increasing rhythm and tempo of her hips. One coherent thought managed to break through the red-hot haze that had overtaken Lisa's mind. *Thank goodness for bench seats and column gearshifts.* However, that ridiculous thought emerged prematurely. Maybe Cathy's foot slipped on the mat under the steering wheel, maybe the hand she had squeezed between the seat and Lisa's shoulder got a cramp. Whatever happened, Cathy's knee suddenly pressed hard against its target. Both Lisa's legs jerked in response, the foot she still had perched on the steering wheel lifted and fell, hitting the horn. Its sounding gave Lisa such a fright she slammed her head against the door handle of the passenger door. She let out another groan, this time a pained "Oof!"

The shock of the blow brought Lisa's undulating hips to a halt and took her hands to her head. As suddenly as the activity in the vehicle ceased, so too did the downpour. The silence was so abrupt it was deafening.

"Lisa," Cathy half sat up, reached for Lisa's head and gingerly fingered the point of contact. "Are you all right?"

Lisa blinked, her head still zinging. "Who are you?"

As Lisa continued to stare blankly, Cathy's eyes opened wide. Lisa eventually grinned, unable to keep a straight face in light of the distressed look she was receiving. "Gotcha."

"Bitch." Cathy laughed along with Lisa, gently stroking her hair and deftly avoiding putting any pressure on the sore spot. Lisa found the touch first soothing, then arousing. It took but moments before the pain of the blow was forgotten and her body again arched and stretched toward Cathy. Cathy met Lisa's mouth, only much more tenderly than before. "Let's get out of here."

"What's wrong with here?" Now Lisa had Cathy in her arms she wasn't about to let her go. And the knee still held so close to her groin was slowly driving her mad. Lisa wrapped her arms around Cathy, drawing her closer. Cathy's breath came in soft puffs, warm over her lips, then moist over her skin as she trailed a series of kisses over Lisa's neck and throat. Lisa groped for the edge of Cathy's T-shirt, desperate to feel Cathy naked in her hands. "Sweet God Cathy, I want you."

The moment Lisa's hands slid under Cathy's T-shirt to circle the firm flesh of her waist, Cathy's soft puffs escalated to a pant. Then suddenly, the warm breath and kisses were gone. Cathy lifted herself into a half-sitting position, eyes alight with desire, but also shining with the determination Lisa had long ago become so familiar with. "I want you too Lisa. But not here."

"Where then?" Right here and right now seemed the only viable option. Lisa switched her attention from Cathy's eyes to her lips. She wanted to kiss them again.

"How about my place?"

After a short silence Lisa nodded, reluctantly admitting the possibilities offered by a bed far outweighed the immediacy offered by the bench seat of her utility. Plus, she also admitted as she realized she could not see out of the windscreen, once home they could fog up the windows all they liked without running the risk of getting arrested. "Okay."

Lisa pushed open the passenger door and half hung out of it as

Cathy climbed over her. Still lying on her back, Lisa held out her hand. "I'm going to miss you on the long, lonely drive."

Cathy laughed as she accepted Lisa's hand, kissing the palm. "I'll see you in about ten minutes." She tipped her head to one side, her eyes questioning, and asked, "Do you remember where my place is?"

Lisa gave a disparaging look. Of course she remembered. Cathy's address, like every other detail about her, was tattooed into her memory. Cathy, interpreting Lisa's look as a yes, gave Lisa back her hand and hurried to her car. Lisa sat up, slammed the passenger door closed and shunted over to the driver's side, turning the key in the ignition. In an effort to clear the fog from the windows she turned the air conditioning on full blast.

Once there was some semblance of visibility through the glass, Lisa slid the column shift into reverse. She checked her rearview mirror and slung her arm over the back of the bench seat, easing off the clutch as she pulled out of the bay. Her peripheral vision caught the dark blue BMW as it turned out of the parking lot. Lisa shivered and her heart fluttered. Ten whole minutes before seeing Cathy again. It seemed an eternity.

Lisa had no idea if it took more or less than ten minutes to get to Cathy's home. As her indicator flashed her intention to turn into Cathy's driveway she was suddenly aware she had no notion of how she had gotten there. She certainly didn't recall the drive.

What she did recall were her thoughts as she unwittingly guided her vehicle along the wet and no doubt slippery roads. Her thoughts, as so often in the past weeks, had been centered on Cathy. However, where her thoughts of the past weeks were subject to a degree of censorship, self-preservation demanding she close her mind to recollections of the physical, now the change in circumstance allowed her thoughts to flow unchecked. And as soon as the first thought seeped through, it seemed it opened a floodgate.

Memory took Lisa back to those first days, to the first time, when Cathy caught her in the shower. Back then, Lisa was as green as they came, but somehow she knew what to do, needing no map to guide her through the uncharted territory. Making love with Cathy was so easy, and felt so right. Yes of course they needed clues from the other, they guided with a touch here, a word there. And they backed it all up with practice, and lots of it.

There was no doubt their physical connection had been incredible. It stretched beyond those first halcyon weeks that lovers throughout history have experienced. The weeks where they were both literally unable to keep their hands off each other, rushing to Cathy's place in between classes, barely making it through the front door before shedding the clothes that suddenly seemed such a hindrance. They were the days where sometimes class was missed altogether, where the company of others was shunned, and time spent apart was a torture. And, as with lovers throughout history, they survived the shift that inevitably has to occur, returning to day-to-day life and its responsibilities.

Not that the return to the day-to-day signaled a plateau in their sex life. If anything, as they become more familiar with each other, more attuned to each other's needs and desires, it seemed their lovemaking moved to a whole new level.

For that's what it was. Lovemaking. It had never been just sex with Cathy. It was the love between them that made it so good. When they were both driven almost wild by their passion for each other, it was love that tempered their touch so the line between pleasure and pain was not crossed. When the tempo was slow and more measured, it was love that had sometimes seen one or the other, or both, so overwhelmed they were reduced to tears.

It remained that way between them almost until the end. Almost until the end they shared a level of intimacy that, had Lisa known at the time was such a rare and precious commodity, she may have taken more care to nurture and embrace it.

Feeling again the surge of regret for her carelessness all those years ago, Lisa wiped her mind clear of the past. The past was gone and she could do nothing to alter it. All she could do was make the most of the present. Another surge, this time not even closely related to regret, coursed through Lisa as she realized the present was taking her to Cathy's arms.

As expected, when Lisa completed the turn into Cathy's driveway, the front gate was open, as was the garage door. Lisa drove straight in, parking her Ute next to Cathy's BMW, at the same time thinking how well the two vehicles sat together, a pleasing juxtaposition. Cathy was waiting for her, the door to her home already open.

Lisa rounded Cathy's car, noting as she went that the front gate was closing. The garage door also began its descent.

"Am I locked in now?" Lisa asked as they entered the stairwell. Cathy closed the door behind her. "Afraid so."

Good, Lisa thought. They held hands as they ascended the stairs.

"Would you like a drink or something?" Cathy asked as they approached the first landing.

Lisa changed her grip so their fingers interlocked. "No thanks."

They reached the first landing. Cathy nodded to the living area. "Would you like to watch TV, play cards, listen to music?"

Cathy's hand was clasped a little tighter. Lisa wasn't fooled for one moment she was here to play *Snap*. "Not really."

They started up the next set of stairs to the top level. "Well, would you like me to show you the best view in the street?"

Lisa felt Cathy's hand pulsing against hers, first loosening, then tightening her hold. The action was so overtly sexual Lisa heard her own voice husky with want. "Where's that?"

They stopped at the second landing. "From my bedroom window."

Lisa's lips twitched at the thinly veiled pretense. Their slow climb up the two flights of stairs had almost driven her to distraction. She wanted to run the length of the hallway and throw herself onto the bed, but instead she gripped more tightly to Cathy's hand, using it as her anchor. She smiled and nodded although her voice again gave her away. This time it broke. "Okay."

On the journey from the bedroom door to the window Lisa

vaguely noticed her surrounds. More of a suite than a bedroom, the room was huge. A gaping archway opened to a bathroom decked from floor to ceiling in sandstone colored tiles. The details Lisa missed, but she was sure she spied a raised spa in there. The next door was closed, and due to the lack of a conventional wardrobe, Lisa assumed it was a walk-in. To one side of the heavy, full-length drapes was a sitting area with a couple of single armchairs and a low coffee table. A king-sized bed dominated the far wall, but even that didn't appear oversized given the dimensions of the room. Lisa was acutely aware of this last piece of furniture as Cathy played out her charade to the end, drawing aside the drapes with a flourish.

"Ta da!"

Light, although muted because of the dullness of the day, flooded into the room.

Cathy turned toward Lisa, a hint of a smile crossing her features. She nodded toward the window, "What do you reckon?"

Lisa's eyes didn't waver from Cathy's face. Cathy was right, the view was spectacular. "Absolutely stunning."

"No, don't." Lisa stayed Cathy's hand when it appeared she was reaching to close the curtains again. Her every sense was heightened, nerve endings tingling, alive. She certainly didn't want to waste a single opportunity to use all of them. "I want to see you."

It was with some surprise Lisa realized just how nervous she was now the moment she had dreamed of had arrived. The way she felt was in complete contrast to the minutes spent with Cathy in the cabin of her utility. Those minutes had been driven by a blinding need, her actions instinctive and unthinking. But now she had had time to think. During the drive to Cathy's home, her memories were unleashed, and their slow journey from the garage to the bedroom only served to heighten her expectations. Expectations Cathy no doubt shared.

Lisa didn't want to feel this way. She didn't want the flock of butterflies in her stomach, didn't want the sudden doubts of her abilities, didn't want to worry the years that had stretched between them may have brought changes. That what had worked so well in the past may not incite the same reactions today.

Cathy smiled again, a soft, almost shy smile. She moved closer, moved so they were almost close enough to touch. They both reached for the safety of each other's hands, and then stood still, eye to eye, silent except for their breathing.

Lisa looked deep into Cathy's eyes, more than a little relieved to see some of her own nervousness reflected back at her. At least she wasn't the only one.

Cathy relinquished her hold of Lisa's hands and Lisa held her breath as fingertips trailed up her cheek and across her eyebrows.

"Have I ever told you, you have the most incredible eyes?"

Lisa laughed softly. Cathy must have told her that a thousand times before. "Once or twice." She caught one of Cathy's fingertips between her teeth as they passed over her lips.

"Lisa—"

Lisa swirled her tongue over the end of Cathy's index finger. She was in olfactory heaven, Cathy obviously having applied her signature perfume to her wrists. Lisa was convinced YSL had created this fragrance with Cathy's body chemistry in mind. The reaction of the perfume on her skin was pure magic, a scent that assaulted Lisa's senses, quickening her pulse and warming her blood. "Yes?"

"Do you think maybe you could kiss me now? I think I'll die if you don't."

Lisa stopped her finger sucking, a rush of absolute joy evaporating all nervousness. The woman who stood before her was just too gorgeous for words. And, Lisa decided yet again as she made the one final step so their bodies touched, so incredibly sexy.

"I love you Cathy," Lisa whispered as she slid her hands around Cathy's waist.

From the moment her lips met Cathy's the slow burn inside her ignited. She couldn't get enough, couldn't taste enough or touch enough. Lisa's hands were everywhere, torn between lingering over each curve or continuing their journey, eager to reach the next. With each touch, she remembered. But with each touch it also felt new, like the first time.

Lisa groaned as her fingers found nipples, hard as pebbles, through the material of Cathy's T-shirt. She swept hands up and under Cathy's cardigan, slipping it from her shoulders. Reluctantly, she left Cathy's lips for the time it took to lift the T-shirt over her head. Lisa took a sharp breath as flesh revealed what her mind's eye had so perfectly drawn. Breath still held in her lungs, she reached to cup Cathy's breasts, feel their weight, delight as they molded to her hands. Cathy would argue they were too small, Lisa would argue back they were perfect. And to her they *were* perfect, firm yet yielding, and so incredibly sensitive. Lisa buried her head into Cathy's neck, trailing kisses down and over her shoulders, past her collarbone. If she just touched here, skin puckered as Lisa ran fingertips around deep pink areola, and if she just tasted there, Lisa gathered a nipple into her mouth, nipping with her teeth as her tongue flicked over and over . . . Lisa could feel her breath hot against Cathy's skin as she experienced the reaction she sought, Cathy letting out a slow moan and pressing Lisa's head harder to her chest.

Hands that clutched at Lisa's hair slid down her spine, the touch sending her into shivers. The same hands slipped under Lisa's jumper, pulling at the hem of her T-shirt.

"Lift your arms."

Lisa's jumper and T-shirt were whisked from her body in one deft movement. They were no sooner tossed to the floor than arms circled Lisa's back, fingers quickly finding the catch to unhook her bra. It, too, was tossed aside.

They stood just far enough apart to study each other. Lisa saw Cathy bite on her lower lip, eyes intent on Lisa's breasts. Lisa, for her part, could not make up her mind where she wanted her eyes to settle. Like her hands before, they darted up and down, wanting to study every square inch, but not wanting to linger for fear of missing some special patch of skin. It took little time for Lisa to realize sight was not enough. Her hands reached out to Cathy again, drawing her close. Their breasts pressed together, softness on softness.

"Cathy—" Lisa felt she would drown in the sweetness of Cathy's mouth, felt she needed nothing more to survive than the touch of Cathy's tongue against her own. Her arms wrapped more tightly around Cathy as their kiss deepened. "How I've missed you."

The renewed urgency in Cathy's kiss was Lisa's reply, as was the hand that slid from Lisa's waist to begin work on the buttons of her jeans.

Lisa found the hot spot between Cathy's thighs and her head swam at the groan, not quiet at all, that escaped from Cathy's mouth into her own.

Aware her knees were about to crumple under her, Lisa mumbled into Cathy's mouth, "The bed. Let's go to bed."

"Bed." Cathy repeated, her voice agreeing but her body defiant, pressing harder against Lisa's hand.

Lisa found herself in the midst of a beautiful quandary. *Bed or floor? Bed or floor?* Either option promised delights. If she kept her hand where it was they would end up on the floor. If she could gather the last vestiges of her self-control they could make the few steps to the bed. The lure of the bed won. Lisa lifted Cathy off the floor.

"I *can* walk now you know." A bubble of laughter emerged as Lisa took small backward steps.

"I can put you down if you want." A few more little steps and the bed was almost in reach.

"Don't you even think about it Lisa Smith." Cathy wrapped her legs more securely around Lisa's waist, her fingers curling up and through Lisa's hair.

Lisa felt the hairs on her nape stand on end. She let her knees bend as they hit against the mattress, taking Cathy with her as she fell backward onto the bed. Lust, longing and love coursed through her veins as Cathy straddled her hips. She guided Cathy back to her lips. "Kiss me."

They somehow maneuvered through the frantic scramble to remove the last of their clothing. One of Cathy's shoes now poked from the pair of jeans that had landed unceremoniously on top of it, the other goodness knows where, probably near the window from the sound of leather hitting glass at around the time it was thrown. The clock radio was almost shrouded from view, covered by a leg of the jeans that hung precariously over the bedside table. Lisa could just make out the last digit, but time was immaterial to her. At the moment she didn't care of the hour, the day, or even what planet they were spinning on. All she cared about was the woman who lay beside her, eyes closed as she moved under Lisa's hands.

Once naked, Lisa and Cathy had shared a moment of stillness, eyes wandering down the length of each other's body. The look they exchanged as their eyes met was combustible. For the second time that afternoon they hurled themselves at each other, bodies colliding, soon becoming a tangled mess of limbs as it seemed they both tried to make up for the past eleven years in a single moment.

Cathy's hand had come tantalizingly close to the place Lisa most wanted to be touched, but it slipped away to clutch at Lisa's back as Lisa slipped first one, then two fingers within her.

"Oh . . ." Cathy pressed herself harder against Lisa's hand, eyes closing as she opened her mouth to again greet Lisa's tongue.

Lisa kissed her deeply and thoroughly, enraptured as memory became reality. She remembered everything, the increasing rhythm of Cathy's hips, how her hand would cup Lisa's cheek as they kissed, how Cathy's tongue would be on fire, invading her mouth as she drew closer. She recognized the change in form and texture, muscles tightening around her fingers, the thrusting against her hand becoming more pronounced, then suddenly stilted.

"Look at me," she urged.

Lisa felt her heart would burst as she met eyes that strained to stay open in the moments before the body rush, eyes that were almost black, pupils so dilated the iris was insignificant. They closed again as Cathy's back arched and a cry emerged, fingers pressing hard into Lisa's skin before fluttering limply away.

"Oh Lisa." Cathy's body dissolved into the mattress and Lisa nuzzled into Cathy's neck, trying to hide the smile that spread across her face, the smile that said she was more than a little pleased at her success. She still lay on her side, fingers held captive as Cathy closed her legs around her hand. Lisa felt she could lay like this forever. Almost.

Cathy read her mind. Or maybe she read her body, Lisa none too subtle in the wriggle of her hips and the leg she flung over Cathy's thigh. Cathy twisted and slithered until she lay on top. Lisa's once captive hand was released, only to be recaptured as it was held above her head. Cathy's eyes flashed as she slid her free hand downward. "Lisa." The tip of her tongue teased at the corner of Lisa's lips. "You're so wet."

"Your fault entirely." Lisa lifted her head from the pillow to try and catch Cathy's tongue. But she was too late, Cathy already working her way down Lisa's neck, lips leaving a moist snail trail as they passed between her breasts and across her stomach.

Lisa's hands sifted through Cathy's silken hair as she opened herself to receive the most intimate of lovers' kisses.

And she remembered. Oh, how she remembered. She remembered the mouth that encased her fully, the tongue that glided in long, knowing strokes. She remembered the hand that reached to grasp her own as that tongue darted and glided, seeking, finding, and settling into a delicious rhythm. But oh, the gathering of Lisa's body was so fast. Cathy too felt the approach and she slowed. But for Lisa it was too late. Her hand swept down to Cathy's shoulder, giving the two short taps that meant *don't change a thing*. And oh yes, Cathy remembered the signal, one of many they had devised for the moments when speech was impossible.

Not too long later Cathy slithered back upward. Her smile was wicked and her eyes glinted. She didn't say it but Lisa could read the *that was quick* in her expression. Lisa ran hands weakly up and down Cathy's back, her heart still pounding.

Lisa's pulse raced as she tasted herself on Cathy's lips and tongue, and she gasped as Cathy was suddenly within her, fingers swirling against walls that still throbbed in the aftermath of her orgasm. "You'll be the death of me Cathy Braithwaite."

"No I won't." Cathy settled on her side, thighs parting in response to Lisa's insistent fingers. She shuddered at the contact, eyes flashing as she once more sought Lisa's mouth. "I can almost guarantee you'll survive."

Cathy was right. Lisa did survive. Outside, the first storm of the season raged then slowed then raged again. Rain lashed at the windows and the wind whipped the ocean into a frenzy. The front would pass and all would become relatively quiet, until the next squall approached the coast.

Inside, a similar force of nature was occurring. Frenetic need would slow to tender kisses and gentle caresses, softly spoken words of love and encouragement. Then, without warning, passions would flare again. At these times, bedclothes and pillows fell to the floor, made redundant as two bodies sought only contact with each other.

Throughout, Lisa wondered at the absolute pleasure she extracted from being at one with this woman. Regret at the wasted years again surfaced, but she would not allow it to take hold. All that mattered was she was reunited with Cathy now.

Cathy lay on her side, for the first time in years able to indulge one of her favorite activities, watching Lisa sleep. It had been dark for hours so the light was restricted to that which came through the sliding glass doors leading out to the balcony. Even that was dim, a cloud filled sky eliminating the moon and the street lights shining below their third-story level. Despite this, Cathy's eyes adjusted and she was clearly able to make out Lisa's form in silhouette.

She took one last lingering look, and then slipped off the bed, pausing to pull the sheet from the tangled mass on the floor and gently cover Lisa with it.

Cathy was poking around in the refrigerator when she sensed another presence in the kitchen. She swung around to find Lisa leaning against the island bench. Her hair was sticking up at awkward angles, her T-shirt not only on inside out, but backward, and she was rubbing tired eyes into focus. Cathy thought she had never seen anything more appealing.

"I thought you were sleeping." Cathy kicked the fridge door shut, arms laden with the fixings for ham, cheese and tomato sandwiches. She smiled as she dumped the provisions onto the bench.

"I was." Lisa rounded the counter and hugged Cathy from behind, resting her chin on Cathy's shoulder, "I was dreaming some incredibly sexy woman was in the kitchen rustling up gourmet fare." She whispered into Cathy's ear, "Looks like my dreams have come true."

Lisa's breath tickled and Cathy shivered, "Well, you're spot on with the incredibly sexy bit, but I can't say ham, cheese and tomato is exactly gourmet."

"It will be with a dash of my favorite."

Cathy pointed her knife toward the pantry. "There should be a jar in there somewhere."

"A jar of what?"

Cathy knew Lisa wasn't suffering short-term memory loss, she was being quizzed. Cathy didn't mind. Lisa could play twenty questions all night and Cathy would put money on getting all the answers correct. All the questions relating to their past that is. The present was a different matter. But she was working on it, delighting each time some new aspect of Lisa revealed itself. Cathy put the knife well away from the edge of the counter and spun around in Lisa's arms. "Dijon mustard."

"You remembered." Lisa appeared surprised but pleased.

"Of course," Cathy said, and patted her on the bottom. "But it isn't going to walk out of the cupboard by itself. Go make yourself useful."

Cathy returned to her preparations as Lisa padded across the floor. She smiled when Lisa exclaimed from inside the walk-in pantry, "Shit Cathy, you've got enough stuff in here to see you through a nuclear winter."

There was a whole lot Lisa did not yet know about Cathy either. Including the fact she was now quite proficient in the kitchen, a complete contrast to the student who struggled to boil an egg. Lisa had done most of the cooking back then, slowly teaching Cathy the basics until she was at the point of making a decent pasta or baked dinner. It occurred to her she was not exactly showcasing her skills at present, but hey, she was starving. So too apparently was Lisa, who, Dijon collecting completed, settled into one of the chrome stools on the other side of the counter. She rested her chin on her knuckles and watched the preparations with hungry eyes.

"I didn't think I could ever eat again after such a big lunch, but now I'm ravenous."

Cathy glanced up and winked. "Must have been all that exercise."

Her wink was answered with a knowing smile. "Must have."

Unable to resist, Cathy tossed a tomato in her hand. "Would you like this on your sandwich or served in a glass on the side?"

Lisa went as red as the tomato before covering her face with her hands. "Shit. I still don't believe that happened."

Cathy sniggered and Lisa looked at her through parted fingers. "Shut up Cathy."

Cathy couldn't help herself. Laughter burst forth as she remembered the incident. Unlike Lisa, she had seen the tomato take off, flying in a high arc before it plopped neatly into the unsuspecting diner's glass. "I'm sorry Lisa." Her knife was placed in the middle of the bench before she did herself or Lisa an injury with it. "It's just . . . you should have seen the look on your face."

Lisa removed her hands from her face and tried for a glare. But Cathy saw her mouth twitch up at the corners. "Shut up Cathy," she repeated, a giggle emerging even as she spoke.

Lisa's laugh was a catalyst for Cathy's, which in turn was a catalyst for Lisa's. Soon they were both clutching at their stomachs, tears rolling down their cheeks.

"Stop it!" Cathy begged, a stitch forming in her side. She couldn't even look at Lisa now, each time she did a new batch of the giggles emerged.

"You started it," Lisa retorted, wiping at her eyes. "Don't look at me. My sides hurt."

It took a good few minutes for Cathy's laughter to subside sufficiently that she considered it safe to resume her food preparation.

"Cathy—"

"Hmm?" Cathy adjusted the knife across the now completed stack of sandwiches, remembering Lisa preferred hers cut on the diagonal. Lisa had always insisted they tasted better cut that way. Cathy thought it absolute rubbish, but it was an idiosyncrasy she could live with. At least she ate her crusts.

"You know, the whole tomato thing was your fault."

Cathy left her knife poised above the sandwiches. "How do you figure that?"

"Well, you nearly gave me a coronary with your little announcement."

Cathy shrugged, still disbelieving she had actually said it. Well, no she wasn't really. She'd needed to say it, so she had. "I figured with all the misunderstandings lately, it was probably better just to be direct."

Lisa raised her eyebrows. "Well you couldn't have got much more direct if you tried." She flashed a winning smile and said, "Not that I'm complaining though."

Cathy sighed happily and turned her attention back to the cutting board. The knife sliced cleanly through the four rounds, which she divided evenly between two plates.

"Thanks." Lisa accepted the proffered plate but left it untouched as Cathy pulled up a stool to sit beside her. "Cathy—"

"Yes?"

"Were you planning to tell me you were . . . umm . . . single again, or were you going to leave me to figure it out for myself?"

Cathy smiled despite the twinge of sadness. She still felt very bad over her treatment of Toni. That, plus the fact she was mourning the loss of her best friend, was the reason she had ignored her instincts, the ones that kept leading her to the telephone over the past days, fingers ready to dial Lisa's number.

"What did you want me to do Lisa? Walk up and say hi, I'm single again, do you want coffee or shall we just go straight to bed?"

Lisa grinned wickedly as she picked up a sandwich. "I could have lived with that."

Cathy called Lisa a shocker. Lisa just grinned again and said that was why Cathy loved her. Cathy didn't disagree, but she couldn't resist one more little dig.

"Not only are you a shocker, but you can't dress yourself. You look absolutely ridiculous with your T-shirt on backward like that."

"Is it?" Lisa frowned downward. "So it is." Her T-shirt was pulled over her head and unceremoniously tossed to the floor. Lisa ran fingers through her hair, eyes bold as she considered Cathy. "Better?"

"Much." Whether from the coolness of the kitchen or from Cathy's stare, Lisa's nipples hardened before her eyes.

"You know what," Cathy scraped her stool away and groped for her plate. "I think we should take these upstairs."

"Who's the shocker now?" Lisa placed her plate on top of the jeans on top of the clock radio. She eased Cathy's housecoat from her shoulders.

"I am." Cathy let her housecoat slip to the floor. She just couldn't get enough of the woman who stood before her. Love and lust intermingled to form a potent mix. "But it's entirely your fault."

"Entirely." Lisa agreed, eyes smoldering.

Hunger for food forgotten, Cathy pushed Lisa onto the bed. She climbed on top, straddling a leanly muscled thigh. The muscle rippled as Lisa shifted so her knee was slightly bent.

"How's that?" Lisa placed hands firmly on either side of Cathy's ribcage.

"Perfect." Cathy shuddered as she began to glide and grind, closing her eyes and abandoning herself to the pleasure that only came from complete release. It was something else she had not indulged for years, Lisa the only one Cathy had ever felt so at ease with to really let herself go.

It was a very powerful feeling, and very freeing.

Lisa placed her now empty plate onto the bedside table. She patted her tummy and said, "That was yum."

"Glad you liked it." Cathy's empty plate was stacked on top of Lisa's.

Lisa wriggled underneath the covers, snuggling into Cathy and arranging her pillows just how she liked them. Then she realized she hadn't cleaned her teeth. She imagined dental decay setting in by morning. "Do you have a spare toothbrush I could use?"

Ten minutes later Lisa was much happier, as they both took a trip to Cathy's opulent bathroom. Lisa immediately adopted one of the two basins as her own. She spat toothpaste into the basin and splashed water over her face, feeling right at home in her new surroundings.

Cathy laughed delightedly when Lisa announced this fact.

Back in bed, Lisa again snuggled into Cathy. "Speaking of home . . . Which house are we going to live in?"

Cathy laughed again. "You are such a lesbian Lisa."

Lisa knew Cathy was referring to the old "Lesbians pack up the U-Haul on the second date" joke, but she'd let Cathy say it anyway. She opened her eyes wide, "Why?"

"It's not even the end of date number one and already you want to pack up the U-Haul."

Lisa poked Cathy in the waist, eyes sparkling with mischief. "My, my, we've changed our tune haven't we? It was only . . . what . . . a week ago, you thought I was—"

"Shut up." Cathy clapped her hand over Lisa's mouth. "Are you ever going to let me live that down?"

Lisa pried Cathy's hand away. "Probably not." In one deft motion she rolled Cathy onto her back, straddled her stomach and grasped both of her wrists to pin them above her head.

"Well I'll just have to tell everyone about your attempts at teaching a tomato how to swim."

Lisa half smiled at what promised to be a well-worn joke, her thoughts turning to something that had been bothering her since the whole gay/straight debate in her lounge room. "Cathy, there's something I just can't figure out."

"What?"

"When did I say I was through with women in front of you? I've been racking my brains and I just can't think of a time."

Cathy blushed and it took Lisa a good while to coax the truth.

"You little sneak!" Lisa pretended offense, but really she was more than a little pleased Cathy was interested to the point of eavesdropping.

Sensing Cathy was still mortified by her actions, Lisa decided a little confession of her own was in order. "Anyway, I beat you to the sneaky thing. Joel and I were hanging round Toni's back fence the night you decided to drop in."

"Really?" Cathy's eyes widened. "Why?"

Lisa related the cat collar episode and the trek down the lane to check on Virgil's welfare. Lisa slid off Cathy and threw her head into a pillow. "I still can't believe it's only been five weeks since then."

"Do you think we've gone at it too fast?"

"Oh no." Eleven years was not exactly pushing the speed limits.

"I was more thinking of all the stuff that's happened. If you think about it, we're lucky we're here at all."

"I'm glad we are."

"Me, too." Lisa agreed wholeheartedly, reaching to look under her jeans to check the time. It was past midnight. Luckily she and Joel had tomorrow off, their next job scheduled to start on Tuesday. Lisa had planned to spend Monday catching up on their paperwork. Maybe she could pop into the offices and take Cathy out for lunch? If she managed to get out of bed before midday. "I just hope you can put up with someone who's usually in bed by ten on a work night."

"Gee, I don't know Lisa," Cathy looked at Lisa aghast, but the twinkle in her eye betrayed her. "Sounds pretty dull and boring to me."

EPILOGUE
Eleven months later

Cathy watched the ripple of back muscle as Lisa reached for the shorts lying on the floor next to the couch. Lisa pulled a wallet from one of the back pockets. "Heads or tails?"

"Heads, please."

The shorts were returned to the pile of clothes that had been discarded not long after dinner. Lisa turned a dollar coin over in her hand. "Best two out of three?"

Cathy shook her head. "Let's make it one toss. Winner makes an immediate decision."

"Okay," Lisa nodded her assent.

"And don't even think about saying something like *I decide to go with whatever you decide*, if you win," Cathy warned as Lisa placed the coin on her thumbnail.

Lisa just poked her tongue out in reply and tossed the coin.

Two sets of eyes followed its passage toward the ceiling and back to Lisa's outstretched palm. It was immediately covered with Lisa's other palm. "Do you want to change your call?"

"No way," Cathy tugged at Lisa's hand, eager to see who was finally going to decide which house they were to live in. After eleven months of shuffling between their respective properties, it would be nice for them to settle in the one place and really make it a home.

"Just show me the coin honey," Cathy said.

It was tails. Cathy smiled. She had lost. "So, where's it to be? Your place or mine?"

Lisa threw herself back onto the couch. "I think . . ." There was a long moment of silence as Lisa sat up again and took a good look at her immediate surrounds, and beyond the expanse of windows to the night. "I think . . ." There was another pause, and this time the tilt of Lisa's head showed she was listening to the sound of waves crashing against the beach. "I like it here."

"You're absolutely sure?"

"Positive," Lisa nodded, a slow smile creeping across her features. "I like having my own basin in the bathroom."

"But all the work you've done—" Cathy visualized Lisa's home, with the polished boards, careful paintwork, meticulous tiling in the kitchen and bathroom—all the little decorator touches that had been thoughtfully and lovingly applied. "Your heart and soul are in that house."

Lisa's reply was immediate. "My heart and soul are where you are Cathy." Her soft expression turned wicked, and she grinned, "And besides, I can turn my renovating eye to that patch of desert out the back you dare call a garden, and of course, it won't be too long before those tiles in the guest bathroom are completely outdated—"

Cathy resisted the urge to smile. She conceded the state of the strip of yard at the rear of her house, but the second bathroom, along with the kitchen, had been overhauled only two years prior. "What about your rock doves?"

There was a thoughtful silence. "Do you think Toni would mind feeding them if I bought her the seed?"

This time Cathy could not help but smile, delighted Lisa had even considered the idea. Eight months ago, when Toni walked back into the accounting offices after an extended absence, she never dreamed this day would come, when the three could be friends. Toni warmed to Cathy slowly, finally stepping beyond the confines of her office and accepting the repeated invitations to lunch and making an occasional appearance at Friday afternoon drinks. Encouraged, Cathy invited Lisa to attend one of these Friday afternoon sessions. It was a disaster. Toni dawdled in her office for a good fifteen minutes, and when she did join the group congregated in Cathy's office, she and Lisa exchanged curt greetings then both descended into moody silence. Not to be defeated, Cathy invited Toni to dinner at her house. She also invited Van and Steph, who provided most of the conversation throughout the entrée and main courses. The breakthrough came over dessert. Lisa's ears pricked up at Toni's description of the *Pump* classes held at the gym she had recently joined.

"What's *Pump*?" she had asked. On discovering it was a cardio and weight workout performed to music, she wanted to know, "Can anyone attend or do you have to be a member?"

Cathy nearly fell off her chair when Toni suggested, albeit reluctantly, if Lisa may like to meet her for the ten o'clock class the next morning.

Cathy packed Lisa off the next day with the sincere hope she and Toni did not start throwing weights at each other. To her relief, Lisa returned in one piece, and to her delight, Lisa announced the class great and Toni okay. Since then, schedule permitting, Lisa met Toni at the gym at least once a week.

Still, Cathy was somewhat surprised Lisa thought of Toni for the task of feeding her beloved family of rock doves. "I'm sure she wouldn't mind. Ask her tomorrow."

"I will if I get the chance."

"Why wouldn't you get the chance? Aren't you meeting her at the gym?"

"Yeah," Lisa nodded, wriggling until she lay lengthways on the couch. She pulled Cathy on top of her, a laugh in her voice as she whispered in her ear, "But I reckon tomorrow Toni's finally going to ask Heather out."

"Really!" Heather was the *Pump* class instructor with fabulous biceps.

"Uh-huh," Lisa nodded into Cathy's neck and whispered in a definitive tone, "and I think Heather is going to say yes."

Cathy held herself at arm's length above Lisa, hopeful this may be the case. Heather was the first woman Toni had shown an interest in since . . . "And just what makes you think that?"

"Because, I kind of was speaking to Heather before class last week and kind of dropped Toni into the conversation and Heather kind of looked quite interested."

"Lisa Smith!" Cathy could imagine Lisa being as subtle as a brick in her hint dropping. "You're terrible!"

Lisa laughed out loud, shrugging and pulling Cathy down to her lips. "And you love it."

Cathy didn't argue. She loved everything about the woman who held her in her arms. Instead she just sighed happily and closed her eyes, sinking into Lisa and that very special place they shared together.